Drone Wars: The Beginning

A Novel

By

Mike Whitworth

Published by Doc's Press
www.docspress.com

ISBN-10: 061580697X
ISBN-13: 978-0615806976

Dedication

My wife, Diana, made this novel possible. Without her support, courage, love, and encouragement, I could never have written this story. I love her with all of my heart! Also of immense help were our cats Happy and Dusty, who often took turns sleeping on the desk as I wrote, and our dogs Bear and Misha, who frequently slept at, or on, my feet as I wrote.

The cover art is by the talented Kip Ayers. Thank you Kip for such fantastic work and being so great to work with! See Kip's work at www.kipayersillustration.com,

Author's Forward

This is a novel, a work of fiction, written only to entertain. It is the first in a series of novels about a monstrous conspiracy by a government and its supporters to murder citizens who disagree with their viewpoint and actions, and what happens when some of those citizens survive and take action against that government.

The novel is set in the USA some time in the future. I chose the USA only because it is a place familiar to most readers, and this familiarity allows better plot progression. I have taken much freedom to describe government agencies and titles that do not exist in order to simplify the plot.

The incidents and people described herein are completely imaginary. None of the incidents are real, or ever happened. I sincerely hope nothing like the imaginary incidents described in this work of fiction ever do happen to anyone anywhere.

At this point in time, though, I am not so very sure that someday soon they will not. The technology described in this book is mostly either available now, or is projected to be available fairly soon. As all of us know, technology can be misused by people who have evil intentions as well as by those who simply do not think about the ramifications of what they are doing.

I hope you enjoy this imaginary tale of what our future might become, and I sincerely hope that the bad parts of such a future never come to pass for anyone, anywhere.

I do not advocate violence against government, and I do not want a second civil war in America. I do, however, have a few words for anyone who believes they can control the American People through tyranny of any kind. To you I say, no matter how much you believe you understand the

American People, you don't. No matter how you proceed, you will seriously underestimate the will, creativeness, and fortitude of the American People, thus ultimately creating your own downfall. True Americans, though very patient and peace loving, value liberty, and are neither subjects nor slaves to do any tyrant's bidding. No matter how massive any tyrant's efforts to divide or subjugate them, the American people are a force that can and, sooner or later, will defeat any evil.

Mike Whitworth
April 2013

Chapter 1: ATTACK

"Murder by remote control is still murder." John Debrouillard

<u>Middle-Indiana</u>

The silence, interrupted only by the sound of the hoe striking the earth as I sliced the sparse weeds off just below the soil surface, was both refreshing and calming. As usual, I enjoyed the rhythm of hoeing the garden as much as I enjoyed being outdoors on a sunny Indiana summer day. It took me a minute to notice the buzzing, whirring sound. I turned just as the drone fired. That turn saved my life because the .40 caliber round fired by the drone missed. I dropped the hoe and ran for cover.

The drone followed me flying about six feet above the ground and repeatedly fired at me as I dodged crazily across the garden stomping the plants that I had carefully tended and cared for during the past two and a half months, and some for an additional six weeks in our greenhouse before we transplanted them to the garden.

I stepped onto the 2x10 that bordered one of our raised beds, and the board gave way. I stumbled and fell to my hands, which dove eight inches into the soft, compost-rich soil. Several rounds fired by the drone made pockmarks in the ground just ahead of me. I realized that they would have hit me had I not stumbled.

I rolled to my right as the drone repositioned itself for another shot, sprang to my feet, and dashed across a series of raised beds by stepping only on the boundary boards as though they were narrow stepping stones. The beds were each four feet wide and there was a two-foot-wide path between each pair of beds. The differing length of my steps and varying pace made my motion jagged and more difficult for the drone operator to predict. The drone kept firing, but my erratic motion helped me dodge the bullets.

I made my way to the portable building we used as a shop without getting hit and dove through the open door. The drone kept firing at me but, with the four and a half foot span of its four-rotor system, it couldn't come through the door after me. The bullets had no trouble passing through the thin metal walls though. I quickly turned my heavy workbench over and crouched down behind it.

The Roubo-style workbench top was made of a 6-inch-thick slab of glued-up hard maple and stopped the bullets. I was glad now that I liked to work wood using hand tools where such a heavy bench was needed. A typical, plywood-topped bench used by most power tool woodworkers would have left me riddled with holes by now.

I had read where this model drone carried a .40 caliber, semi-automatic pistol equipped with a laser sight and a one hundred round drum magazine, but I thought they were only used overseas by the military. I had no idea how many bullets the drone had already fired, but it was a lot. After the drone fired maybe 20 more rounds almost randomly into the building, the rolling staccato of gunfire ceased. I jumped up and dashed across the shop to the door. The drone was hovering about seven feet off the ground not four feet from the open shop door. I imagined I could see its cowardly, psychopathic operator sitting at his desk controls somewhere safe as I grabbed the 12-gauge shotgun from the pegs over the door and brought it to bear on the drone all while expecting to be shot. I had to act though because my wife Susan was in the house, and I didn't want the drone to kill her too.

The shotgun was a Remington model 870 pump that held five rounds. I fired all five as fast as I could work the action. On the fifth round, the drone veered away and crashed in the yard.

I felt a momentary elation but didn't take time to enjoy it. I ran for the house holding the empty shotgun. Susan was in the house canning sweet corn we had picked that morning and I wasn't sure if the drone I shot down was the only one. Susan was coming out of the house as I crossed the yard.

"What happened?" she asked. I could tell she was shaken by the tone of her voice. "What was that thing?"

"We have to get out of here, Sweetheart," I said. "We have to go now." That was when I heard them.

This time there was more than one. I glanced across the cornfield that abutted our backyard. The sky just above the six-foot-high corn was black with drones. As they came closer, the sound grew louder until it drowned everything else out. I dropped the shotgun, grabbed Susan, and started for the house just as the roar of 50-some-odd drones, all firing their .40 caliber guns at once from two hundred yards away, began. Susan jerked, and I almost carried her into the house, down the hall, and lowered her through the trap door into the root cellar as the bullet storm ripped through the house. I felt a blow on my right calf and another on the top of my right shoulder as I dropped through the trap door after Susan.

The root cellar wasn't there when our house was built. Two years before, we cut a trap door through the floor in the small bedroom that served as my office and excavated the root cellar below the house proper, one five-gallon bucket of dirt at a time. We chose to put the root cellar under the house for several reasons. First, during the winter we wouldn't have to go out into the cold or snow to retrieve our home-canned food or our stored carrots and potatoes. Second, our one-acre lot was small enough as it was and we wanted to use the space an outside root cellar would have taken up for growing edibles or other useful things. Having the root cellar under the house also made it a quickly accessible tornado shelter, which was nice since Indiana has more than its share of tornados.

Our lot, zoned rural residential, was mostly gardens and various edible plants grown in raised beds, with fruit trees, bees, chickens, and rabbits. Our lot was a hard-won, edible landscape with a dose of permaculture. The root cellar was lined with hundreds of jars filled with food that Susan had canned from our gardens and small orchard. She had also canned more than a hundred quart jars of chicken and rabbit meat. We grew and raised about 90% of our own food, and I worked from home as a consulting hydrogeologist, as well as sold wooden dough bowls and handcrafted furniture that I made during the winter months in our 12 by 32 foot, wood stove-heated workshop.

After we dug the root cellar, we lined the walls with rubber roof membrane and then poured one five-gallon bucket of hand-mixed concrete at a time into the forms. When the 10-inch-thick concrete walls and footing below, all reinforced with rebar, had cured, we sealed the inside with a thin coat of hydraulic cement. The root cellar had two rooms. The first, which we were in, had a concrete floor, and the second had a dirt floor that helped to stabilize the humidity for storing root crops like potatoes, sweet potatoes, apples, and carrots, etc. through the winter. The floor of the dirt-floored room was two feet lower than the floor of the other room. I had installed an automatic sump pump just in case of flooding. So far we had no flooding problems. Since the basement was dug into clay-rich glacial till, I didn't expect any, but it pays to be careful.

Both root cellar rooms were capped with a steel-reinforced slab of concrete, 12-inches thick, supported by 12-inch steel I-beams. Part of that stoutness was to transfer the weight of the center support piers for the house above to the new footings poured for the root cellar, and part was to add sufficient mass so that the root cellar could double as a fallout shelter. When we built the two-room root cellar, I thought we were going overboard, but Susan encouraged me to take my time and do it right. Building the root cellar took us over a year. I don't think the neighbors even noticed, but then we were careful not to tell them or let them see what we were doing. I bought the steel beams when the neighbors were all on vacation and hauled them home on our 16-foot utility trailer. It was almost all Susan and I could do, even with come-alongs and a winch, to get them off the trailer and under the house into position. At the time, we didn't dare ask anyone for help.

It was just operational security, or OPSEC. Susan and I are preppers. I had been worried about the economy for a few years and when I mentioned to Susan that we should store some food and supplies just in case we had an economic collapse or an EMP event, she encouraged me, and then led the way in planning the gardens, fruit trees, and chickens. The bees and the rabbits were my idea. The small rack of firearms on the wall next to the canning jars was Susan's idea, even though when we married she didn't like guns.

I slammed the trap door shut above me, glad that we had lined it with ¼" steel plate and three layers of Kevlar. Susan stood against the storage shelves holding her side. She didn't look good. I helped her through the door and down the steps into the second room and set her down on a wooden bench I made for her to use while sorting through the lower storage bins. It was then I saw the blood on her side and chest. Her last words to me were "I love you Sweetheart. Kill the bastards for me, please!" Then she slumped over into my arms. Her life passed while I held her. I hugged her tightly to me, and my tears started to flow as the house above was macerated by thousands of .40 caliber lead bees.

As I stroked her head, I remembered our first sweet potato crop and her bubbly excitement and enthusiasm as we dug them up. I turned the sweet potatoes up from the earth with a shovel, and then she pawed through the dirt with her bare hands, holding each one up for me to see as if it was a rare diamond or emerald, all the while happy and smiling and suggesting ways we could cook them.

After maybe 10 minutes, I managed to get up and went back into the concrete-floored room and took a 9mm Browning High-Power, that had belonged to my Father, a Beretta Bobcat in .22 long rifle, and a stainless steel .223 Ruger Ranch Rifle from the gun rack. The rifle had also belonged to my Father. New sales of all three semiautomatic firearms like these were banned. Until now at least, the feds had stopped short of house-to-house confiscation and had just said that semi-automatic weapons owned before the law was passed must be registered and proof of purchase provided. I had no proof of purchase, and even if I had, I would never have registered my weapons. Registration has been the first step to gun confiscation and genocide in every tyranny of the last century.

Back in the dirt-floored room, I grabbed one of the bug-out bags we kept there. In the bug-out bag were Dave Canterbury's five C's of wilderness survival, three ways of making fire (combustion), a couple of reflective space blankets for cover, a billy can for a container, some parachute cord, and tarred bank line for cordage, a Mora knife for a cutting tool as well as a canteen full of water, some survival food bars, a first aid kit, some fishing tackle, a compass, a small flashlight, and full magazines of ammo for the guns. I also had a Swiss Army Knife and a small sharpening tab with a diamond grit plate and a ceramic rod in my pocket. The sharpener also used to have a ferro rod for striking a spark to start a fire, but it broke off one time when I dropped it. I never got around to getting another one.

I slipped the High Power into my waistband and clipped the inside-the-pants-holster to my belt and jeans. The Beretta I dropped into the bug-out bag still in its pocket holster. I took one last look at Susan's body slumped on the bench.

"I will get the bastards for you, Sweetheart, every last one of them. I promise!" I said as I took one last look at the love of my life slumped dead on the bench. I wanted so much to bring her back; to return to the mostly carefree days of growing fruits and vegetables and raising chickens; to return to the happy times we had shared, but I knew those times were gone now forever—all because some asshole in our government was afraid of people who were self-sufficient, or had opinions differing from the mass of sheep posing as citizens of our once great country. The sheeple some called them. Well, I was no sheeple and, although I had never been a violent person at any previous time in my life, I now knew that the capacity for great violence had always lain dormant within me. Susan's murder brought it welling up from depths I never before knew existed.

I moved a rack of bins aside—it rested on concealed rollers so it moved easily—and crawled into the escape tunnel.

I had just finished the escape tunnel about six months before. It was shored, floored, and walled with treated lumber. The bottom of the tunnel sloped from both the entrance and exit to a low spot located about midway along the length of the tunnel. The space below the floorboards was filled with gravel, and I had installed an automatic sump pump at the tunnel's low point. The sump pump drained into a flowerbed in the yard. There were also LCD lights, with battery backup, installed along the tunnel to light the way.

Susan had requested the tunnel. She said that if times got bad, we might have to leave our home and she wanted a concealed and safe way out. She was worried that if the government ever declared martial law that we might be forced to go to a FEMA camp. I have always had a moderate case of claustrophobia, but I dug the tunnel for Susan anyway. I wouldn't let her dig because I thought digging the tunnel was too dangerous. She carried dirt though; as ever, always determined to help.

Susan thought FEMA camps would be used to guillotine, or otherwise kill, and cremate 'useless eaters.' She said, because we were just regular, everyday citizens without much money, the government would probably be happy to kill us off so the powers that be would have more of the Earth's resources for their own use. I wasn't sure that I agreed with her, but I wasn't sure she was completely wrong either. I had always heard that "power corrupts, and absolute power corrupts absolutely." In my lifetime, I had yet to find any evidence that statement was not true.

I read somewhere that the president locked himself in his study and reviewed the films of overseas drone strikes like they were some kind of death porn. I had not known that American citizens were being attacked with drones here at home on our own soil until now, but I hoped that son of a bitch of a president was watching when I took down the first drone.

When Susan and I started prepping we were both overweight and out of shape from living a typical American lifestyle. All the work I had done, and cutting out all wheat, GMO corn, almost all sugar, both diet and regular soft drinks, and eating our own chemical-free produce and meat now had me fit and strong. Instead of the 290 pounds I used to weigh, I was now 220 pounds of pretty solid muscle on a six-foot frame. I had even started jogging about a year ago.

Once in the tunnel, I switched the LED lights on and crawled forward. Near the end of the tunnel, I stopped to check on my leg and shoulder. One round had passed through the meat of my right calf but, as best I could tell, had not hit the bone. I stopped the bleeding by placing gauze pads on both the entry and exit wounds. Then I tied strips from the torn-off leg of my jeans around my calf to hold the pads in place. The strips worked better for this than paracord or tarred bank line from the bug-out bag.

The hit on my shoulder was just a big nick so I covered it with a gauze pad and some tape. Neither wound hurt very badly yet, but I figured they would soon enough. I swallowed three painkillers from the first aid kit in the bug-out bag.

The tunnel exited into a clump of bushes next to the cornfield at the edge of our lot. I crawled to the end of the tunnel and waited until I could no longer hear the drones. Then, I slid the hatch aside. It didn't open upwards, but instead slid sideways into a cavity, so it wouldn't draw attention when it was opened.

I looked carefully toward our house. There was nothing but a pile of rubble where our cozy 1,200 square foot house once stood. There must have been more drones than I thought, or else some of the drones were larger than the one I shot down and carried more ammo. I was surprised no explosives had been used, at least I hadn't heard any.

I was doubly glad that we had not filed for a permit for the root cellar and tunnel construction, and that we had done both in secret. Much of the dirt had gone into some of the many wooden-sided, raised beds in our gardens, and some had been dispersed into the cornfield behind us at night, one or two buckets at a time, usually after midnight.

I quickly slipped into the corn and headed across the field toward the creek. I was limping on my right leg, which, despite the painkillers, was really starting to hurt now. It would be dark in another two hours, but I couldn't wait and be trapped here. I knew the authorities would be on the scene in just a few minutes. I did not want to be caught.

I figured the morning news would say that a rural couple was killed in a gas explosion or that a homegrown terrorist cell blew themselves up making a bomb. I was glad the neighbors on both sides of us were gone that day. Otherwise, I assumed they would most likely be killed as part of the cover-up.

I made my way to the woods that bordered the creek. I was hoping whoever sent the drones was so convinced that we were both dead that they would not be using the satellites to look for me right now. That would come later though, when they discovered the root cellar and the tunnel. Between now and then I had to disappear, and that is not an easy thing to do in a world filled with electronic surveillance.

My cell phone was still in the house, or what was left of it, and I carried no electronics on me. My driver's license sat in my wallet securely wrapped in several layers of tinfoil, just in case it contained an RFID chip. I had only a non-RFID debit card and maybe a hundred dollars in my wallet. However, I grabbed the plastic bag of emergency cash that we kept in the tunnel. It held about $2,000, in 20s mostly. Not nearly enough for what I had to do now, but I had it to do anyway.

I jogged and limped through the woods to the creek. We were in a mild drought this summer so the creek was low. It mostly just came up to my ankles as I walked along the creek bed. I stayed in the water for over a mile and a half, reconnoitering carefully when I neared the bridge on the county road to be sure no one was stopped there before I walked under the bridge.

I was very careful to always walk in flowing water. I was now wet to my armpits from crossing several deep holes.

The guns and bug out bag were dry because I held them over my head in the deep spots.

When I came to the fishing hole, I climbed the bank, and made for Henry Butler's place. Henry was a farmer and a friend. He was one of those people who seemed like a real grouch until you get to know them. The first time I met him at the annual neighborhood picnic he made fun of my shiny new pickup truck and told me that only sissies drove fancy trucks.

I looked at him and said, "Well, just what are you so fucking grouchy about?"

He looked at me for a full 30 seconds, and then smiled and said, "Fuck if I know?" We have been friends ever since.

Henry stood an inch or two taller than I but didn't carry the muscle I did. He was maybe ten years younger than I was. We shared the same political views, more or less. At my and Susan's urging Henry and his wife Martha were now quietly prepping as well. Prepping was not a huge change in lifestyle for a farmer anyway, or, at least, that was what Henry said.

I carefully made my way across Henry's back field and then, after watching carefully for anything out of place, toward the back side of his house. One time I thought I heard a drone but decided it was just a small plane. Once I reached Henry's back yard, I knelt in the bushes and tossed some small pebbles I had gathered in the creek against his window until Henry appeared on the back porch with a shotgun.

"Henry, don't shoot!"

"Hey, I know you," Henry said. "What's wrong, Man?" I stepped out of the bushes and walked across the scorched grass carefully staying under cover of a couple of trees until Henry could see me. "Geez, what the hell happened to you?"

"Henry," I said. "Please don't ask any questions. Believe me, you don't want to know. I need to borrow the Beast. I may not be able to get it back to you." The Beast was Henry's pride and joy, a 1961 ¾ ton Chevy pickup that he had completely restored, and then carefully dented, weathered, and scratched up to fit his idea of what a good pickup truck should look like.

Henry hesitated only for a second. "I'll get the keys." Henry went into his house and came back out ten minutes later. Martha was with him. Henry handed me the keys and Martha handed me a large paper bag.

"You may need this," she said.

I took the bag and said, "Please, for your own safety, you didn't see me. You accidentally left the keys in the Beast and when you get up in the morning, after sleeping very late, you will report it missing."

Henry looked me in the eye. After a few seconds, he said, "No. Martha and I are going in the car tonight to visit her sister—a spur of the moment thing. We will be gone for a week or 10 days. Maybe the Beast will be gone when we get home? If so, I will report it then."

"Thank you Henry. Thank you Martha."

"You would do it for us," Henry said.

"How is Susan?" Martha asked.

"You don't want to know," I said.

I think Martha could see the pain in my eyes. "Oh," she said. "Oh my."

"Please, for your own safety, don't mention this to anyone. Not in email, text, on the phone, or in person, ever."

"Did this have to do with that loud roar we heard earlier?" Henry asked.

I nodded but said, "Please don't ask."

"Well, we were inside anyway and didn't hear a thing."
Henry looked at Martha and winked. "Had the TV too loud,
you know. Take care Old Son, and stay away from those
fancy trucks."

I nodded then turned and limped across the dry grass
doing my best to stay under cover of the trees while heading
to the barn where the Beast was stored. I noticed Martha
was crying on Henry's shoulder and his eyes didn't look dry
either. If anyone saw him I knew Henry would want him or
her to think it was over the loss of the Beast, but I knew
better.

I put the rifle behind the seat, threw the bug-out bag
onto the passenger seat, and climbed into the Beast. Henry
was right, of course. Compared to my more modern pickup
truck, the Beast did almost everything better—except gas
mileage.

Henry had pulled the original engine and dropped a
modified 454 cubic inch Chevy under the hood, replaced
the brakes with modern disc brakes, installed power
steering, and added a 100-gallon auxiliary gas tank in the
truck bed. The Beast was also four-wheel drive and now
had a 4WD shifter in the cab. It also had a front, bumper-
mounted, 12,000 lb. winch, and another winch just like it
mounted on the rear bumper. As always, Henry had both
gas tanks full.

Maybe the biggest advantage of the Beast was that it
wasn't computerized and carried no electronics at all. That
meant that it couldn't be tracked electronically. Only by line
of sight, automated tag ID software used with traffic camera
feeds, or by satellite if you knew where to look. To the best
of my knowledge, the feds had not started requiring RIFD
chips on vehicle tags yet.

I started up the Beast and drove away. I felt really bad about taking the Beast away from Henry, but I didn't know what else to do. I mourned Susan as I drove well within the speed limit to the interstate highway. Part of me still couldn't believe what had happened. I calculated I had maybe two hours before the feds figured out that I had survived. I hoped it would take them a while to expand the search. I thought I might have as long as six hours before they broadened the search, if I were lucky.

I drove generally south on the interstate for two hours and then pulled into a truck stop. It was now past 9:30 P.M. and completely dark. I parked in the back part of the parking lot after making sure there were no cameras and waited until no one was watching. I then slipped out of the Beast and, using my Swiss Army Knife, removed the tag from the pickup truck beside me, as well as the tag from a truck two spaces over, nearly breaking the big screwdriver blade on the second tag. I switched the second tag onto the first truck and then quickly got back into the Beast with the first tag and left.

While on the interstate, I avoided stopping at rest stops because the Federal Transportation Security Police (FTSP), otherwise known as the 'Granny Gropers', had been setting up checkpoints at interstate highway rest stops in recent months. I suspected it would not be long before they were setting up permanent checkpoints in the middle of the major highways, instead of just at random rest stops. Fortunately for me, they had not done that yet.

I saw only one unarmed federal highway drone silhouetted against streetlights as I passed through Indianapolis, but it ignored me. The only stop I had made so far was to steal the tag, even though I had to pee so bad my tonsils hurt.

Three hours out I turned onto the back roads. I stopped and switched tags on the Beast so that it would be harder for the feds to track me using license plate scanners if they had figured out I was now driving the Beast. I dropped the original tag from the Beast into a creek a few miles further along.

I also dug into the bag Martha gave me. Inside were eight large sandwiches, a gallon jug of water, some first aid supplies, and a roll of bills held tightly together with a rubber band. The roll contained $432, probably all the cash Martha and Henry had on hand. The bag also held a clean white tee shirt and a pair of jeans; Henry's no doubt. I checked the waistband. They were a size too big, but that was better than a size too small. An hour later, I stopped in a secluded spot and changed clothes. The tee shirt was too tight across the shoulders, but otherwise it was fine.

I wolfed down two of the sandwiches Martha had given me. They were good, but I was stressed enough I almost couldn't taste them. I had not had a single bite of wheat, or a wheat-containing product, in just over three years. I had read that GMO wheat, especially the newer, shorter varieties that almost all the farmers grew now, is just a chronic poison that slowly kills whoever eats it. Since I had stopped eating wheat, other GMO products, and drinking soda, I had lost weight without effort and my health had recovered. I felt like I was 25 years old again. For this reason, I believed what I had read about the wheat. However, the sandwiches were all I had and I needed to eat for the energy—at least that is what I told myself. Perhaps it was just old habits emerging under stress, perhaps it was hunger; I really wasn't sure.

I put the rest of the sandwiches, the roll of bills, and the first aid supplies in the bug-out bag. I read about some folks who stuff their bug-out bags to the max. We kept ours half-empty because we felt they would attract less attention that way.

I dug a hole with the Swiss Army Knife and my hands and deeply buried my old jeans and denim shirt. The blade was dull when I was done, so I quickly sharpened it on my pocket sharpener. I like to always have a sharp knife.

My eyes teared-up at the thought of what Henry and Martha had done. Of course, I was still crying over Susan too.

Yes, I would kill the bastards. Every damn one of them! I remembered when Congress passed the bill that allowed our government to kill our own citizens with no due process. I also remembered this president saying he would never use that power. What a lie that was!

I wasn't sure why the government tried to kill me, but I had my suspicions. Although, if they chose to kill me, a pretty small fish, then there must have been others before me. Many, many others—all lost on the back pages of local newspapers and most likely never reported in the mainstream news. Hell, I didn't even vote, I just had a few strong opinions.

I wasn't sure where to go. Then I remembered Roscoe. That was it. I would go see Roscoe.

Roscoe was a blogger and a prepper. I enjoyed reading his blog and made it a point to seek him out once when Susan and I were on vacation in the West. Roscoe and I hit it off well from the beginning. That both surprised and pleased me. It surprised me because Roscoe and I had very different backgrounds. Roscoe grew up well off and was retired from the military. He had seen combat in several theaters. What he had seen around the world might have been what turned him against what we both perceived as fiscal irresponsibility and massive encroachment on individual liberty by our government.

I, on the other hand, grew up poorer than a church mouse and worked hard to earn three college degrees. I was the first person in my family to earn a college degree. For many years I taught at the university before I became disenfranchised by the all too common, over-the-top political correctness and game playing at the expense of scholarship and education. At Susan's urging, I took early retirement, and we bought our small house in the country.

In any event, Roscoe was the best chance I had for finding some help in hiding from whoever was after me until I could figure out how to mount a counteroffensive. Other than Henry, Roscoe was the only other prepper I knew.

I kept driving south and then skirted the southern border of Illinois. I don't like Illinois. They have too many draconian rules for me. Illinois also had more surveillance drones in the air over the highways and more FTSP checkpoints than any other state in the Midwest.

When I could, I turned right and drove north into Missouri. I drove on back roads all the way, navigating with a good paper atlas that Henry kept in the Beast. Henry called the atlas his old fashioned GPS. I kept driving north until I reached northern Missouri and then started working my way generally northwest. By now the sun was rising and I looked out over green pastures and rolling, forested hills. My leg ached, and my shoulder hurt, but I was glad to see the sun come up.

I thought I should ditch the Beast and find other wheels, but I couldn't bring myself to do it. In Nebraska, I drove into a medium-sized town and stopped at the ubiquitous big box store.

When I entered the store, I coughed a lot, and kept my head down and my hand over my mouth. I also stuffed some paper in each cheek before I went inside. I didn't know if it would work, but I had at least read about a few ways to prevent digital facial recognition. The feds have almost everyone's face on file from the new driver's license pictures, so it wasn't like they didn't have my picture, but maybe losing the weight would also be a help?

I bought ten cans of ugly, rust-preventing spray paint. I paid cash and didn't talk to the cashier at all. Despite the fact I paid with cash, the teller didn't seem to think of me a terrorist even though the government said that people who pay with cash might be terrorists. I guess she just didn't feel threatened by a few cans of spray paint. I also bought a cap and sunglasses. I wore the cap and sunglasses out of the store with my head down to keep the feds computer facial recognition algorithms from identifying me from the overhead store cameras.

About a hundred miles away, under some dense trees, I spray painted the Beast and buried the cans. Now the Beast didn't look like a dented and scratched old green truck, it looked like a patchy brown and green scratched and dented old truck. I kept the cap and sunglasses on while I was driving in case there were cameras along some of the back roads.

Nowadays, for the feds to search for someone was as easy as setting up a computer algorithm to process the incoming data stream at the giant central federal spy center; the center that our government built using a few billion of our tax dollars to spy on us, the citizens who provided all the money from their hard work, yet were not even told about it. The center wasn't officially acknowledged to exist, but the information had leaked, nonetheless.

It was in the wee hours of the morning when I got close to Roscoe's place a few miles out of Ten Sleep, Wyoming. I parked about a mile away and limped toward his house on foot, carrying the bug-out bag and the rifle, with the Browning holstered inside my pants under the tee shirt. I was still wired from everything that had happened, but I was wearing down fast.

Roscoe's house was dark. No lights that I could see. I was careful as I crept close. I could just make out the house by starlight and—it was destroyed, completely destroyed, just like ours. I hoped Roscoe made it out, but I doubted it. I knew he did not have a basement.

I had read where the feds wanted 50,000 drones flying the American skies. I was starting to believe they already had more than that—perhaps many, many more. Even if they didn't, it was undoubtedly easy enough to move a hundred or so of the smaller drones across the country by plane as needed. The drone operators didn't even need to move with them. As I understood it, the drones could be remotely operated anywhere in the world if they were equipped to operate using satellite communications.

There was nothing I could do here, so I left. So far, I only had to fill the truck up with gasoline once. I chose an outlying station and paid cash for the 108 gallon fill up— over $500, plus another hundred to keep the clerk quiet about the cash transaction.

I would need to fill the tank again before too long, but filling up with gas at a conventional gas station was a real risk. I knew almost all the more isolated ranches kept an elevated fuel storage tank containing at least a few hundred gallons of gas on site. I wondered if I might find a ranch where they would sell me gas and keep quiet about it. Most of the ranchers I had met over the years have been pretty good about minding their own business.

Sometimes a risk simply must be taken. Then again, maybe I took the risk because by now I was too tired to think clearly? I drove west out of Ten Sleep and began to look for ranch roads. I passed by a couple and then, after maybe 15 miles, turned onto one that looked a little more rundown than the others.

The ranch house was about six miles down a very rough and winding gravel road. It was old and a bit run down. There were two barns, or machine sheds, each three or four times the size of the house. I needed the 4WD for the first time on the way to the ranch house.

I pulled up in front of the house and got out of the truck. I had taken about three steps when a musical voice said, "Hold it right there Mister."

I half turned to see whom the voice belonged too. There stood a trim and quite attractive lady of indeterminate age dressed in jeans and a western shirt holding an AR-15 rifle. There was a very slight smile on her face. About 30 feet behind her two cowboys were approaching. Both carried AR-15 rifles as well, and they were pointed at me. I figured I was screwed.

"Search his truck, Jerry," the lady said.

I slowly put my hands in the air and said, "I don't mean anyone any harm."

Jerry searched the truck and found the bug-out bag and the rifle behind the seat. He carried them to the lady for her inspection. She glanced at the rifle and shuffled through the contents of the bag. Looking up, she asked. "Are you a prepper?"

I nodded my head.

"You in trouble?"

I nodded again.

"Ok, hand that pistol in your waistband to Jerry and come inside." I did as she asked and limped after her into the ranch house. Jerry and the other man were right behind us. Now they had their guns and mine too.

She motioned to a chair. "Sit there." I sat. "What happened to your leg?"

"Gunshot," I said.

"Who?" She asked.

"I don't know. It was a drone," I replied.

Jerry smiled and said "Well, Toni, I think we have a real terrorist on our hands here. What did you do to get shot, fella?"

"That part I am not sure about," I answered.

"Are you being followed? Are you wanted?" Toni asked.

"Yes to both, I suspect."

Toni turned to the other cowboy. "Will, take his truck and drive it to Boise. Ditch it but good. Jerry will be along in two days to get you. You guys set up a place and time between yourselves."

"Yes Ma'am," Will replied. He and Jerry conferred for about 30 seconds. Then, Will handed his rifle to Jerry, and walked out the front door.

Toni looked at me. "You were wise to use an old truck with no GPS."

I shrugged.

"Jerry, go get Doc to look at his leg, please."

"I don't think that is wise," I said.

"It's OK," Toni said. "He is cool." She smiled just a little bit. OK, tell me your first name and your story. I don't want to know your last name yet."

"Plausible deniability?" I asked.

"You might say that," she smiled a tiny bit more.

I told her who I was, including my last name—I have always had trouble with authority—most of my history, and about the drones. I didn't mention Susan. It was just too difficult.

Toni listened and then asked, "Where is your wife?" while pointing to the wedding ring on my finger.

"She didn't make it." I choked on the words, but managed to get them out. Toni's gaze softened a good bit, and she didn't ask any more questions. We waited quietly until Doc arrived.

Doc was about five-eight and a whole lot younger than I thought he would be. He assured me he had graduated medical school, although he had not yet finished a residency. He looked at my leg, re-bandaged it, and gave me a small bottle of antibiotic pills to take twice a day. He also stitched up the nick in my shoulder. He said it took fourteen stitches. I was glad he numbed it first.

Toni watched the whole time but said nothing.

When Doc was done, I asked Toni, "Are you going to turn me over to the feds?"

Doc sniggered, and Toni said, "No, I think you may just be one of us."

"Who are us?" I asked.

Toni smiled. There was something in her expression I couldn't get a read on. "People like you," she said. "People just like you."

Chapter 2: PEGGY

"Evil is as evil does." John Debrouillard

<u>Colorado</u>

Peggy Bronson slowed down for the stop sign and came to a dusty stop on the dirt road. She waited for the wispy tan dust to settle and, once she could see all was clear, turned right onto the paved road.

Peggy had been glad to see her sister and her dad. It was more difficult to visit now that she lived so far away, but she managed it twice a year, even though her sister had yet to come visit her. It had been a year since her mom's funeral.

Peggy thought her dad was handling the loss fairly well. Her sister didn't agree with her. She thought he was handling it poorly. Peggy suspected that might be because her sister, ever the center of attention, didn't like the way their father had become more introverted after their mother's death. Most likely, her sister saw their father's introversion as an inconvenience.

Her mom had always been the one who pressured Peggy about finding a good man and getting married. Now her younger sister, though unmarried herself and still living at home, was doing the same thing. That irritated Peggy more than she thought it should. Nonetheless, she was now headed home a day earlier than she had planned.

She drove for a while, alternatively thinking about an algorithm she was working on for her employer, and trying to come up with a killer comeback the next time her sister asked her about getting married. She slowed down to navigate an abrupt curve in the road thinking that it wasn't her fault she had not yet found the right man—or was it? Was she being too picky? Was she refusing to settle for a less than perfect man? She didn't think so.

As she rounded the curve, she saw what looked to be a small predator drone swooping down toward a red car coming her way. She had seen pictures on the internet of the predator drones used by the military and the president when he assassinated terrorists overseas. She had always thought they were much bigger than this one. This drone was only about as long as a car. As best she could tell, it had a wingspan of about 12 feet.

She stared in both amazement and horror as the drone fired a missile. The exhaust trail was unmistakable. It looked just like it did on the movies. The missile hit the red car while it was still moving. The car was almost completely demolished by the explosion and what was left of it slid to a stop. The flames were dancing six feet above the hulk of what had been the car.

Peggy was afraid any people in the car were dead or horribly injured. She swerved off the road to avoid the wreckage and came to a stop only 75 feet from the burning car. She could feel the heat from the flames as soon as she opened her door. Debris from the blast had pinged off her car and even pocked the windshield in two places.

Just in case anyone in the car was still alive, she put her car in park, got out, and walked cautiously toward the wreckage despite the heat. She was afraid of what she might see. She had read where some of the terrorists who were targeted overseas were torn limb from limb by drone strikes. She wasn't sure she could handle seeing something like that. As best she could tell, there was no way anyone in the car could possibly have survived.

Out of the corner of her eye, she noticed the drone was returning. That scared her. She ran back to her car, got in quickly, started the engine, and drove away. The drone followed.

She hoped the drone had carried only one missile. She couldn't see a second missile attached to the bottom of the drone, but she randomly swerved the car hoping to avoid a missile impact in case she was wrong. After a couple of miles, she decided that either the drone had carried only one missile, or she was simply under surveillance.

Peggy considered herself just a normal citizen. She was not politically active, nor had she ever been arrested for anything. In fact, she had never even had a speeding ticket. She was, however, like most people she knew, at least somewhat distrustful of the government.

She knew that many politicians seemed far more concerned with pleasing large corporations than protecting citizens. Why else would the feds stand behind GMO corn after that scientific study showed lab rats developed tumors when they ate it? She also knew that the government was prone to cover up things the powers that be did not want the public to know. Therefore, she began to worry that witnessing the drone strike made her a target. From what she had read, drones like this one cost too much for anyone except the government to operate.

One of Peggy's friends, Alec Davis, a retired shopkeeper who was overtly anti-government, although in a non-violent political activist fashion, once told her that the powers that be were perfectly willing to incur collateral damage to achieve their goals. Alec explained to her that collateral damage was the death of citizens and the destruction of private property. Alec was a solid citizen and had always proven himself to be trustworthy. She believed him—especially now.

Peggy saw an intersection coming up and turned left onto a county road. In her rearview mirror, she watched the drone follow her. Of course, it was possible that the government might let her go—maybe with only a warning to not say anything about what she had seen. However, she wasn't at all sure of that. Her friend Alec had informed her that 4,500 innocent civilians had been killed by U.S. government drone strikes overseas. If those innocent civilians didn't concern the government, she doubted they would care about one insignificant American citizen such as herself either.

She drove faster. The drone picked up it's pace as well. That was when she knew she was in trouble. She decided that she needed to evade the drone if she didn't want to become collateral damage. Luckily, she knew the area, having been raised in the general vicinity, and was able to navigate the back roads without a map. Peggy knew there was a national forest about eight miles from her present location. She thought that the forest might be a good place to lose the drone.

The drone followed her every turn. Peggy drove faster and faster. Her hands gripped the wheel so hard they hurt. She concluded that the government might send another drone, this one with a live missile, to kill her. She was hoping she would have time to reach the national forest and evade the drones under cover of the forest canopy before that happened.

Peggy wasn't sure what, if any, remote sensing equipment the drones carried beyond a camera. She hoped the drones were not equipped with infrared scanners that would allow them to follow her under cover of the forest.

Just as Peggy entered the national forest, she glanced in her rear view mirror and saw another drone coming to join the one that was still following her. Peggy pushed her accelerator closer to the floor. The tires now squealed around every turn she made climbing the forested mountain. Here, the forest cover was still patchy. Gradually, the tree cover increased, but she still caught glimpses of the drones following her. Now the second drone, clearly armed with a missile, had taken the lead. She saw the first drone turn and fly away.

Peggy decided she had an urgent need to convince whoever was behind the drone's cameras that she was dead before the drone made her so. That was when she decided to crash her car; her brand-new Lexus that she had wanted so badly and saved five years to buy. However, Peggy wasn't a fool. She knew her life was worth more than any car, at least to her. She watched for her opportunity.

The road grew steeper and continued to wind up the mountainside in increasingly abrupt hairpin turns. To her left the slope began to drop off almost vertically. That left

Peggy in a quandary. To escape the car she needed to exit the driver's door, yet that was the side of the road closest to the steep slope that dropped several hundred feet or more down the mountain. After going around an inside bend, the answer came to her.

She slowed down as she drove into a tight bend to the right that was well covered by overhanging pine trees. She carefully opened the driver's door with her left hand and held it just barely open.

As she turned left into the next curve in the road she kept her car as far to the right as she could. Once she was well into the curve she opened the door, turned the steering wheel hard left, rolled out of the car, and slammed the door behind her in one fluid movement. She had always been athletic. Now she was very glad of her ability.

The gravel was hard. She cried out in pain as she hit and rolled almost to the drop off. The car swung to the left ahead of her and went over the edge. She heard it crashing through the trees below.

She quickly got up and managed to scramble into the bushes and worked her way up the steep mountainside a few feet. Settling behind a thick bush and making herself as small as possible she saw the armed drone fly by and dip down the mountain. She was shocked when she heard the explosion.

It took her a while to understand that the drone had fired on her car where it came to rest below on the mountainside. She had been hoping that this was all in her imagination, and the drone was not really after her. Now, she knew differently. She was relieved to see the drone fly away. She was so scared she was shaking.

Ten minutes later she realized that she better do something. The only thing she could think of was to hide deep in the woods. She was sure that government police would be along at any minute. And if they caught her, she was sure they would kill her.

Her purse and her cell phone were still in what remained of her car, so she couldn't call anyone. Fortunately, she was wearing jeans, a thin red plaid flannel shirt, and tennis shoes instead of a dress and heels, but she had nothing in her pockets and no food, no water, and no means of communication. It would be dark in about six hours. It was going to get cold after the sun went down, probably below freezing, especially up here on the mountain.

DIS Drone Base No. 3, Oklahoma

Clayton Jackson sat in a comfortable chair. He liked to think of it as a real pilot's seat. The wrap-around-screen in front of him required his complete attention. The video from the on-board cameras filled the screen so well that it seemed as if he was sitting in an actual cockpit in the drone, even though the drone had no cockpit.

It was good to be operating so close to the front again. Flying a drone located halfway across the globe was a bit difficult because of signal latency, or delay. It worked OK for intel flights, but was less than satisfactory to him for strikes.

He liked the strikes. Man, how he liked the strikes! He loved the feeling he got when he loosed a missile on target and then saw the explosion. He loved the feeling of knowing he had killed someone, or maybe even more than one. His best to date was six confirmed kills with a single missile. He thought of that mission every single day. Every single day he also thought he had the very best job in the world.

He had heard of the new quad-copter assassin drones armed with either semi or full auto .40 caliber guns. Man, how he wanted to operate those. Rumor was that the pilots of those drones could actually see the blood splash from the bullet strikes. He wanted that so bad he could taste it.

He focused on following the car. He couldn't see the driver, but the message that had flashed across his screen 30 minutes ago said to acquire the target at drone 8947's position and eliminate the driver of the dark blue Lexus. The message said the driver was a 36-year-old blonde woman of medium height. He again wished that they would tell the pilots the names of the victims. He would love to know the names of the 103 people he had killed. Somehow, it seemed it would be so much more satisfying to know their names.

Following the car as it climbed the winding road up the side of the mountain, he held off firing his missile for two reasons. First, there was tree cover over most of the road. His on-screen computer indicated that he had a 70% chance of striking his target with the intermittent tree cover. Standard operating procedure required a minimum of 95% before firing. Second, the map of the terrain that flashed on the top of his screen showed that soon the road would exit the trees. There, with no cover, his chance of a successful strike would closely approach 100%.

He was surprised when the car swerved out from under heavy tree cover, went off the road, and down the mountainside. He quickly flew the drone into position and released the missile just as the car came to rest. It was a perfect hit, as always. His many years of computer gaming had not failed him yet.

He couldn't officially count the kill until the review team looked at the mission imagery, but he was sure he had fried that blonde bitch to a crisp. It gave him a warm feeling inside. He wondered what this one had done against the government. They never told him, but he imagined various terrorist plots and assassination attempts.

He whipped the drone out of its dive and climbed until he could fly above the mountain back to base. It would take him about 45 minutes to fly the drone back to base and land it. If he were lucky, he would immediately have another assignment and another drone at his command. Once, he got to fly five complete missions in his eight-hour shift. Most days it was one or two—but he could hope. He had another five hours to go on his shift.

And nothing. Not even a surveillance run. That sucked. Thirty minutes before his shift ended, his screen flashed a command for him to report to supervisory control. That didn't sound good at all, he thought. Usually, they just flashed congratulations for the confirmed kill across the screen.

He got up and ambled toward the door to supervisory control, nodding occasionally to another pilot when they were unoccupied enough to notice him. The room was wide and long. The dull roar of the heavy-duty air conditioning created a deafening background noise. He was used to that now, and it didn't bother him. However, after eight months as a drone pilot, he was still amazed at how many pilot stations there were in the room. He had estimated over 400 once, and a couple of times the stations had been completely occupied. Today, pilots filled only about 30% of the chairs. It must be a slow day.

He entered the supervisory control room. The Day Watch Supervisor Alan Melding looked up. He saw a tall, thin youngster wearing Bermuda shorts and a lightweight hoodie. Most of the pilots wore the hoodies because of the air conditioning, but very few wore shorts. The shorts made this kid stand out, as did his success record. In eight months, he had 103 confirmed kills.

That was why management had believed it was unnecessary to send a backup drone to eliminate the witness. This was the first time Jackson had missed a kill. Alan had warned them of the possibility, but they had cited budget constraints, and now he had to deal with the problem.

"Clayton, you had your first miss. The subject was not in the car when your missile struck it. The Image Review Team flagged this one because they couldn't see the driver as the car went off the road. We just got word from the Dirt Recon Team sent to investigate that the subject escaped into the mountains on foot."

Clayton looked somewhat shocked.

"Don't worry kid," Alan said. "Sometimes it happens even to the very best, like you. Why a while ago, we had a subject escape a sixty quad-copter-drone strike. We got his significant other, but he got away clean. Now that was really something. Apparently, the guy had an escape tunnel we knew nothing about."

"Sixty quad-copter-drones? Wow, I would have loved to have seen that."

"I will show you the film sometime. It is now mandated viewing for all drone operations management personnel."

"Man, that guy must be some kind of terrorist?"

"Yeah," the supervisor nodded, "that is our only long-term target miss to date. But, we will get him," he paused. "Don't worry about the target you missed today. That was just a collateral damage incident. We sent a ground hound after her. He will have her in no time. Those hounds are incredible. They have not missed yet.

"I don't even know what a hound is," Clayton said.

"Maybe it's better you don't know the details," Alan replied. "But, don't worry. With a record like yours you may well be management material in a few years. Then, you will have a higher clearance, and you will get to learn about a lot of things that most people could not even imagine."

Clayton smiled. "I am not sure I could give up piloting."

"Spoken like a true patriot," Alan said as he rose to shake the young pilot's hand.

Colorado

Peggy knew she had to keep moving. There had been no time to hide her tracks. Other than brushing them out with a branch, she had no idea how to do that anyway. She only knew what she had seen on TV and in movies. She also knew that Hollywood often sacrificed technical accuracy for profit and that meant that she didn't even know if what she had seen would work.

Limping a bit, Peggy alternately walked and jogged deep into the forest. She had torn the sleeve from her shirt and bound her left arm where it was badly scraped from hitting the gravel.

Peggy wasn't sure who would be after her, but after nearly being killed by a government drone, she was convinced that someone, or something, would. She no longer trusted the authorities. Her world had been turned upside down in less than an hour.

She had read occasional internet rumors about government drone strikes on home soil, but she just thought those were the ravings of conspiracy theorists and the lunatic fringe.

Her sense of safety was now completely gone. She realized that her previous feeling of security was just an illusion and always had been, but she missed it more deeply than she would have ever imagined possible.

Peggy pushed herself and kept moving ever deeper into the forest. She had watched a single episode of *Dual Survival* once with a boyfriend. That was her only introduction to the topic of survival in the woods. She knew from watching that episode that shelter was more important than food or water at first. The hippie-looking guy had made a point of that on the show. He seemed very convincing, so she decided she should stop moving a couple of hours before dark and either find shelter or pile up leaves and sticks to make a shelter like they had done on that show. They called it a debris hut, but it just looked like a pile of leaves and sticks to her.

She didn't know how to make fire, but she was hoping if she could find shelter out of the wind, she could survive the night without it. She knew the morning weather report at her father's house had said that the low tonight would be about 40 degrees. That meant high in the mountains, where she was now, the temperature might drop as low as 30 degrees. That wasn't very cold when you had warm clothes, but all she had on were the jeans and light flannel shirt she had been wearing. Even her jacket had gone down the mountainside with her car.

As she continually pushed deeper and higher into the mountainside forest, she lamented losing her suitcase. She would have loved to have any of the clothes in the suitcase now, fashion be damned.

The really scary part was that no one would be looking for her. She had been visiting her father and sister in the rural Colorado area where she and her sister had grown up and had been on her way home to Ohio, where she worked as a computer programmer, when she had encountered the drones. Her father and sister wouldn't expect to hear from her until late tomorrow at the earliest, and none of her family or friends would expect her to be deep in the forest high on a mountainside. There was no one at home waiting for her either. At the moment, she both felt good that no one would be worried and also regretted that same fact.

Peggy kept moving up the slope. She suspected that if she didn't use the full capacity of her brain and her physical ability, she would be dead before nightfall.

Chapter 3: REFUGE

"Illegitimate governments fear accurate and critical thinking above all else." John Debrouillard

Wyoming, near Ten Sleep

I was still groggy when I awoke. Toni had shown me to a bedroom. I fell asleep before I could even get my boots off. When I woke, my boots were on the floor beside me and I was covered with a blanket. I had no idea what time it was or how long I had slept, although I knew I had slept for a very long time. My leg hurt and so did my shoulder, as well as several muscles that I thought had no reason to.

It all seemed like a dream. I looked around at the bedroom filled with western-style furniture, so different from the Shaker-style furniture I had built for our bedroom at home, and realized it had not been a dream. Susan was dead. As that thought permeated my consciousness, I started to get mad at the people who took her from me. I remembered my promise to Susan, and I, who had never fired a gun at anyone in my life, vowed again that I would do my best to kill every one of them—no matter whom they turned out to be.

I bent, pulled my boots back on, and tied the laces. Then, I walked out of the bedroom door and down the hall.

"Good. You are awake," the young doctor smiled. He looked just as implausibly young as he did earlier.

"How long did I sleep?" I asked.

"Thirty-seven hours," he replied. "But, the sedative I gave you probably helped."

"I don't remember that," I said.

"I gave you a shot after you fell asleep."

"Doc, you are sneaky," I said.

"You don't know the half of it," he replied. "Sneaky is the new survival skill."

"Gee, I think evading drones is right up there."

"You bet," the Doc replied. "Some of us are getting good at that too."

"Doc, sometimes you speak too quickly. It is a bad habit," Toni said as she entered the living room. "Remember what George Washington said: 'Be courteous to all, but intimate with few, and let those few be well-tried before you give them your confidence.'"

"That is still good advice today," I mused. "I suspect if I had not posted adverse opinions to some of the recent government actions, my wife would still be alive."

"I think you may be right," Toni agreed. "However, I am afraid that our 'benevolent' oppressors will not stop with those that are simply a bit vocal about their opposition. I am afraid that the trend is soon going to be about discerning thought crimes and then eliminating potential opposition before they even know they are truly opposed."

"That sounds a lot like selective genocide," I said.

"It is," Doc said. "And I think is has already started on a small-scale."

I looked at Toni. "Don't you think you are trusting me too quickly with your opinions?" I asked.

"That would have been true before I had you checked out," Toni agreed. "While you were asleep, I had a complete background check run on you. I am not worried. In this case, posting your opinions online helped me decide."

"You should be worried if someone tracks that background check back to you."

"It can't happen," Doc said. "Don't worry about it."

"What happens next?" I asked.

<u>Reston, Virginia</u>

"Where is he? Why haven't you found this one? Are you incompetent?"

"Now Boss, just take it easy. We have five analysts searching through the entire national incoming data stream and three programmers working constantly to refine the search algorithms. The target has not used a cell phone or sent an email, nor do we detect him at any physical location. We tried to activate the transmitter on the RFID chip in his state driver's license, but he must have shielded it or buried it somewhere. We are back searching through all the data recorded by traffic cameras, store cameras, and others in a 30-mile radius as well. We will find him. No one can hide from us."

"It has been three days and nothing. That target just vanished from a house that was absolutely demolished by gunfire from our drones." The Boss, LaDonna Perkins, Manager of Target Information Acquisition for the Department of Interior Security, Drone Operations Division, settled herself deeper into her chair and glared at her subordinate. She was proud of her previously perfect record of target data acquisition for the quad-copter, assassin drone group and totally pissed off about the first target miss due because of data acquisition failure. She looked at her subordinate again. She saw a nerdy-looking man of about 40 who, at the moment, seemed nervous. "Did you know that the target had a basement and an escape tunnel that were not in the records?"

"No Ma'am, I didn't." Greg Rhodes shifted in his chair thinking that the pre-strike survey group had failed, not his group. Greg's group only did data search and target location. However, he knew better than to say anything to Ms. Perkins. Ms. Perkins had a notoriously bad temper and was not noted for logical responses when she was angered. Right now Ms. Perkins was angered.

"Well, OK then." Ms. Perkins seemed slightly mollified at Greg's deferential manner. "Listen. We need to find this guy ASAP. It is of critical national importance. Why, if word gets out among the domestic terrorists, our reputation may be damaged. Did you know that this guy even managed to shoot down a quad-copter-drone, with a shotgun, no less."

A flicker of worry that he might have chosen the wrong career flashed through Greg's mind. If the domestic terrorists could shoot down a drone, could they come after us? He vanquished the momentary worry from his mind and asked, "That has never happened before, has it?"

"No, it hasn't," Ms. Perkins said. "And I won't ever let it happen again. From now on, we will use four times as many analysts for target data acquisition, so we can be far more thorough."

"Won't that be expensive?" Greg asked. He knew the budget was big, but he also knew that Ms. Perkins was often after him to keep costs down and to do more with less.

"Of course it will be expensive. However, I feel that it is necessary and I have requested the additional funding for next year. Speaking of budget, I want you to put three more analysts on this—and make sure you have your very best analysts working on this."

"Yes Ma'am," Greg said, relieved that the conversation seemed to be ending. "Don't worry Ma'am. We will find him."

Wyoming, near Ten Sleep

"You know they will be after me," I said to Toni. "Isn't that a risk to you?"

"You have strong luck," Toni said.

"I don't think so," I replied, thinking of Susan.

"I understand," Toni said, "but hear me out. You are the first actual target they missed—don't laugh, but target is what the government calls you and everyone else it has assassinated here at home. Not only that, you brought down a drone and managed to disappear, and all that acting alone. The really lucky thing is that you came here."

"That was just chance," I pointed out. "I was tired and trying to find some gasoline away from the surveillance grid. All I knew was that most ranchers are fiercely independent folks who don't like government, or other, intrusions."

"There is truth in that," Doc said.

"Tell me what you know of government surveillance," Toni requested.

It seemed a reasonable request so I said. "I am no expert, but here is a summary of what I know, mostly from reading science reporting and alternative news sites on the internet. Our government monitors our cell phone calls, emails, and internet posts. I also understand that any purchases made with credit cards, debt cards, or store customer appreciation cards can be tracked by the feds. I also know that there is a network of digital cameras, especially in urban areas, which send data to software with facial recognition capability. I know that they can use satellite imagery to identify license plates on moving vehicles in some cases and that they have the technology to bounce signals off windows that allow them to hear what is being said inside a building."

"That's far more than most of the sheeple are aware of," Doc said. "But then, you are awake. Oh, by the way, the windows in this house are made of three-quarter-inch thick tempered glass with a soft, clear plastic center. They can't eavesdrop through those."

"Kind of like a cone of silence," I said. Toni smiled. "I am just barely awake, not nearly as much as I thought before. For example, I didn't know that our government was killing citizens with drones here at home, and I, for sure, didn't realize that people could be killed just for comments made on blog sites. I have never even espoused violence against the government, of any sort."

Toni smiled. "I have read all your online comments. I know that to be true. The government, the powers that be, does not fear violence from you. Your entire history shows you are not a violent man. What they fear is your ability to come to logical and accurate conclusions from relatively sparse sets of facts. You see right through their camouflage and tell people the government's real motives and predict their course of action all too well. You are very well known by your pseudonym throughout the awakened world. Your comments have caused more people to wake up than you know."

"Yeah," I said. "A handle of 'RetiredProf' is incredibly scary. I should have thought of that."

"The question we have is what do you want to do now?"

"Simple," I replied. "I want to kill everyone who was involved in any significant way in the murder of my wife."

"I think that goes all the way up to the president," Toni said.

"Then, if that is so, and I get the chance, that SOB is as dead as the drone operators."

"And you are not a violent man," Toni laughed. "Well, turn about is fair play and, in this case, would be admired by our Founding Fathers. Just how do you think you are going to do this?"

"I would very much like to do it face to face. However, the thought keeps running through my head that 'to live by the drone is to die by the drone'. As to precisely how, right now I have absolutely no idea."

Toni smiled, "Then let us help."

Looking at Doc, I asked. "Who are us anyway?"

"I think you will be surprised," Toni smiled. "I think you will be very surprised. You do need to know though, that we may need you as much, or more, than you need us."

Reston, Virginia

"We have him!" The data analyst jumped up from his chair and shouted at the top of his voice. "We have him!"

"Who?" The supervisor called from across the room.

"The target who took out the drone and got away."

"That's great!" The supervisor said, now looking over the analyst's shoulder as he sat down again in front of his computer screen. "Where?"

"Not too many miles out of Ten Sleep Wyoming."

"Geez, how in the hell did he get from mid-Indiana to Wyoming without us knowing? I didn't think it was possible that anyone could take out one of our drones, and I certainly didn't think it was possible for a target to move that far, that quickly, undetected."

"It's okay boss. We have him now!"

"How did you find him?"

"Sir, I had a hunch that he would take a local vehicle from somewhere in Indiana and move as quickly across the country as he could. Therefore, I searched through satellite imagery, using an algorithm that I wrote, to read the license plates of every vehicle on back roads in every state bordering Indiana. I located an old green pickup truck with an Indiana tag, as well as 23 other potential targets. I used my algorithm to track all of them. The 23 other potential targets were all tracked to various locations and the occupants confirmed not to be our target. The old green pickup truck showed up again in Oklahoma with a different tag number. One that was not registered to it."

"That green pickup truck was registered to a neighbor of the target's who lives about two miles away from him. Those neighbors are not now at home and have not reported the truck missing. We found them visiting relatives and interviewed them. They said they did not know the truck was missing. The man became distraught when we told him that his truck had been stolen. We don't think they had anything to do with the target's escape."

"Using the satellite data, I followed the truck's path through old data until the driver stopped to get gas. Although the target was attempting to mask his identity by wearing a hat and carefully staying undercover, we got one photo that allowed me to tentatively identify the target by general build."

"I continued following the truck via old satellite images. It pulled into a ranch not too far from Ten Sleep, Wyoming. The truck left there soon after and headed toward Boise, Idaho; however, the driver was not our target. Therefore, since no other vehicles have left the ranch, our target must be still on the ranch. I have had constant satellite surveillance on the ranch. We are attempting to bounce signals off the windows and decipher what is being said inside the house."

"Great work! Send me the location data and I will set up the strike."

Washington, D.C.

"Yes Mr. President," the secretary of the Department of Interior Security said. "We have ten mini-predator drones in the air and on the way for the strike. They will be there within the hour."

"Good. Kill that son of a bitch and everybody in the house," the president said. "Let me know when they are dead. There better not be any mix-ups this time. Oh, and send me the film as usual."

Wyoming, near Ten Sleep

An alarm sounded from another room. Toni and Doc looked up quickly and immediately got to their feet. Toni looked at me and said, "It's time to go. Let's get moving."

I got up and followed them to the garage. Doc picked up my bug out bag and my firearms on the way and handed them to me. There was a tricked-out GMC pickup in the garage. It had a full-length bed and a crew cab. The bed had a tonneau cover. The wheels were oversized, and I suspected the engine was as well. Doc got into the driver's seat. That surprised me. For some reason, I had figured Toni would do the driving.

Doc fired up the truck as I got into the back seat and we roared out of the garage almost before the door was completely open. The rough ranch road that I had driven, at best, at 20 mph, Doc took at over 80 mph. I was afraid for my life.

When Doc turned onto the paved road he floored it and I noticed that the speedometer rose to 140 mph. Doc drove at that speed nonchalantly. That scared me bad enough. Then I realized the speedometer went to 180 mph. I glanced at Toni. She did not seem the least bit worried.

We had been driving for about 50 minutes when I saw the drone. I pointed it out to Toni, but she did not seem overly concerned. "That looks like a predator drone," I said. Toni turned leaned back into the back seat area and glanced out the window.

"I don't think I can shoot these down with this rifle," I said.

Toni laughed. "I agree with you. Don't worry, we have another way. It's a way that we have not had to use yet, but it was well worth the investment."

"Only if it works," Doc said.

"I assume you have tested it somehow?" I asked.

"It's not as if we have had our hands on mini-predator drones to test it on," Toni said. "I am reasonably sure it will work. At least it should."

"That is reassuring. Just who are you people?" I asked.

Doc said, "Sometimes we are not too sure ourselves."

"I have to admit, I have never met a doctor before who doubles as a race car driver."

Doc laughed. "Just a hobby."

DIS Drone Base No. 3, Oklahoma

The supervisor stood behind the mini-predator drone operators. He watched each screen in turn. For 52 minutes, he anticipated the appearance of the pickup truck that satellite data had shown leaving the ranch. He was beginning to sweat. His superiors wanted this target gone so badly that another five predator drones were on the way to destroy the ranch house, just in case. However, those drones were another supervisor's responsibility. That relieved him, because he could now focus all his attention on removing the target and any other occupants in the truck.

He had heard that this target destroyed one of the quad-copter assassin drones with nothing but a shotgun. He had not known that was possible. Neither had the design engineers, several of which had already been demoted or fired over that incident. The quad-copter assassin drones were now being redesigned to resist shotgun blasts but it would be quite some time before the new models could be put in the field.

He didn't think it was possible that anyone could take a mini-predator drone out, despite the fact that Iran had managed to hack and capture a military predator drone a few years ago. However, there was the case just a few hours ago where a target had escaped a predator drone strike. That was a first as well. Things just seemed to be going wrong lately, and he didn't like it. He didn't like it at all.

Then, the pickup truck appeared in the screen. He watched carefully as five of the drones acquired the target and, on his command, all fired at once.

Chapter 4: GROUND HOUND

"Nothing is as easy as it seems." John Debrouillard

<u>Colorado, The Front Range</u>

He hitched his small assault pack higher on his back and shifted his rifle to his left hand while he searched for tracks. When he found the partial imprint of a small running shoe, he knelt and sniffed making sure his shoulder cam had a clear view. The scent came clearly to his droid-enhanced nose. It reminded him of slightly sweet, stale sweat with a hint of petunias. The slightly sweet smell was fear. He knew that scent and its variations very well. So far, every one of his targets had given off some form of that scent. The smell of petunias was from the perfume she wore. That scent would stay on her and be detectable by his enhanced nose for weeks.

He almost laughed out loud when he saw the tracks. There had been no attempt to cover them. He was dealing with an amateur—but then, they all were. Just once, he would like the challenge of targeting a well-trained adversary. So far, he had not encountered one. He stood, sniffed the breeze, and started off after his target with steps as light and easy as a professional dancer.

He was a tall wiry fellow with closely cropped black hair. A large scar ran almost the entire length of his right forearm. He glanced at the scar and thought, as he often did, that the injury, which at the time he thought might get him booted out of military service, was in fact, his greatest blessing. He remembered.

He had been on patrol along highway A1 out of Kandahar near the old British fort at Malwand when an IED flipped the Humvee. A big piece of shrapnel sliced his right forearm open to the bone. They medevac'd him and two others back to Kandahar. The other two died and he was sent stateside; he couldn't even remember their names. He knew that military teams were supposed to be tight and loyal to one another, but he didn't like any of the guys on his team. He was glad that two of them had died.

He was lying in the hospital bed. His arm hurt. They had him doped to the gills with painkillers. Still, the pain was almost unbearable, yet he was alert. The man in the dark suit was surprised to see that.

"How are you feeling, Corporal?" the man asked.

"Passable," Greg replied. His military training and natural distrust kept him cautious and wary. In his experience, both in and out of the military, no one who wore a suit was to be trusted.

The man opened a folder and glanced inside. "Corporal, how would you like the opportunity of a lifetime?"

His curiosity aroused, he said, "Huh?"

"You have no living relatives, and you scored exactly as we need on your personality test."

Greg looked quizzically at the man in the suit. "But they nearly didn't let me in the service," he said. "They said that I was almost a psycho."

"They were wrong. You are a total psychopath," the man in the suit smiled. "And that is exactly what we need."

Once he was told about the opportunity and he had accepted their offer, they modified him. The process took over a year. They implanted sensors in his nose and wired them directly to his brain. The sensors increased his ability to detect scents almost on par with that of a bloodhound. He took to that so quickly and so well that they told him he must have been a dog in a previous life.

In his left eye, the doctors implanted an infrared sensor that allowed him to detect body heat. That one was difficult to learn to use and it left him with an ever so slight blind spot on his left side. Of course, he didn't tell them about that because he feared they wouldn't let him stay in the program.

In his right eye, the doctors implanted an automatic device that gave him artificial night vision. As the light outside dimmed, the device kicked in and it was never dark for him. That did negatively impact his three-dimensional vision at night because he had to close his left eye when he used the night vision and his right eye when he used the thermal vision. The tiny batteries for those devices were implanted in his neck. Each was good for a year or more before he needed simple outpatient surgery to replace them.

And then, when he recovered, there came one year of training in tracking. He liked that. But, what he really liked was the killing. They gave him six weeks of training in how to do the killing. Both he and they knew that the killing was the real reason he had agreed in the first place.

Now, he was a Federal Ground Hound Striker. He was no longer in the Rangers. In fact, he was no longer in the military at all. The odd thing was that he didn't mind a bit.

Peggy paused to catch her breath. She was about half a mile up slope from where her car went down the mountain. She was in real trouble, and she knew it. This was the worst scrape she had ever been in. She was pretty sure that if someone would spend tens of thousands of dollars, or more, to try to kill her with a drone, they would spend even more money to make sure the job got done, even though she was only a single insignificant witness to a domestic drone strike. She had no idea who had been in the red car. She told herself she was willing to keep quiet about it, but it didn't seem as if she would be given that opportunity.

Logically, there must be someone or something else coming after her soon. She didn't think drones would be good at finding her on the wooded mountain slopes, but she wasn't sure. Her knowledge of drone and remote sensing technology was limited. She also thought it was possible, maybe even most likely, that they might send human trackers after her. As far as she knew there were no robots with an adequate operational range to follow her up the mountain.

When it occurred to her that they might send humans, she at first thought she might be able to reason with them. After a bit of thought, she knew that was extremely unlikely. She wasn't sure how much time she had, but she knew she had to run. Not only run, but also disappear. She didn't think she knew how to do that, but she was determined to try.

It seemed odd to her that a quote from Robert Heinlein, the science fiction writer, flashed into her mind so clearly that she could see the words on the page:

"At least once every human should have to run for his life, to teach him that milk does not come from supermarkets, that safety does not come from policemen, that 'news' is not something that happens to other people. He might learn how his ancestors lived and how he himself is no different— in the crunch his life depends on his agility, alertness, and personal resourcefulness."

Having a vision that clear was unusual for her, but she was stressed, and she guessed it was not too surprising that stress brings out strange things in people sometimes. She thought about the words that flashed so clearly before her mind's eye. She was someone who had always bought milk and groceries from the store with little thought as to their origin. She had also believed that policemen were there to protect her and other citizens. And now the government—for who else could spend the kind of money that those predator drones cost—was trying to kill her. She didn't think the local police would lift a hand to protect her from that.

At this point her life depended only on her own resourcefulness, alertness, and agility. She was truly on her own for the first time in her life. She wanted to panic, but she gritted her teeth and kept moving, trying to think about the tidbits she had heard, seen, or read about tracking and wilderness survival. Like most people, she found most of her information came from old TV shows she had watched. Now, she was thankful that her dad had liked the old western reruns so much. She just hoped the writers of those old shows knew what they wrote about.

She also realized for the first time in her life that knowledge was really hers only when it was available in her own brain. At the moment, she had no books, no internet, and no one to call. She wished she had paid more attention in school and memorized more useful knowledge instead of just letting it wash out of her head while thinking that if she ever needed the information, she could just look it up in a book or on the internet. She also realized for the first time that knowledge alone wasn't enough. Skills had to be practiced to be there quickly when badly needed.

Peggy pushed ahead, moving more carefully now while she formulated a series of possible plans. Her dad had been a soldier in Vietnam, a Marine she thought, although he very seldom talked about it. She did remember him once saying that no battle plan ever went off exactly as planned. That spurred her to think through as many options as she could come up with. Her mind was now working faster and more clearly than she ever remembered being capable of. She hoped she would be resourceful enough—and lucky enough to survive. Another thing her dad once said was that luck plays a role in any endeavor, although the goal is always to minimize the need for it.

The Hound strode along at a slow but steady pace. He knew this target would not likely be a challenge, but he enjoyed being outdoors and, most of all, prolonging the anticipation of a kill. He smiled to himself. This one he might even do things to. That was allowed only when there was no chance of discovery. He thought this time would qualify since the location was so remote. It had been quite a while since he last had that opportunity. Such a sweet young girl she had been, and so scared. He could still remember the strong sweet smell of fear that was so uniquely hers. The experience was still fresh in his mind, and he enjoyed reliving it as he stalked yet another target.

This target was obviously inexperienced. She had made no effort to hide her tracks, and the waffle-sole of her fashionable running shoes made clear prints in the dirt of the trail where it wasn't covered with the forest litter of pine needles and leaves. Where the trail was covered, the scuffmarks allowed him to read her movements like he was reading a book, and one with large print, no less.

He strode onward but still more slowly than usual. He calculated his target was about two hours ahead of him. He could close that gap in about an hour and a half if he picked up the pace just moderately, but he savored the game and the anticipation.

He was in the best condition of his life and could run for hours at a time, even in rough terrain, without becoming winded. He often wondered if the regimen of pills and injections that they had him on had anything to do with that? Of course, he didn't care. He loved what he was doing so much that they could do anything they wanted to him as long as he could kill, and sometimes rape, and torture his targets. He smiled. There was nothing he would rather be doing.

Peggy considered her situation as she walked deeper into the woods. If they sent a tracker, they might use dogs. Somehow then, she must mask her scent and leave no tracks. The problem was that she had no idea how to do either. She did, however, remember one thing that her father had told her. He said that when she didn't know how to do something to just use her brain to figure it out. She thought her only chance of survival now was to be smarter than her pursuers. She knew she was fairly smart from her time in school, but she had never been tested like this. She wasn't sure she would, or even could, succeed, but she was determined to try.

Now, she was getting mad. She was rapidly getting over the shock and the un-realness of it all, and she was getting madder by the moment. For the first time in her life, she was mad at the people who made up the government. For the first time in her life, she also feared her government. Another quote popped into her mind, and she wondered where she had seen this one before.

"People who relieve others of their money with guns are called robbers. It does not alter the immorality of the act when the income transfer is carried out by the government." Cal Thomas

Now, she understood that every monetary payment by citizens to the government was backed up by the threat of a government gun, and so, increasingly, was infraction of even minor laws punished the same way. She was not sure that was what the Founding Fathers had in mind. In fact, she was pretty sure it was exactly this they were fighting against during the revolution against English rule.

Well, if the Founding Fathers could fight, then she could too. The government had already destroyed her life just because they were crooked, but she could not let them win easily. She knew her father would understand, but she wasn't sure about the rest of her family.

Now to the practical, she thought. How to hide her tracks? She knew that walking in a stream was often used to hide tracks in the western movies she had watched, so it followed that she needed to find a stream. She turned and walked diagonally downslope from the ridge she had been climbing toward the small valley to her right because she knew that streams were almost always in valleys. She was thinking about how to hide her smell as she walked.

Logically, smell was just the detection of molecules emanating from her skin, from her perfume, etc. which were left behind her in the air. She decided she must stop as many of these molecules as possible from leaving her person. That would be difficult because the shirt and jeans she wore were porous enough for molecules to easily escape. She needed to cover herself in something that had a very low permeability. She remembered from a geology course she was required to take in college that wet clay was smear-able and had a very low permeability. If she could smear clay on thickly enough, it might just work. She started looking for clay as she walked toward the small stream in the incipient mountain valley below.

She reached the stream and noticed that dusk would be on her in an hour or so. The water was moving quickly, but was not very deep, nor was the stream very wide, only six feet across at its widest point.

She strode into the stream without hesitation and began walking downstream because the wind was blowing more in that direction and she figured it would be harder for any bloodhounds to follow her. After a while, she found some grayish clay in the stream bank. She didn't know what type of clay it was, but she knew it was clay. It would have to do.

The Hound picked up his pace. It would be nice to catch this target just before dark. Then, he could set up camp and have his way with her all night before dispatching her in the early daylight. He knew how to drag things out and enjoy the fear the targets always had. He had done it before. The memories were good; the memories were really good. He had to be careful that they didn't distract him from following the trail.

The trail showed she had turned toward the small stream in the valley below. "All the better," he smiled to himself. That would make it easier for him. They always thought that taking to water would lose him, but it never did. His enhanced nose took care of that. Her trail was easy to follow, and he made good time as he approached the stream.

He had been on the trail for more than four hours when he lost it. He stopped and sniffed. The faint odor of perfume was gone, as was the sweet scent of fear. He had lost the target's scent. That had never happened to him before. He would have to track conventionally. He closed his left eye because it was beginning to get dark, and he wanted clear vision. He kept moving. In a few yards, he came to the stream. The water was shallow, and he could see a single mark that indicated she had gone downstream. He stepped into the stream. Now, he got a whiff of his target again, and he relaxed. She was just ahead.

In a few minutes, the smell became stronger, and the water grew deeper. Soon, he could see her on the left bank. She was sitting with her back to him, all hunched over. It looked like she had gotten herself soaking wet and very muddy. The water was cloudy, probably from her falling in the stream, he told himself. He slowed his pace and moved quietly toward her anticipating the fun he would have. He left his rifle slung across his back, his pistol in its holster, and extended his hands. They were all he would need for this one.

He was within two paces of her when a muddy, gray apparition rose up out of the water to his left and swung a rock at his head. He felt the impact and all went black.

When Peggy found the clay, the plan came to her. She took off her clothes, filled them with leaves, sticks, and mud, and placed them so that to anyone coming down the stream it would appear as if she was just sitting dejectedly.

Despite the cold, for it was about 40 degrees, she stood naked except for her shoes and smeared the clay as thickly as she could over all of her body. It was difficult to smear it into and thickly over her hair and over her face and head, but she knew it was necessary. The process left the stream quite muddy. She found a softball-sized rock that she could grip well with both hands and sat down in the water against the stream bank. She dug out a section of the bank so her head and shoulders fit perfectly into the depression, and then smeared clay all over her face and the edges of the hole for her head and shoulders. When she was done, she didn't think anything was detectable except her eyes. She had even been careful to smear a thin layer of clay over her eyelids.

She had been sitting in position holding the rock under the water for almost 30 minutes, fighting harder than she could ever remember just to keep from shivering, when she heard him. She closed her eyes and waited, listening with the one ear not filled with clay. When he was close, she opened one eye and saw that his attention was focused on the dummy she had made. His hands were stretched out toward the dummy as she rose from the water and, using all her strength, smacked him in the forehead with the rock. He went down against the bank, but she kept pounding the rock into his skull until she was positive he was dead. She was surprised there wasn't a dog with the man. She knew by the uniform that this was a government man sent to kill her.

She threw up. The spasms racked her until she thought her ribs would break. It took her about 15 minutes to recover enough to stand. Shivering, and chilled to the bone, she washed herself off in the stream as best she could. Then, she emptied her clothes of the mud, sticks, and leaves, and washed them out in the stream. After wringing her clothes out, she put them on and began rubbing herself all over to get warm. Her mind was just as numb as her body.

She thought about taking his pack and rifle, but she figured the government might have tracking devices somewhere in his stuff. Besides, she didn't know how to use a gun. When it occurred to her that others might come after her too, she decided it was time to leave. She started wading downstream in the creek figuring that walking in the water might delay any other trackers who might be after her. She knew she had to get somewhere warm as quickly as possible and she knew she needed fire, but she had no way to make one.

After careful consideration, she decided it was worth it to go back the few steps necessary and see whether the tracker she had killed had any matches in his pack. She thought that it was remotely possible that something like an RFID chip might be installed in the matches, or the matchbox, but she calculated it was well worth the risk. Without fire, she believed she would die before morning.

With effort, she turned the dead tracker over and opened his backpack. She got the dry heaves and had to wait a few minutes until they passed. After rummaging around in the backpack, she found a cheap plastic cigarette lighter. She quickly pushed it into her pocket and started back down stream. She thought about taking the knife from his side, but she was afraid that it might be chipped.

After about an hour and a half of walking, always in the stream and mostly by moonlight, she noticed a deep hollow in the rocks above the stream. She was freezing and shivering almost non-stop. She felt almost sick. Therefore, she decided she would stop in that hollow and build a fire for the night. She just hoped that she could get a fire started.

She remembered from the one episode of *Dual Survival* that she had watched on TV that she needed a bundle of dry, fine plant material to start the fire. It was mid-summer, and she didn't see any dead grass in the vicinity. She remembered that one of the actors on the show had mentioned using dry bark to start a fire. She looked around and found a dead tree where the bark looked dry. She peeled some off and put it in her still damp pocket all wadded into a ball so the center would stay dry. At least she hoped it would. Then, she looked around for a rock that she might be able to break and produce a sharp edge that she could use to shred the bark.

Sometimes she thought the only thing she had ever learned in geology lab was how to break a rock. The instructor was always asking them to knock a piece from this rock, or that rock. In the process, she had learned which rocks broke with sharp edges. When she found the one she wanted, she also picked up a larger rock to break it with. She did not remember the names of either of the rocks she picked up, she just knew that one of them would produce a sharp edge.

After climbing the slope to the hollow, and collecting some firewood along the way, she snuggled into the back of the hollow as far out of the wind she could get. She then, after several tries, knocked a sharp chip from the smaller rock and shredded the bark from her pocket with the flake. Carefully copying the way she'd seen the guys on *Dual Survival* do it, she lit the nest of shredded bark that she had made with the lighter and blew on it. It caught quickly and burned well. She was surprised. She had a small fire going in a few minutes. She waited patiently until she could add some larger pieces of wood to the fire.

She knew a relatively big fire would be detectable for quite some distance if it could be seen, but she needed one for warmth. She built the fire as far back into the hollow as she could and still leave room for her to be between the fire and the rock wall. She also, just as she remembered the guys on *Dual Survival* talking about, stacked some larger rocks on the side of the fire away from her to reflect more heat from the fire in her direction. In about 20 minutes she had a pretty good pile, one high enough to hide most of the fire from anyone who might be walking along the stream.

In about an hour, she was warm and cried herself to sleep. She woke once in the night and thought she heard a helicopter off in the distance. When the sound quit, she put some more wood on the fire and fell back asleep, exhausted.

Washington, D.C.

"With a rock. Just a fucking rock?" The president paused and turned in his chair for effect. "You have to be fucking kidding me! You mean to tell me that a 36-year-old computer programmer who has never even been on a camping trip in her life and, to our knowledge has never even fired a gun, managed to take out our top ground hound striker with nothing but a fucking rock?"

"Yes Mr. President," the man in the carefully tailored suit replied.

"So tell me just how much did we spend on this ground hound?"

"Mr. President, Sir, I believe it was in the neighborhood of 32 million dollars."

"Let me be sure that I understand this. An unarmed, 5'4", 115 pound woman with no hunting, fishing, shooting, martial arts, police, or military experience took out our armed, bio-enhanced, 6'5", 200 pound, military-trained, psychopathic killer ground hound?"

"Yes Mr. President, Sir. That is correct."

"So what are you going to do about this?"

"Mr. President, we have three more hounds on the ground and they should eliminate the target by noon today. She is in a very remote area. There will be no witnesses."

"For your sake, it needs to happen just as you say it will. You are excused." The president gritted his teeth as the secretary of the Department of Interior Security quickly left the oval office.

Chapter 5: DRONES DOWN

"Determination to win is more important than having the right weapon." John Debrouillard

<u>Wyoming</u>

I saw the flashes as the drones fired. Toni saw them the same time I did. She was holding a small black box in her hands and quickly pushed a button on the box. I heard a small explosion in the very back of the truck. As I watched, it blew through the truck bed cover and a huge cloud of glitter flew hundreds of feet into the air behind us.

One by one, the missiles detonated in the air, distracted by the chaff thrown up out of the back of the truck.

Doc cheered, and drove faster. "Hey, Jonas' stuff worked!"

"What if they send more missiles?" I asked.

"We mounted five of those babies in the truck bed. We have four left," Toni replied. "I hope that will be enough because that's all we had room for."

Doc said, "Since no one has used this tactic before, at least the best of our knowledge, I doubt that they will be able to mount more than one more missile attack before we can go to ground."

"What are you going to do? Drive this truck into a rabbit hole?" I asked.

"You might say that," Doc laughed.

"I hope those guys haven't figured out exactly what happened. If they have, they can simply fire off one missile at a time, and when the chaff shots are gone, so will we be," Toni said.

We traveled about 15 miles before I saw five more drones approaching from the rear. Toni was watching forward and left. I was watching rear and right. We weren't sure which direction the attack might come from. "More drones approaching from the rear; five of them," I told Toni.

"Oh, shit!" Doc said.

"I echo that," I said.

Toni said, "Me too."

I saw a flash as one of the drones fired. "Here comes another one," I said.

Toni waited until the missile was closer this time before touching off another round of chaff. Like the others, the missile exploded in the air. I watched as another drone moved slightly ahead of the others and fired its missile just as the previous drone turned away. Toni sent another round of chaff skyward and that missile exploded as well.

"Three missiles were now pointed at us and who had only two chaff shots left. Do you think we can make it to the rabbit hole before we get roasted, as our new friend so perceptively suggested?" Toni asked.

"I don't think so," Doc replied grimly. I noticed the speedometer was pegged at 180 mph and Doc was fiercely concentrating on his driving. I was past scared.

DIS Drone Base No. 3, Oklahoma

The supervisor watched as the five missiles fired simultaneously. He felt gratified that the escaped terrorist and his accomplices would soon be dead. He was as surprised as everyone else in the room when the chaff erupted into the air from the back of the truck. He watched in disbelief as the missiles, one after another, exploded harmlessly in the air. Those missiles were supposed to be chaff-proof. He saw what happened, but he still didn't believe it. This group of terrorists had some incredible technical capabilities.

Quickly he called for five more drones. He didn't see how these terrorists would have any more of that 'magic chaff', but just to be sure, he only called for a single missile launch when the next five drones were in place. The result was the same as before. Once the missile came close, something exploded in the back of the truck and threw a glittering cloud into the air. Again, the missile blew up harmlessly in the air. "Damn," he thought. "How much of that stuff was in the bed of that truck, anyway?" He immediately got his boss on the phone to request more drones.

Wyoming, Approaching the Rabbit Hole

"Here comes another one," I said, still looking out of the back window. Toni waited until what seemed like the last possible second and then sent a cloud of glittering chaff into the air. The missile exploded so close to us that the explosion rocked the truck and Doc nearly lost control.

"Watch it," he said. "That was too close."

"And here comes another one," I said.

This time Toni sent the chaff into the air a little sooner and, even though we felt the explosion, it wasn't as bad. "That was the last chaff shot," Toni said. "And there is one more drone following us."

"I am sorry I dragged you guys into this," I said.

Toni turned her head and looked at me. "We were in this before you ever came along. It's not your fault, if that makes you feel any better?"

"Well, it might if we survive this," I smiled. Doc was silent and totally focused on his driving.

"The government doesn't give up easily," I said. "Well, neither do I." Even though I figured I was about to die, I was just now starting to get mad. I picked up the Ranch Rifle and turned in the rear seat. Using the butt of the rifle, I smashed the rear window. Reversing the gun I aimed at the last drone.

"You must be one hell of a shot with that little rifle?" Toni said.

"Not really," I replied. "But then, I might just get lucky." I aimed carefully, or at least as carefully as I could, considering the bouncing of the truck, and fired off one round. There was no effect. I figured I missed.

Doc was pushing the truck as fast as it would go. "I hope they hold off a bit," he said. "I think I know a shortcut. Aim at the missile," Doc said.

I did as Doc suggested and aimed at the red nose cone on the missile. As best I could tell the missiles were about four inches in diameter. That meant I was trying to hit a four-inch diameter bull's-eye at over four hundred yards from a truck going about 180 miles an hour down a paved road. That was an impossible shot. But then, I was getting pretty mad and impossible just seemed difficult right now.

I estimated the ballistics of the .223 round, the distance and angle to the drone, and fired another round. This time I hit the drone.

"Wow!" Toni said. "That is incredible shooting."

I fired again. This time I missed. "Doc, slow down a bit if you can."

"You bet." Doc slowed down to about 80 miles an hour. The drone slowed as well and maintained position behind us.

I re-estimated my shot and then relaxed and let my subconscious takeover. This time when I fired the drone exploded.

"Way to go!" Doc shouted.

Toni's mouth fell open. It took her a few seconds to regain her composure. "I think that must be the finest shooting I have ever seen!"

"Let's get the hell out of here," Doc said.

We drove, again at 180 miles an hour, for another 20 minutes. There were no drones following us now, and I think we all relaxed a bit. Doc slowed down as we approached a curve and, without signaling, turned right onto a dirt road on two wheels. The road was rugged and rough but Doc still drove over 80 miles an hour.

"How long before they pick us up again with drones?" I asked.

"I estimate about 30 minutes," Toni replied.

"Is that enough time?" I asked.

"It should be," Doc said.

After about ten miles, Doc turned onto another dirt road and drove another mile. Then, he turned onto an even rougher road that was not much more than a track. By now he was only driving 15 or 20 miles an hour and was in four-wheel-drive. The track led to a mine opening in the side of the mountain. Doc drove the truck into the opening with no hesitation. He pulled the truck about 100 feet into the old mine and stopped.

DIS Drone Base No. 3, Oklahoma

The supervisor watched the operator's screens as another missile fired from a drone. Again, the glittery cloud exploded from the back of the pickup truck, and the missile exploded prematurely. "Damn! Who are these people?" He shouted. The drone operators in front of him were startled and some even looked up.

"Fire another one," he said, tapping another operator on the shoulder. The drone operator complied. Another missile was launched. Again, a glittering cloud of chaff exploded from the back of a pickup truck, and the missile exploded in the air without damaging the target.

The supervisor kept his cool, although later he wondered how he did, and said, "Don't fire the last missile yet. Let's keep eyes on the target, and wait until we have reinforcements. I have another five drones authorized. Their operators will be here any minute. Then we will blow those terrorists to vapor. The drones who have fired their missiles are also returning to base as quickly as possible to be reloaded and will be back on target, if needed, as soon as they are capable."

"Sir, I think they're shooting at my drone?" The operator with the last live missile said.

"With what?" The supervisor asked.

"A rifle, I think, Sir?"

"Nobody could hit anything with a rifle out of a moving truck at that distance," the supervisor calmly stated. Just then, the drone exploded. Everybody in the room was speechless as they stared at the main screen after it went blank.

"We need eyes on the target!" The supervisor shouted. "Turn the last four drones around and reacquire the target."

"But Sir, those drones don't have any missiles," one of the operators said.

"We need eyes on the target until we can get more armed drones to the target. Do it now. Do it now!"

The Rabbit Hole

We got out of the truck, grabbed our gear, and headed deeper into the mine. Doc led the way with a powerful flashlight. We walked about 200 feet before Doc led us into a side tunnel. After a while, Doc turned into another side tunnel. Eventually, I lost count of the turns we made. We had been walking for about 35 minutes when I begin to see daylight ahead.

"We're almost there folks," Doc said.

Doc strode out of the tunnel opening with no hesitation. Toni also showed no concern. I followed, wary as usual, carrying the Ranch Rifle for comfort, if nothing else. We walked along a game trail for about a mile. The trail was well hidden under the trees. Of that I was glad. That meant that if they were going to track us, they would have to use a thermal imaging satellite, rather than one that just carried a camera. I remembered reading that the government did not have full coverage with the thermal imaging satellites yet. In fact, I thought they had said that it would be another year or two before they did? Of course, they might get lucky as I had with the shot at the drone, but I hoped not.

Doc stopped. "Here we are," he said.

"Where is here?" I asked.

"In the middle of nowhere, it appears," Toni smiled.

Doc began bending some small pine trees over so that Toni and I could see the vehicle that was completely concealed by the small trees and a camouflage tarp. The trees were green, and had been planted around the vehicle. Doc said, "We put the car here about five years ago, just in case."

"And you think it will still start?" I asked.

"It should," Doc said. "There's a small solar panel set up to maintain the battery and our people have changed the fuel in the tank every six months and performed maintenance."

"I repeat, just who the hell are you people?" I asked.

"It pays to be prepared," Doc grinned. Doc pushed his way through the small trees, took a key hanging on a chain from his neck and opened the car's trunk. I gathered that one key would open the trunks of many, if not all, of the vehicles that these people had scattered around. Doc took a couple small bow saws from the trunk and handed one to me. "Let's cut some trees out of the way so we can get on the road."

It took us about 15 minutes to saw the small pine trees off at the ground, and drag them out of the way. We climbed into the vehicle, a 5-year-old Chevrolet sedan, and Doc turned the key. The engine roared to life and Doc wasted no time in getting us out of there. I didn't see any sign of a road but Doc drove anyway, weaving his way between trees and over terrain where most people would need a four-wheel drive. After about a mile, Doc turned onto a dirt road and before too long we were on a paved back road heading sedately for somewhere else.

"Where are we headed?" I asked.

Toni turned and looked at me from the front seat. "Somewhere as far away from drones as is possible," she laughed.

Chapter 6: SANCTUARY

"Luck comes only to those who never quit." John Debrouillard

Conference Room, The White House

Men and women in suits, ties, and various appropriate attire trickled into the conference room. One by one, they chose their seats. Some nodded to one another while others were quietly focused inward. The mood was somber. No one spoke. After all had taken their seats they waited silently for almost 20 minutes. Then, a very large Secret Service agent stepped into the room and said, "Please rise. The president is here."

The president entered the room. It was easy to tell that he was agitated. He strode to the head of the table and majestically paused. He was a tall, fit man with a momentarily stern visage. Looking one by one at the members of his entire cabinet, he said, "Just what is going on? First, a 5'4" untrained and unarmed woman takes out one of our best ground hounds, and with no assistance whatsoever. That in of itself is absolutely incredible. What is worse, she is still at large!"

"Also, we have a man, also untrained—never having served in the military—who managed to take out a quad-copter assassin drone with a shotgun. What's more, this guy escaped the following 60 quad-copter assassin drone attack through a tunnel dug from a basement that we didn't even know existed."

"Now, for the really bad part. When we found him, way out in Wyoming, which I'm here to tell you is a long way from Indiana, he managed to hook up with a hard-core resistance cell. Our intelligence indicates that he should not have even been aware of the existence of this particular cell, yet he managed to avoid detection and go directly there. And, if I am to believe what I was just told, the resistance in that cell is now using chaff to destroy the chaff-proof missiles used in our domestic predator drone strikes. They took out nine missiles using chaff shot into the air from crude mortars in the bed of a pickup truck. And we should've had them," the president paused for effect. "We should have had them. We had ten mini-predator drones on this mission, and we think they were out of chaff after missile number nine. We should have had them. And then, this untrained civilian shot one of the drones down from a moving vehicle—with a fucking rifle, no less. And now we have been looking for them for almost 30 hours now. They vanished. No trace. How is that even possible?"

The secretary of Defense, a short, plump, effeminate, and graying man, spoke. "But Mr. President, Sir, my technical advisors tell me that is impossible for someone to shoot a drone down with a rifle, except perhaps for the most highly trained of marksman. Is this man a trained marksman?"

The president looked at a man in the room that most of his advisors did not know. "Ladies and gentlemen, I want to introduce Mr. Saperstein. He is the new White House intelligence liaison to our domestic intelligence gathering effort that spans many different agencies. Mr. Saperstein, will you answer the question?"

"Yes Sir, Mr. President!" Saperstein was medium-height and tending towards portly. He also wore thick glasses and exhibited a studied look of nerdy elegance. "Ladies and gentlemen, to summarize the data we have on this target, I present the following: This target was slated for removal for influential comment posts on various antigovernment internet blogs. As far as we know, he never advocated or took overt action, or for that matter covert action, against the government. However, his views are decidedly anti-government, as well as specifically against this administration. Our analysis showed his ability to predict our plans in his posts was extremely high. I mean this guy was right on the mark so often it was plain scary. Therefore, either he was lucky, had access to a well-connected whistle blower, or was well connected to the resistance. If indeed he was connected to the resistance, or a whistle blower, we could find absolutely no evidence of that connection."

"If I may interrupt?" The secretary of Defense requested. "Is it possible that this target was just an unusually discerning, regular, everyday citizen with an anti-government bent?"

"Sir, our analysts do not believe that is a statistical possibility," Saperstein answered.

Saperstein continued. "The target never served in the military or in law enforcement. He has never been a member of a militia, a shooting club, or even had a hunting license."

"We do not know how he obtained his shooting skills and there is no evidence that he has extensive practice with firearms. Therefore, we must consider the possibility that the weapons he used were somehow enhanced over typically available civilian models."

"We recovered the shotgun he used to shoot down the quad-copter assassin drone. As best we can tell, it is a standard Remington model 870 12-gauge shotgun of the kind used by hunters. There do not seem to be any modifications. Other than the fact that it has a relatively long barrel, it is a very typical shotgun."

"However, we have not recovered the rifle he used, nor do we have any record of him purchasing a rifle. In fact, the only guns we have a record of him purchasing are a .38 caliber revolver and the shotgun. We also recovered the .38 caliber revolver, the shotgun, as well as several other unrecorded firearms from his residence, or, I should say, what remained of his residence."

"We have analyzed the imagery from the drone strike, and we believe the rifle he used to shoot down the drone was a Ruger Mini 14 or Ranch Rifle in .223 caliber. These rifles do not have a reputation for accuracy. Therefore, we must assume that the resistance has modified some of these weapons somehow."

"How is it possible for one of our mini-predator drone missiles to be set off with a rifle bullet?" the president asked.

"Mr. President," Saperstein responded. "We are using contact fuses on these missiles to save money."

"Well see that this problem is fixed," the president said.

"Yes Mr. President," Saperstein said, "it will be done."

The president raised his arms and then motioned downward with them. "Please be seated ladies and gentlemen. We have a lot of work to do today."

Leaving Wyoming

We drove across the country. Their planning impressed me. Doc removed ball caps from the trunk of the car, put one on, and gave the others to Toni and me. The ball caps appeared to be perfectly normal. Toni showed me a switch inside the cap and told me to turn it on.

"These caps are equipped with small LED lights that blind surveillance cameras so your face cannot be identified. The batteries are sewn into the caps and should last about 100 hours."

We switched to a second car. This car was parked in the parking lot of a small plumbing business located on a side street in a small town.

There were new clothes in the trunk for each of us. We took turns changing clothes in the bathroom of the plumbing establishment. No one else was in the building. I assumed they must have left through the back door when we arrived. OPSEC again, I suspected. The clothes appeared to be chosen to change our look and did a pretty good job of it.

When we switched to a third car, there was an additional car waiting with a driver, a blue Ford sedan. Doc got into the passenger seat of the Ford and waved goodbye to Toni and me as they drove away. I was a bit puzzled, but not particularly surprised.

"You drive," Toni said. "I'll tell you where to go."

Toni and I drove for about 14 hours, taking turns driving while the other napped. I was worried about being stopped, but with the change of clothes came new ID. And it looked good—actually it looked official. I wondered for the umpteenth time just whom I had fallen in with?

Once, when we stopped at a gas station, I saw a federal cop staring at us. That made me nervous. Toni ignored him. I had my Browning tucked into my pants under my shirt and wondered if I might need to use it? I had just finished filling the car with gas when the cop walked toward me. I did my best to ignore him. Toni had gone into the gas station, which like all gas stations today, was really just a quick stop, to buy bottled water.

The cop walked within two feet of me, nodded, and kept going. Relieved, I smiled, and nodded back. I hoped he could not tell my knees were shaking. Just about that time Toni returned with the food and drinks, and we left.

"Did he get a good look at your face with his lapel cam?" Toni asked.

"Yes he did," I replied.

"Time to make a change," She said. Toni took a cell phone from her purse, dialed a number, and before it was answered, hung up.

"What was all about?" I asked.

Toni smiled. I found I really liked it when she smiled. Toni was a very attractive woman. Even in my state of shock over the loss of Susan and the events that had occurred since, I could tell that. But it wasn't her attractiveness that got through to me; it was the fact that her smile had a slight mischievous bent. That simply intrigued me. She said, "We need a change of car and outfit."

"And you did that without even talking to anyone?" I asked.

"Well," Toni replied. "You know all personal calls are monitored by our illustrious, although less than legitimate, government. Why should we give them anything to go on?"

Toni gave me driving directions for the next hour and then motioned for me to pull into a small restaurant parking lot. That surprised me, because we had been avoiding restaurants the entire trip, just as I had when I was running from the drones, Toni seemed to think the fewer stops the better. That's why I was surprised when we stopped at a restaurant a little while after we had eaten sandwiches from an ice chest left for us in the car.

The restaurant was small and old. It seemed to have had more than one owner in the past because the sign supports were too big for the current sign. The restaurant was called Aunt Myrtle's Diner. We got out of the car and entered the restaurant. I held the door for Toni, and she walked in ahead of me. I thought she would choose a table. Instead, she walked straight through the dining room into the kitchen. I followed her. In the kitchen she turned to me and said, "Don't worry, this place is safe."

Apparently, Aunt Myrtle was a 6'6", 360-pound guy. He hugged Toni warmly and shook my hand. "Everything is set up and ready to go. There are changes of clothes and hats for both of you in my office, and here is your new ID."

My new ID said I was a retired cop. Myrtle reached into his pocket and pulled out a 9 mm Beretta. Looking at me, he said, "Give me your pistol and take this one. You will get yours back later. Cops, even retired cops, don't carry Brownings."

I shrugged, removed my Browning from my waistband and handed it to him. He handed me the Beretta, and I checked to see if a round was chambered, tucked it into the inside the waistband holster and dropped my shirt over it. Aunt Myrtle smiled and said, "Now don't use it unless you have to."

Toni went into the office and came out looking entirely different. In fact, she looked about 10 years younger and had a different looking hairstyle. I guessed it was a wig. Aunt Myrtle laughed and said, "Now that's the girl I don't remember."

I went into the office and found the set of clothes waiting for me. They were unlike the jeans and oxford shirt I would normally wear, but I figured that was good and put them on anyway. Just like the other set, they fit perfectly. I wondered again how these folks communicated so well without the government snoops knowing. I also picked up the hat, which looked like something out of a *Raiders of the lost Ark* movie, and joined Toni and Myrtle in the kitchen.

Aunt Myrtle said, "Well, you look different too," he laughed. His laugh was deep and genuine, as was the smile on his face. "I think that's a good thing."

Toni turned to me and said, "We are going to separate now, but I will see you at our destination." She stepped over, stood on her toes and kissed me on the cheek. "Be careful now, you hear?" Then, she turned and determinedly walked out of the kitchen through the back door, only glancing back once. A couple of minutes later I heard a car start and drive out of the parking lot.

Aunt Myrtle draped his huge arm across my shoulders. "Don't worry kiddo. You're going with me." We waited in the kitchen for about two hours. I fell asleep on a stool until Aunt Myrtle woke me. We went out the back door into the parking lot and got into a rather unremarkable car. I was surprised that Aunt Myrtle fit inside, but he did, although I am sure not very comfortably. In the ensuing seven-hour drive, I got to know Aunt Myrtle a bit and discovered that I really liked him. He was almost as old as I, and was retired from the military. He laughed when he told me that and said, "I've gained a bit of weight since then."

"So, tell me about the Myrtle moniker," I asked.

"My real name is John," he said. "Same as you."

"So, why don't you go by John?" I asked.

"When I retired from the military, I was only 38 years old. I joined the Army at 18 and got out when I had 20 years in service. I cast around for something to do for a month or so and ended up with a job as a dishwasher in the diner. There was a real Aunt Myrtle then. She was an odd old lady, to say the least, but I liked her, though few others seemed to. She was a loner, like me, and didn't have any family. When she died, I was cooking for the diner. She left me the place on the condition that I never change the name of the diner, so I didn't. The patrons started calling me Aunt Myrtle as a joke and it stuck. Now I answer to Aunt Myrtle, although I prefer just plain old Myrtle. Somehow, it suits my sense of perversity." Myrtle smiled at me. "Besides, with my size, not many guys are willing to pick a fight about it. Too bad, I love a good fight."

"Where are we going anyway, Myrtle?" I asked.

"I can't tell you, John. OPSEC, you know," Myrtle replied.

"I understand," I said. "I am just curious."

"I would be too in your situation," Myrtle laughed. "Anyway, we are almost there."

I looked around. We were in just about the last place I would suspect could provide a haven for these folks, but I had been surprised a number of times by them already. The piney woods flowing past the window looked different to me than what I was used to in Indiana. We were somewhere in the central part of the state of Mississippi. For the most part Mississippi looked like anywhere else in the US; the stores and restaurants were the same old chains in the towns we drove through, although the towns seemed a bit more spread out than in Indiana. Everywhere that I looked, there were mostly pine trees. Myrtle said that making paper was big here and most of the pine trees were grown to make paper.

I guess I had always assumed that any underground resistance to the government would be located either in the American Redoubt (Wyoming, Idaho, and Eastern Washington), or at least in a state like Michigan, where militias are common.

We drove for another hour and then stopped in the parking lot of the mall on Highway 98 (Hardy Street) in Hattiesburg, Mississippi. Myrtle said, "Just leave your stuff in the car and follow me. Our stuff will be with us by tonight." I followed Myrtle into the mall. We walked from one end of the mall to the middle and then sat down at a table in the food court.

After looking carefully around and nodding ever so slightly at a man who passed by our table, Myrtle said, "wait here, John. Someone will get you in just a few minutes. I will see you tonight. Don't worry, and don't panic. You are safe," Myrtle laughed. "Just don't take your hat off, even though the cameras in this food court are not working at the moment."

I waited for about ten minutes. I watched everyone who passed by trying to not let anyone know I was watching. Then, Toni walked up to my table and sat down.

She was wearing a blonde wig that made her look different, but it was Toni. She was also carrying an armload of shopping bags from various stores in the mall. She smiled at me when she sat down. I was surprised to find that, not only was I glad to see her, but that I had also missed her when she was gone. That both bothered and surprised me. I was still morning Susan. I had no room in my life right now for anyone else.

I thought about Susan while Toni chattered about this store's sale and that store's sale, a dialogue, obvious to me anyway, designed to make her and, by association, me seem to be completely unremarkable citizens, or sheeple.

I noticed that Toni was wearing a wedding ring and an engagement ring on her left hand. She had not been wearing them before. I also noticed that her rings matched the white gold band that I still wore. Toni must have noticed my glance.

"Security is in the details, John," she said very quietly. "There are no working cameras, or microphones in this spot right now, but the cameras and microphones in the rest of the mall are just as active as ever, and feed directly into the government database. We have found that sometimes it is the smallest of details that can fool the feds. Just pretend like you are married to me when we walk out. Just for the cameras, you know."

I nodded, still thinking of Susan. I did note a sort of wistfulness in Toni's expression that seemed a little out of place. Thinking about that I realized that she knew a lot about me but I knew very little about her—yet I willingly trusted my life to her.

Toni stood and rummaged in one of her bags. She came up with a dark blue lightweight windbreaker and another ball cap. This cap was green and said *John Deere* on the front. I shrugged into the windbreaker and switched hats, after flipping the hidden switch inside the new one. Toni smiled approvingly. "Let's go, Sweetheart," she said.

I was a bit shocked by her use of the term sweetheart, but I figured it was just part of the cover, so I got up and walked along beside her. As we left the food court, I noticed that three rather average-looking men were following us, not obviously though. Before everything that had happened, I doubted I would have noticed. I tapped Toni on the shoulder and ever so slightly pointed at one of them with my chin. Toni's eyes widened a bit, and she stood on tiptoe and whispered in my ear.

"They are ours. Relax if you can and laugh like I said something funny." I laughed a bit. Toni smiled at me as if I was the center of her universe, and I marveled at her acting skill. She almost had me fooled, so I thought she could fool the cameras very well.

We walked all the way to the other end of the mall and exited through the J. C. Penny store. I walked alongside Toni and she went straight to a suburban-looking, crossover vehicle. One of those things that city people thought was a real backwoods vehicle, and rural folks thought was a useless city vehicle.

Toni got behind the wheel, and I got into the passenger seat. For such a large car, there was remarkably little room in the cab. I figured these things were marketed to women and midgets, or something. I missed my pickup truck and wondered again what had happened to the 'Beast'. I knew Henry was missing his truck too. I owed him my life as well as a truck.

We drove for about 30 minutes, mostly in silence, although Toni glanced at me from time to time. We were out in the countryside now. I noticed a railroad overpass coming up. Somehow I wasn't surprised when Toni stopped the car under it. There were no other cars in sight.

"We get out here," she said.

I opened the passenger door and stepped out. A man about my size, wearing the same kind of jacket as the one I had on, was suddenly standing there. He took the hat off my head, handed me his, and got into the passenger seat with just a wink. I noticed a lady dressed the same as Toni, and about her size, also suddenly appeared on her side of the car. She traded places with Toni. Toni smiled as they drove away leaving us standing under the railroad overpass.

"Just wait a bit." Toni smiled at me. "Everything is good."

A white trade van approached about two minutes later. It was moving slowly. Once under the overpass, it stopped and the back door swung open. Taking my hand, Toni led me into the back of the van. The man inside smiled and closed the door behind us. Again I wondered at the size of the group I had stumbled onto. They seemed to have endless resources, not that I minded at the moment.

Toni and I sat on folding chairs in the back of the van. The fellow who had opened the rear door for us had crawled back into the passenger seat in the cab and was having an animated conversation with the driver about deer hunting. Toni held her finger to her lips to indicate we shouldn't talk. That suited me quite well. I had a lot of thinking to do about what had happened, how I would get the bastards who had killed Susan, and, oddly enough, about Toni. She had shed her blonde wig and looked normal again, but no less appealing. I wondered if I were undergoing some sort of transference from Susan to Toni. I vowed to myself to honor Susan's memory.

I did have to admit to myself that it seemed strange that I, who, until recently, had never fired a shot in anger, nor even used my fists in a fight, was doing my best to figure out how to kill people. Not only to kill the drone operators, I also wanted to choke the life out of whoever had given the order for the attack with my own hands—even if it was the president of the country.

Somehow, my life now didn't fit with my previous anti-war, anti-violence stance. Although I had a few guns, inherited from my father, when Susan and I married, I had seldom fired them before Susan and I began prepping. I think I kept them just because they had belonged to my father. I couldn't even begin to picture myself shooting anyone. I often hoped when I was younger that I would never be in a position to need to use a gun on another human being. I greatly admired the folks who said to always turn the other cheek.

I now realized I had been wrong; that sometimes violence is not only justified, it is necessary simply because there are evil people in the world who can be stopped by nothing else. I realized that there is no difference between defending yourself when attacked by a mugger who wants to take your life or when attacked by a government who wants to take your life.

We drove for a while and then turned down a dirt road onto a prosperous-looking cattle farm. The work van drove into one of the machine sheds. We got out when the back door opened. It was Doc who opened the door.

"Glad to see you made it, John," he said. The smile in his voice was genuine. I discovered that I liked this young doctor very much, even if sometimes I feared his driving.

After the van left, one by one, we walked over to the house. It was a sprawling, quasi-Victorian, story and a half monster, with a tiny tower, and an extensive wrap-around porch. It just oozed expensive.

"Welcome home, John," Toni said as she and I walked through the door. Myrtle was there and stepped over and gave me a bear hug that I thought I might not survive.

A small fellow entered the room. He was Walter Mittyish in appearance but walked with a quiet confidence that instantly drew my attention. He strode up to me and extended his hand. "Hi John. I am Lorne Vanders. This is my home."

I shook his hand. "Thank you for the refuge," I said.

"Think nothing of it, John," he said. "What you did was amazing. I suspect you have little idea how much of an impression you made on the government and how badly they want you now. We have been but quiet resistors—until now. Your story has gone viral on the internet, at least the parts of the internet where the government has little control, and is stirring up a hotbed of anti-government sentiment.

"I am more than a little pissed at them myself," I replied. "I assume you guys had something to do with my story appearing on the internet?"

"Yes."

"I know you are probably tired but, if you would like, we can use your skill with that rifle of yours. I just got word that there is something in Colorado that needs to be done. We are flying there in two hours, if you want to come along. We may need to shoot some ground hounds."

"What the heck is a ground hound?" I asked. Lorne explained and the more I heard, the more I felt sick to my stomach. I realized that these ground hounds were not the ones who had killed my Susan, but from what Lorne told me, they would have done so with no hesitation.

"Toni put her hand on my shoulder. "John, the hounds are real. I lost my husband, my sister, and my niece to them a year ago." I looked into Toni's eyes. I could see the pain in her face because I recognized the same pain in my own face every time I looked into the mirror.

"I will go, but I don't have my rifle," I said.

"It is already here," Lorne said. We also have field equipment for you.

"Good!" Doc said. "We need you on this one, I think."

Myrtle said, "I wish I could go, but with my size, I would just be in the way."

"Be careful," Toni said, touching my arm. I was too lost remembering Susan and thinking about what I wanted to do to get even with the government to notice.

Chapter 7: THE MOUNTAIN

"Turning the other cheek never works when you are dealing with psychopaths." John Debrouillard

Colorado: The Front Range

Peggy awoke in the early dawn and realized that she had best get moving. There was frost on the ground, but she was still warm from the embers of the fire in her overhang. Reluctantly, she kicked dirt over the embers and, having nothing to carry except the sharp rock in one jeans pocket and the plastic lighter in the other pocket, quickly set off down the mountain. She knew she needed to get off the mountain as soon as she could because she was poorly equipped to survive in the wilderness, although she was surprised at how proud of herself she was so far. She knew her father would be proud of her, if he knew.

Peggy was cold but walking helped some. She kept walking along the stream for about two miles. There, she noticed that there was a long ledge of bare rock on the left stream bank. The ledge of smooth gray rock ran diagonally up the slope to the ridge. Thinking that the ledge of bare rock might help hide her tracks, she walked into the stream and waded downstream for about ten yards. Next, she carefully took her shoes and socks off, and washed her feet. She then stepped onto a small rock in the stream and, from there onto the rock ledge, being careful not to touch anything except bare rock.

Once on the ledge, she took her shirt off and carefully dried her feet, and then put her not so dry shirt back on, stuffed her socks into her shoes, and tied the laces together so she could hang the shoes around her neck.

Once she was ready, she moved as rapidly as she could along the rock ledge. Walking barefoot on the rock felt like walking on ice, but she kept going. After almost a mile, she climbed to the ridge staying as much as possible on bare rock and brushing out her tracks where there was no bare rock. She doubted it would fool one of those trackers for very long, but she knew she had to keep moving as carefully, yet as far and as quickly as she could.

Once on the ridge, she put her socks and shoes on, walked to where she could not be seen from the other side of the ridge, and started down the next small valley at a pretty good jog. It was a pace she could keep up for quite a while, even in this broken terrain, although it required almost complete concentration from her. She thought she would make it as far down the mountain as she could and then figure out how to hide for the night. She didn't know how she would do that yet, but she knew she was going to try as hard as she was able.

Six hours later she was almost 15 miles farther down the mountain. She was exhausted. Peggy had not had anything to eat since yesterday morning, and she was beginning to weaken. She knew she was mentally tough enough to keep going anyway, but she wasn't sure how long she might have to keep going, and that worried her.

Mississippi

Lorne Vanders climbed into the pilot's seat and began confidently fiddling with the controls. I watched him from the back seat and my respect for the man grew. Doc climbed into the passenger seat and buckled in. Lorne fired up the jets while carefully checking everything out.

"We are going to fly from Mississippi to Colorado in this?" I asked. "How often will we need to refuel?"

"Just once on the way," Doc replied as Lorne stayed busy with the controls.

"That is a very long range for such a small jet, isn't it?" I asked.

"Yes it is," Lorne replied. "This is an Eclipse 550. It has a range of over 1,000 miles and carries up to four passengers. That should be enough though, if the forth isn't as big as you, John."

I could see Lorne's smile so I figured he wasn't too upset by my size. I reasoned the weight limit was why Myrtle wasn't going. After all, he had military training and I didn't. He would be a better team member on a mission like this than I would.

Lorne taxied the jet out of the machine shed, down the driveway, and onto a long, straight stretch of blacktop.

"Aren't you worried about cars on the road?" I asked.

"Lorne said, "No. The road is private and all on the ranch. We built it to look like a blacktop road, but we use it mostly for a runway. It is 3,500 feet long, just enough for this little jet.

"Big place, then," I said.

"Yes," Lorne agreed. "Over 30,000 acres. For Mississippi, that is a huge place. However, on the record, it is divided among several different owners."

"Don't you have to file a flight plan?" I asked.

"Well, we are supposed to," Lorne laughed, "but sometimes I just forget."

Doc said, "this baby has a military transponder, among others, as well as anti-radar devices."

"Yeah," Lorne responded. "If we are careful, and we are always careful, we can make the occasional flight like this one undetected."

"I assume this flight is important?" I asked.

"Yes John," Doc said. "We need to take someone out of the frying pan."

Lorne taxied the plane onto the runway and then took off. It was indeed a speedy little jet. The takeoff forcefully set me back in my seat. Once we reached altitude, Doc filled me in on the mission. As he spoke, I got angrier and angrier with the government. After what I had been through, I believed everything Doc told me.

The jet flew at 450 miles per hour. Counting the stopover at a private airport near Tulsa to refuel, we were over central Colorado in just three and a half hours. I wasn't sure where we were landing when Lorne started the descent, but I knew it would be dark soon. I leaned forward and watched through the window as the nose dipped. After a while, I could see a faint white stripe on the land surface. It looked to be out in the middle of nowhere.

"Y'all hang on now," Lorne said. "This might get a bit rough since the landing strip is 200 feet short of what the specs suggest for this baby."

Lorne was right. The deceleration after the wheels touched the terminal was rough. I felt as if I was going to fly forward right through the windshield from the back seat despite the seat belt and shoulder harness. Somehow I didn't. We stopped with only a hundred feet of runway left.

"Better this time," Doc laughed. I wondered just where and how often these guys flew. And the thought also occurred to me to wonder how they could afford it.

Once the plane was stopped, Doc let the stairs built into the hatch down and we deplaned. I had the small tiger stripe camouflage backpack they had provided and my Ranch Rifle, now freshly cleaned and with four more 20 round magazines than I had left home with. That gave me 160 rounds for the rifle. I also had my Browning High Power pistol and four extra magazines. The .22 pistol stayed behind, but I now had a KaBar combat knife in its place.

I went down the steps first. Doc followed, carrying a small pack like mine, and an AR-15 rifle. Soon after Doc hit the tarmac, Lorne did too. Lorne was also carrying a small backpack, and what looked to be a WWII surplus Garand rifle that seemed almost as big as he was. Somehow I didn't doubt he could use it. That was the type of rifle Audie Murphy used in WWII and Audie Murphy was only a little bigger than Lorne. I had never fired a Garand myself.

We were barely on the tarmac when a pickup truck rolled up and a tall cowboy got out. "Howdy, Lorne," he said.

"Hello Dusty," Lorne smiled. "How ya doing?"

"Pretty well, considering," Dusty said. "We can talk later. Let me get y'all to the hanger." Lorne got into the cab of the truck after handing me his rifle. Doc and I climbed into the truck bed. Doc went first and I passed the rifles up to him, one by one. The rifles were not yet loaded; that made me feel better. I had barely gotten situated before the truck rolled off.

"Gee, this guy drives like you, Doc." I said. Doc just smiled and hung on just like I was doing, only I had two rifles to hang on to while he just had one.

The truck stopped in front of a big machine shed—the kind that back in Indiana we call pole barns. This one was about 30 feet high, 40 feet wide, and 80 feet long. There was a sleek, black helicopter sitting on the tarmac in front of that fancy pole barn. When the truck stopped, Lorne jumped out and was in the pilot's seat in a flash. Doc and I stowed our gear and the three rifles in the outside bin, and then got into the helicopter. Again, Doc rode shotgun.

Without a word, Lorne fired up the chopper and, as soon as the turbines reached speed, tilted the chopper forward and almost catapulted it into the air. Doc was busy with some fancy equipment in front of him and Lorne had headphones on so I didn't try to talk to either of them. We flew for about an hour and then Lorne started circling while Doc studied the screen in front of him.

"I think I have her location. We will have to go on foot about six miles from the only place we can set this thing down and then anticipate where she will go come daylight. We need to find her before the hounds do. There are supposed to be three of them this time."

We landed in a clearing that Doc indicated to Lorne from the map. I gathered Lorne was flying using infrared for visibility because there were no lights lit on the chopper, not even the basic running lights. At least, that's what I thought the goggles were for.

Once we landed we got out and retrieved our gear. Lorne locked the chopper with a key fob that looked as though it went to a Buick.

"I think she will go down the small valley she is in now. She will know that is the way to civilization," Lorne said. "Our background check suggests she has few, if any, survival skills."

"I think you are underestimating her," I said. "I couldn't begin to take out one of those ground hound things with just a rock."

Lorne paused and thought for a few seconds. "You may be right, John," he said and set off down the trail.

There was just enough moonlight to see the trail ahead, although poorly. I wondered why we weren't using night vision, but I didn't say anything. These guys had probably not only checked the stage of the moon but the weather as well.

Daylight came late in the shallow valley. We found where she had spent the night under a rock overhang with a warm fire. Lorne looked at me and said, "John, that was a good call. It won't do to underestimate this one." We followed her trail for a while. Lorne turned out to be a good tracker.

"I lost the trail," Lorne said. "We better split up and circle to see if we can pick it up again."

"No," I said while I was studying the terrain around me. "See that strip of bare rock. It is only on that side of the stream. I'll bet she backtracked on that rock and then followed as much bare rock as she could up to the top of that ridge. It would be faster traveling along the ridge, or just below it on the other side where she would be out of sight from this valley. I am willing to bet we will find her trail again just over that ridge from that rock outcropping. At least, that is what I would do, if I were in her place, and I am no woodsman either."

"Ok," Lorne said. "Lets hoof it up the hill and see if she left a trail there. We won't lose more than 20 minutes if she didn't, and we may gain as much as an hour if she did."

The trail was there. It was easy to follow, for Lorne anyway. I saw only the occasional footprint or scuff mark. Lorne started off along the trail at a fast trot. Doc and I followed.

Reston, Virginia

"We have her on satellite. Let the hounds know her position and direction of movement. I don't care how good they are at tracking. They need to intercept her as soon as possible. I don't want this to become an embarrassment to our agency."

"Yes Sir, Mr. Secretary," the shift manager said. "It is being done as we speak."

Colorado

The three hounds listened carefully as the voice in their earphones gave them instructions. It was obvious that they each were a little disappointed, but they knew better than to disobey orders. The lead hound started off, and the others followed. It would take them about two hours to intercept. They should have her by noon and maybe as soon as eleven.

We had been trotting down the ridge for about three and a half hours when Lorne stopped. Motioning for silence he stopped and pointed ahead. Far down the ridge a single figure was staggering along. There she was, and she looked exhausted. We had just started forward when I saw three armed figures appear about 200 yards behind her. I assumed they were the hounds. I knew we couldn't cover the distance before they could get to her so I raised my rifle to my shoulder, estimated the range to be just over 600 yards, and fired. Much to my surprise, the lead hound fell to the ground and didn't move. The girl stopped, looked back, and then tried to run faster.

The other two hounds ignored their fallen comrade and started after the girl at a run. Lorne took my Ranch Rifle from my hands and handed me the Garand. "The sights are at six come ups. Aim right on. Go prone."

I took the Garand and went prone. The sights were similar to my Ranch Rifle. I fired as soon as the rifle came to bear and that big old 30-06 slammed into my shoulder. The hound in the rear spun as his leg collapsed under him. I fired at the third hound as the second was falling and, even at that range, could see the splash of blood as the bullet struck the back of his head and blew his face off.

We approached carefully. The wounded hound had crawled a little ways and was sitting on the ground trying to stop the flow of blood from his thigh. From the extra bend in his wounded leg, I could tell that the bullet had shattered his femur. He barely looked up as we approached. Lorne fired one round from his pistol through the hound's head and the body collapsed on the ground.

We caught up with the girl, a thirty-something really, I thought. She tried to run from us, but collapsed after 20 yards. She had a rock in her hand and glared at us defiantly as we approached. Doc took the lead.

"Relax, Peggy," he said. "We are friends. We are here to help you."

"How do I know you are not from the government?" She asked. "How do you know my name if you aren't from the government?"

"We are part of a loose organization that is working to resist this unconstitutional government." Doc said. "We found out about you from a mole we have placed in the government. You might be surprised to know how many government employees do not approve of what is going on."

"What is the name of your organization?" She asked.

"We don't have a name," Doc said. "Think of us kind of like the hacker group, Unknown."

"Don't come any closer," she warned, holding up her rock.

I put down my rifle, removed the pistol and knife from my belt, and placed them beside the rifle. I took a sandwich from my pack and then dropped the pack on the ground beside my weapons. Holding only the sandwich, I approached her as she held the rock ready to strike.

"How do I know you won't poison me?" She asked. Without a word, I took a big bite out of the sandwich, chewed and swallowed. Then, I handed the sandwich to her. She took it with one hand and looked for a few seconds into my eyes, and then she dropped the rock and, holding the sandwich with both hands, started eating. Doc tossed me another sandwich. When she finished the one I had given her, I held the other one out. She looked me straight in the eye, and didn't take the sandwich, so I took a bite out of that one too. After I swallowed, she took it and it was gone so fast I wasn't sure I had even given it to her.

Lorne also laid his weapons down and walked close to Peggy and me. "We need to move out now if we are going to get you to safety." He looked at me. "John, can you carry her and keep a good pace?"

"Yes," I said. "I think so."

"Good," Lorne said. He went back and picked up both my rifle and his, and handed me my knife and pistol. I gave him back the knife. I removed the magazine from my pistol, ejected the chambered round, dropped it into my pocket, reinserted the magazine, and handed the pistol to Peggy.

"Can you hold onto this while I carry you piggy back and manage not to shoot anyone?

"Yes," she said.

"If we run into trouble just hand it back to me," I said.

"OK," she nodded.

I stooped down, and she climbed onto my back with the pistol tightly clasped in her right hand. Her finger was off the trigger just like I showed her. We started off with Doc in the lead. I was glad again that I was in pretty good shape, although after two more miles of travel down that ridge, I decided I was really in horrible shape. I ached all over, and I was limping badly. My right calf, where the bullet had passed through, felt as if someone had taken a giant pair of locking pliers and squeezed them tightly around my leg. In other words, cliché or not, it hurt like hell, but I refused to set Peggy down. We stopped once to rest and then cut straight across in the direction of the chopper. Doc was still leading the way with his GPS.

It took us another hour to get to the chopper. I was so stiff and sore when we arrived that I could hardly even set Peggy down. The crease in my shoulder that Doc had sewn up felt like it had ripped open. A glance and the blood on my shirt suggested it had. The last half-mile had been sheer physical torture that I managed only by willpower, and by focusing on my rage against the government. I don't think Peggy was in any better shape than I was when we got to the chopper. Lorne and Doc were still hopping around like bunnies. I decided I needed to lose another 30 pounds, at least.

Lorne and Doc had to help Peggy into the chopper, and, much to my embarrassment, me as well. "Not bad for a big man," Lorne smiled at me. "Not bad at all."

I settled into the seat next to Peggy while Lorne fired up the chopper and Doc studied the instruments. When we were airborne, Peggy turned wearily to me and asked, "Are you ex-military, or something?"

"No," I replied. "I am just a retired professor."

Peggy's eyes grew a little larger, and she said, "No shit? I am just a computer programmer." Soon, she was asleep with her head on my shoulder. I was glad it was my left shoulder. I dozed off not long after.

Chapter 8: THE ORGANIZATION

"There are but few important events in the affairs of men brought about by their own choice." Ulysses S. Grant

Colorado

This time the chopper landed at a small, out of the way airport. There was a car parked nearby. We got into the car, and Doc drove us out of there. We left the rifles and gear, except for the pistols, on the helicopter. After three changes of motor vehicles, and three changes of clothes, we ended up back at the jet. Lorne flew us back to Mississippi by way of California, North Dakota, and Indiana. I slept much of the way and so did Peggy. Once I awoke and noticed Doc was dozing in his seat. Lorne was alert as ever, even though the jet was on autopilot. That Lorne was impressive.

After we landed back at the ranch, Myrtle took charge of Peggy, and Doc showed me to a room in the basement. It was a nice room and had its own bathroom. There were new jeans and a couple of shirts on the bed. I cleaned up, changed clothes, and went in search of something to eat. When I found the kitchen, Myrtle was there happily cooking up a meal.

"Hi John," he said. "I heard you did some really fine shooting. Where did you learn to shoot like that?"

I sat down at the table and Myrtle quickly filled a plate and set it in front of me. Then, he sat down at the table too, "I am not really sure," I replied. "I have always been pretty good with BB-guns, bows and arrows, slingshots, and pretty much anything that shoots. My wife used to say it was because I worked the trajectories out in my head and then trusted my instincts. Even though my dad was a really good shot and liked to shoot and hunt a lot when I was growing up, I never fired a rifle until a few years ago. It just wasn't something that interested me—until now that is," I said thinking of what I wanted to do to Susan's murderers. "I guess it is just a natural talent."

I ate the food Myrtle put in front of me while he talked. I listened as best I could, but I was also wondering what had happened to the old me. The me I knew before would never have been able to eat after killing two people, and putting a bullet into a third, if that me would have even been capable of pulling the trigger. However, here I was, eating with a gusto I had seldom known before. "So, What can you tell me about you guys?" I asked while stuffing some of the best tasting chicken I had ever eaten into my mouth.

Myrtle smiled. I had noticed he liked to talk on the drive we took together, but he had told me nothing about the group. "Now, you take Toni," he said. "She lost her husband, her sister, and her niece to this government about a year ago. Her husband worked for one of the federal agencies in D.C. and found something out that shocked and disgusted him. Something to do with the use of drones, I think. He was going to blow the whistle and make it public, with Toni's encouragement. The government killed him, tried to kill her, and sent hounds after her sister and niece because they witnessed part of the attack. Toni managed to hide for 17 days before we found her. Now, she is one of us, just like you are," Myrtle laughed.

"So what is your story?" I asked.

"My story is neither tragic, nor complex. Lorne stopped in the diner once quite a few years ago and we got to talking. It turned out that we both felt the country was going in the wrong direction. After a couple of visits, Lorne recruited me—willingly, I might add. I am not high in the group, but there are a few things I do rather well.

What about Doc?" I asked.

"Oh, that Doc," Myrtle laughed. "He is something for sure."

"So, what can you tell me about him?" I asked.

"I can tell you only a bit because I don't know everything. Doc is a medical student, although I think he may have just graduated. Lorne recruited him sort of like he did me. Lorne's father and Doc's father were good friends, I think. Doc's father didn't like the way the country was going either. I know that because he told me before he died."

"How did he die?" I asked.

"From prostrate cancer," Myrtle said. "It was sad for Doc to see him waste away like that. Really sad!"

"And Lorne?" I asked.

"Lorne doesn't talk much about himself. I do know that his father was almost as tall as I am, maybe six-four or better, and Lorne is only five-foot-two."

"I thought he was taller than that," I said.

"No, only five-foot-two, maybe even a smidgen under," Myrtle laughed. "He told me once that he has small man's syndrome and that made him over-achieve all of his life."

"He seems pretty normal, if exceptionally skilled, to me." I said.

"He is also rich, I mean almost Bill Gates rich. His dad was rich and Lorne took what he inherited and turned it into a real fortune. The part I like is that Lorne doesn't hurt people just to make money. He is about as fair and generous as anyone I have ever met. He can close deals on a handshake that no one else could."

"I take it you like him?" I asked.

"Yes I do," Myrtle said.

"I like him a lot too," I said. "What's more, my gut says to trust him."

"You can't go wrong trusting Lorne Vander!" Myrtle said. "That is a fact."

"Is that so?" Lorne said, as he entered the kitchen.

"Yes, that is so," Myrtle said. "I have been talking behind your back."

Lorne smiled, "Good. Tell John anything you want. I have nothing to hide—except perhaps from the government." Lorne laughed and sat down across from me at the table. Myrtle looked at him and motioned toward the stove. Lorne shook his head and said, "Maybe later, Myrtle, but that chicken sure smells good!"

"It is!" I said and then stuffed the last piece of chicken on the plate into my mouth. "I am full now. That's for sure."

"That's good!" Toni said from the doorway. I watched her as she walked through the door. She appeared to be more relaxed and rested than the last time I had seen her.

"Where is Doc?" Lorne asked.

"He had to go to Arkansas right after you guys got back. There is a small problem there that he said he would take care of. He said you guys needed your rest after the trip to Colorado." Toni explained.

I looked at Lorne again and wondered if he ever slept. I knew he had been awake now for over 24 hours, and he was still wide-awake and alert. I still felt a bit tired myself, even though I managed to sleep a lot on the plane on the way back to Mississippi.

"OK," Lorne said. "I would like Doc to be here, but we will proceed anyway."

"Proceed with what?" I asked.

"I will fill you in over the next few days," Lorne said. "But first, I would like to know who and what you think we are. I know what Myrtle, Toni, and Doc have told you, but I am very interested in what you think."

"Why are you interested in what I think?" I asked. "I am just a retired science professor."

Myrtle laughed, "Just like I am a ballerina."

I looked at Myrtle and grinned. "For all I know, you dance exceptionally well."

"No," Toni smiled at Myrtle. "Myrtle doesn't like to dance, and he sucks at it."

"You bet I do," Myrtle laughed. "Remember when I fell down at the Christmas party last year and all I was trying to do was a waltz."

Lorne smiled too. "That was a sight to see, but I still have a suspicion it was a deliberate effort on your part to liven up a dead room." Lorne looked back at me. "I think you are far more than a run-of-the-mill retired professor John. I happen to know that you were the top-ranked researcher in your research area."

"Some folks said that," I admitted, "but it wasn't even worth a raise."

"That is because you refused to play politics, John."

"You have checked me out pretty well," I said. I noticed Toni smiled.

"I suspect we know more about you than the government does," Lorne said. "But then, we think you might be far more important to us alive than killing you is to the feds."

"That would have to be pretty important," I said.

"So, tell us who and what you think we are," Lorne smiled.

"Ok," I said. "This may take me a few minutes, but here is what I think." I paused to get my thoughts in order. "I think you are a relatively loose, and headless, group of government resistors and constitutional supporters."

Lorne glanced at Toni, and then at Myrtle. The looks they exchanged seemed to say that I had said something significant." Go ahead Lorne said."

"I think the group organization is somewhat loose because there seems to be no serious command structure. I say this because folks seem to act mostly on their own, more like a mutual aid society, than a rebel army. But, that has its advantages as well." I looked at Lorne. "I am not sure I understand the apparent lack of leadership because I think Lorne is a natural leader and, even though he may have the most resources of any member of the group, I find, that even here in his home, he is quite egalitarian. I think that is the type of leader that would be most effective with a varied and individualistic group such as this resistance."

"I am not the member with the most resources, John," Lorne said. "I am not even in the top ten." I raised my eyebrows at that.

"I will admit that a headless organization is very difficult to destroy, but it also makes it relatively ineffective in choosing and moving toward the most important goals," I said.

"How big do you think we are?" Lorne asked.

"I am not sure," I said. "Based on what I have seen, I suspect you have members scattered throughout all fifty states, and, I suspect, in more than a few foreign countries. Considering how rapidly information seems to pass in your group, and how quickly things seem to happen, as well as the long term preps I have seen, I would estimate that you have well in excess of several thousand members and/or supporters, some who are in positions in the government where they can pass you information. I think it would take that many people, or more, to accomplish what I have seen done so seamlessly." Lorne glanced at Toni and Myrtle and they exchanged that look again.

"Go on," Lorne said.

"I also think you have some sort of secure communications capability that the government is unaware of, or at least has failed to crack."

"What do you think that might be?" Toni asked.

I thought for a minute. "Well, if I had to do something like that, and I was technically capable—which I am not—I would piggyback a seemingly random analog signal on existing internet and cell phone transmissions. That would require developing both the machine language, software, and the proprietary hardware from scratch," I said. "Using off-the-shelf hardware would be far less secure. I would, however, install the proprietary hardware inside common items, such as computers and cell phones so that their use would not draw any undue attention."

"I wish we had thought of that," Lorne said. Again, he exchanged looks with Toni and Myrtle.

"Ok," I said. "If you are not using that kind of com system, then I would expect a coded message system."

"Actually, a coded message system is what we are using. We have to change codes frequently," Lorne said. "Do you think your piggyback idea will work?"

"I would ask some technical folks and see what they think." I said.

Toni nodded at Lorne, "I will check it out. Give me about three hours."

"It will work," I said. "I just don't think it will be inexpensive or particularly quick to develop."

"Do you think the government knows much about us?" Lorne asked.

"I suspect that some, but not nearly all, of your members are watched, and some have been, or will be, targeted for assassination based on actual opposition to the government, or even just the suspicion of opposition. I think the government knows that they have significant opposition among the citizenry, and they are now using every means at their disposal to destroy and silence any resistance. Why else would they use drones to assassinate American citizens?"

"I doubt the government knows how extensive or how well-funded their opposition is, or how easy it is for you to recruit American citizens because of the government's recent all out attack on the Constitution. I think most highly-placed officials tend to be psychopaths and narcissists because those are the personality types that take to the dirty nature of politics most effectively."

"After all, these are the same people who are incapable of understanding how much the people of Pakistan hate us because of the innocent people, especially the women and children, killed in the president's overseas drone strikes— almost fifty innocents for every terrorist as I understand it."

"These people, the powers that be, whether in government, banks, or corporations, simply do not understand, and, in fact, are most often incapable of understanding, the ties that bind the rest of humanity together."

"That lack of understanding is this administration's greatest weakness. That is what you are, or should be, using against them."

Lorne just stared at me. It was Myrtle who broke the silence. "Ok, I am convinced, Lorne. I think you called this one right."

"How effective do you think the government's war against citizen opposition is?" Lorne asked.

"The government collects a huge amount of data on citizens. I am sure the feds record all telephone calls in the US, both cell and landline, and run each of these digital files through voice recognition software in search of key words. Once they identify a citizen who expresses above a certain threshold of opposition to the current regime, I suspect they monitor that person more closely, using computer hacking, surveillance drones of various types, surveillance satellites, bugs, or perhaps even assassinate that person, much like they tried to do with me."

"How would you suggest that the government's telephone monitoring system be fooled while still allowing us to use cell phones?" Lorne asked.

"I can think of several possible ways," I said. "First, all voice recognition systems, no matter how good, have difficulty with some pronunciations. It should be possible to write a software program that garbles either selected words, or perhaps sentences, enough to be unrecognizable to voice recognition systems, or the human ear. A person on the other end of the call could record the call and use the same program to unscramble the message on a computer not connected to the internet."

"Another way might be to overload the government surveillance system with a huge number of untraceable automated calls that use key words and phrases of interest to the government in a random fashion—an old fashioned denial of service attack. I am sure a good computer tech would be able to do the calculations and see if that is actually possible.

"Another alternative might be to use an uncommon spoken language. If the language chosen is only spoken, and has no written representation, and the native speakers are also unlikely to be in opposition to the government, it would be difficult for the government to catch on or crack the code because of their base assumption that speakers of that language are not a threat. That would require a number of translators though so I doubt it will be practical."

"Those are some good ideas," Lorne said.

"Well, they would have to be developed by better technical people than I. I doubt I could do any of those things on my own."

"One more question. Do you remember when Toni made the call when the federal cop saw your face?"

"Yes," I replied. "And probably got me on his lapel camera, which most likely has a direct digital feed into the big government database."

"How do you think Toni's communication worked?"

"I think that Toni had memorized a series of phone numbers. Making a call to any of those numbers would result in a pre-planned action, such as a car, etc., left at a specified location without a word needing to be said."

"Now I am convinced!" Lorne said as he stood and extended his hand. "Your skill with a rifle is amazing, but your analytical skills are truly incredible."

I stood and shook his hand. "Lorne," I said, "I find you to be an amazing fellow, yourself. I have never met anyone quite like you."

"Damn," Myrtle laughed. "What is this? A mutual admiration society?"

"It sure looks like it," I smiled.

Lorne sat back down and so did I. "John," he said. "I believe Toni once told you that you might be more important to us than we were to you."

"Yes," I nodded. "I didn't understand what she meant then nor do I now."

"Well, I will come straight to the point. The time to act against the government is now."

"I don't think a revolution can be accomplished with just guns," I said. "That worked during the revolt against the British, but it won't work now."

"I agree," Lorne said.

"To revolt against a government in a digital age, we must use technology more intelligently than they do. What that really means is, since they have the unlimited budget to develop surveillance and drone technology, etc., that we need to find ways to tap undetected into their surveillance systems and not only find out what they know before they know it, but feed them whatever misinformation we wish. We also need to be able to knock out their surveillance and drones at will, and/or turn their drones and other weapons on them when and where we wish."

Lorne glanced at Myrtle and they exchanged looks. "And that is precisely why we want you to lead the revolution, John," Lorne said.

"You have to be kidding," I said. "I am a retired hydrogeology professor. I have never been in the military, nor am I even a student of military history."

"You look very young to be retired," Myrtle said.

"I took early retirement, so early I am not even drawing a pension," I replied. "I am 51. Like you said, I am lousy at politics."

"I think you are our man," Lorne said.

"Lorne," I replied. "I think you are far better qualified than I. Besides, all I want to do is kill the bastards that murdered my wife."

"John," Lorne said. "The entire upper echelon of our government is behind the murder of your wife, and the murders of hundreds of other innocent American citizens."

"Myrtle nodded, "He is right John. The government is a very rotten place lately."

"We need you, John," Lorne pleaded. "We have a multitude of incredibly talented people, but we don't have anyone who sees the big picture as clearly as you. Nor do we have anyone who can accurately divine the government's intent as you have in your blog comments. We have analyzed your web comments, and you have been 86% accurate with your predictions so far. That is pretty darn incredible, to say the least. We have also read through your research publications, by the way. I won't even pretend to say I understand the technical stuff."

"Does that mean that my encountering Toni on the Wyoming ranch was deliberate?" I asked.

"No," Lorne replied. "That was a stroke of real luck on our part." Lorne glanced at Myrtle and Myrtle nodded.

Lorne spoke again. "We have a lot of very smart and very well-educated people, but we need you to direct them; to give us the big ideas and to be an example that the government doesn't always win."

"I gather that you want to use me in some sort of publicity campaign?"

"Yes, John. In addition to leading us, we want you to be the inspiration that drives the revolution."

"Surely, others have come up against the government and won. What about Toni? What about Peggy? There must be many others? Can't one of them lead?"

"No John," Lorne said. "Not very many people have survived direct government attacks. The three of you are the only ones we know about. You are the leader we want John."

"We are an organization that wants to oust the current illegitimate government and return true constitutional governance to America. A government of the people and for the people, like our Founding Fathers meant it to be. No more executive orders, laws, or Supreme Court decisions that are in violation of the Constitution and in violation of citizen's rights. No more wars that kill our military men and women for profit. No more corporate control and/or influence of the government to further corporate profits at the expense of the health, welfare, and well-being of the citizenry."

"Lorne, I agree that the current government needs to be ousted, and the country returned to constitutional rule. I just don't think I am the one to lead the effort. What would happen if I make a mistake? I am more than willing to help as long as it doesn't get in the way of me killing the murderers of my wife—but to lead?"

"John, we will help you with getting the ones who murdered your wife. We have resources that you don't"

"Lorne, I know that to be true. All I have is a rifle and a few dollars, but I have it to do and that means I will make the murderers of my wife pay even if I have to do it with no more that that."

"That determination is also why we need you, John," Myrtle said. "You have the determination of 100 men."

I looked at Myrtle and said, "Maybe so, but not the good sense."

"John, you won't be alone in this. We have a council who will help. I am on that council," Lorne said.

I raised my eyebrows. "How many on the council?" I asked.

"Five," Lorne said. "I want you to meet with the council."

Lorne was a hard man to say no to. I agreed to meet with the council.

Chapter 9: PEGGY WAKES

"It's this simple people: Government can't allow anything to exist that it does not control." Jessie Ventura

<u>Mississippi</u>

Peggy awoke in a darkened room. She didn't know what time it was, or even remember exactly where she was. She did feel safe though. She wasn't sure who the men were that rescued her from the mountainside in Colorado, but she was certain they did not intend to hurt her. They had killed three more of the trackers who were following her. In doing so Peggy was positive they had saved her life. She knew she would not have been able to prevail against the three trackers—ground hounds her rescuers had called them. She was convinced it had just been luck that had allowed her to escape the first tracker. She was sure she had killed the first man who was tracking her, and that bothered her. But then, she knew that the tracker would have killed her, just like the government tried to kill her with the missile fired from the drone.

Peggy got up and found a change of clothes neatly stacked on the dresser. She examined them. There was a pair of jeans, a western style blouse, and a selection of underwear and socks. On the floor was a new pair of sneakers, still in the box. Everything was her size. After fumbling around the room a bit, she found the bathroom, and took a long, hot shower. She was still both mentally and physically exhausted, and thought a shower would help.

After she showered and dressed, she left the bedroom and realized she was lost. She had been so tired when they showed her to the bedroom that she had failed to notice how she got there. She walked down the long hall until she found a set of stairs. She climbed the stairs and found herself in a large den on the floor above. The light coming through the windows told her that this was probably the ground floor and that she had been in the basement before.

"I am glad you are awake," a lady said from where she was almost lost in an overstuffed chair.

"Just barely," Peggy replied.

"You have been through an ordeal," the lady smiled. "One that most people would not have survived. No wonder you are beat."

Peggy walked across the room feeling a myriad of aches that the shower did not take away, and sat down in an identical large, overstuffed chair next to her. She felt as lost in the chair as the other woman looked, but it was the most comfortable chair she had ever sat in. It was almost like floating on a cloud.

She studied the lady in the other chair for a minute. She saw an unusually beautiful woman with dark hair, wearing slightly loose jeans, and a green plaid western shirt tucked into her jeans. She was trim and appeared to be about the same height and build as Peggy, although it was hard to tell with her sitting in the chair. Peggy wondered for an instant if she was now wearing this other woman's clothes. She also felt a fleeting jealousy that the other woman was much prettier than herself. The highest complement Peggy ever got was cute. No one had ever called her beautiful. "Who are you?" Peggy asked. "Who was it that rescued me? Where am I?"

Toni smiled "My name is Toni. The government killed my husband, sister, and niece, and then tried to kill me too because my husband found out about the drone assassinations of American citizens on American soil by this administration, and tried to blow the whistle. My husband, my sister, and her daughter were killed by ground hounds, just like you almost were. I escaped and hid out until these people rescued me. I am now one of them. Except for them, I have no family left."

"Who are you people?" Peggy asked. "I will understand if you think you can't tell me. Obviously, you are a member of a group of government resistors."

"How do you feel about that?" Toni asked.

"If you had asked me that question a week ago, I would have said that you were terrorists. Now, I am not so sure that it isn't our government who are the terrorists," Peggy responded. "It still seems surreal to me."

"I understand," Toni replied. "I felt that way at first too."

"How long has the government been killing American citizens?" Peggy asked.

"I am not sure, but we think it has been going on for about three years now," Toni said. "So far there are just some rumors floating around on various web conspiracy sites, and neither the news media or the majority of citizens seem to be aware of the murders."

"And the government covers the murders up?" Peggy asked, slowly shaking her head. "What has our country come to?"

"A rather corrupt state, I am afraid," Toni replied.

Both Toni and Peggy turned their heads as John and Lorne walked into the room. Peggy recognized them both. She saw the slight smile on Toni's face as her eyes focused on the taller of the two. Apparently, Toni was interested in the big guy. Peggy studied his face briefly but couldn't discern if he returned Toni's feelings.

Peggy suddenly realized that she didn't even know the names of her rescuers. As they walked toward her, she looked them over. The smaller man walked with a quiet confidence that drew her attention and made her wonder who he was. In spite of a 'less than tough' appearance, he was an attractive man and she felt herself drawn to him. She figured appearances were deceiving, at least in his case from what she had seen on the mountain.

The bigger man was the one who fed her the sandwiches; the retired professor who didn't look old enough to be retired. She remembered how comfortable and safe she had felt with her head on his shoulder in the helicopter and how he had carried her for miles to safety when she was too exhausted to walk. After several years of uninteresting dates and no relationships, she felt attracted to both of these men. Those feelings surprised her and she even blushed a bit. Neither of the men noticed but she saw

Toni's look and knew that she had picked up on it. That was one perceptive lady.

From watching how comfortable the two men were with each other as they walked side by side into the room, Peggy felt that they must be great friends. She could tell neither was gay, and she could tell that both were too preoccupied to pay any male attention to either of the women in the room. A slight smile came to Peggy's face. That most likely meant that both were intelligent and cared very much about something of importance. Neither seemed to be a chaser, and Peggy knew that even if men were seldom interested in her, most men would instantly respond to a beautiful woman like Toni. The fact that neither did meant to Peggy that they both had depth of character.

Then, she noticed the wedding ring on the taller of the two's finger, and an unexplained sadness gripped her. She instantly realized that it was he she was really interested in, and how futile that interest was. She could never be the other woman, and she got the impression that for this man there would never be 'another woman'.

As they got closer, Toni rose from her chair and took the taller man's hand with both of hers. Peggy noticed that the ring on Toni's left hand could be a match for the one he wore. Could Toni be his wife? But her husband was dead. Had she and John recently married? Something wasn't right though. She wasn't sure.

Peggy said, "John, I am glad you are going to talk to the council. You have my support too," Peggy then knew. The man, John, didn't belong to Toni, even though it was clear to Peggy that Toni would prefer it if he did. But, the ring... The ring said he belonged to someone else.

Lorne walked over to Peggy, who had, by now, also risen from her chair. She realized that she was several inches taller than he was but, despite that, she could not think of him as small. She had never met a short man with such confidence before, and she could tell it was not a misplaced confidence. She had met supremely confident psychopaths before, but this man's confidence, unlike theirs, was quiet and competent. She knew he wasn't a psychopath, even though she had seen him shoot the wounded tracker in the head.

Maybe that was it though. The taller man had a sick look on his face when he saw the dead trackers, and saw the wounded one shot. The smaller man reacted more like an experienced special forces soldier inured to violence, even though Peggy couldn't recall ever having met anyone that looked less like a special forces soldier.

"Peggy," the smaller fellow said. "I am Lorne Vanders. The big guy here is John. You may remember us from the mountain. Welcome to my home. Don't worry. You are safe now. I assume Toni already told you a bit about us."

"Not really," Peggy said. "We haven't had much time to talk. And I do remember both of you. Thank you so very much. I owe my life to both of you."

Toni chimed in, "We spoke only a bit, but I think she will do just fine with us."

"You realize you can't go home now?" Lorne asked.

"Yes," Peggy said. "That is hard for me to believe but I knew that was true even when I was on the mountain. I just regret that I won't be able to get my cat. I left her in a boarding kennel when I drove out to see my sister." A small tear flowed down her cheek. "I should have already been home and picked her up."

"Can you get someone to pick up her cat?" John asked. "I know it is a real risk since the cat may be monitored by the feds for that very thing."

"I will look into it," Toni said. "You and Lorne need to get to the meeting."

Lorne said. "At best I only tolerate pets, but your cat is most welcome if Toni can recover it." He looked at Toni. "We need you at the meeting too, Toni. Can you get the ball rolling on the cat before we leave?"

"I know who to contact," Toni said. "I will need fifteen minutes."

"Toni, if you can recover the cat..."

"Her name is Loco," Peggy said. "She reminds me of Marilyn Monroe in the old movie *How to marry a millionaire*, so I named her after her character."

"OK, if Loco can be recovered, I think she needs to be checked for RFID chips or other locating and/or transmitting devices—over a full frequency scan. Can that be done?" John asked.

Lorne smiled, "Yes, John. We have a guy that I think can do that. Now folks, we need to go meet the council, and yes, you too Peggy. Are you up for another plane ride?

"As long as Doc isn't flying," John laughed.

"Who is Doc?" Peggy asked.

"He is the other fellow who was on the mountain with us," John said.

Lorne said, "He will meet us when we see the council."

Peggy looked John in the eye and asked, "Is he a retired professor too? I think he is much too young for that."

"No, he is a medical doctor," Toni answered.

"I think he is pretty good too," John said. "At least with stitches."

"And bullet holes," Toni said. "Peggy, did you know that John was shot twice just days before he carried you off the mountain?"

"Yeah," Lorne laughed, "not bad for a big man, not bad at all."

Lorne slipped into the pilot's seat, and started the preflight checklist—something he had ignored on the previous flight, probably because of the urgency. Toni helped Peggy into the front passenger seat. John got into the one of the back seats, and Toni climbed into the other back seat. Once the plane was airborne and conversation died down, Peggy fell asleep in her seat. Soon after, John dozed as well. Lorne had not revealed their destination to them but John doubted they were going directly there anyway. That didn't seem to be Lorne's style, nor was a direct approach safe.

John awoke when Lorne said they were landing soon. Toni's head was on his shoulder, but all he could think of was Susan. Her memory was an ache in his soul because he missed her so much. The hatred of her killers rose to the front of his mind again, and with another woman's head on his shoulder, he began to work out different ways to kill Susan's murderers. There would be no bringing them to justice in the court system. They were the ones who ultimately controlled the justice system anyway. In this case, revenge had to be direct. No one was going to right this wrong except John.

Once they landed, they split into two cars. John rode with Lorne, and Peggy rode with Toni.

"Where are we going?" John asked.

"To a ship offshore in the Gulf of Mexico," Lorne laughed. "Not so very far from where we started. Insurrection is hell, isn't it?"

Chapter 10: THE MEETING

"Sincerity can sometimes be better expressed down the barrel of a rifle." John Debrouillard

<u>Gulf of Mexico</u>

I looked at the wake of the boat behind us as Doc pushed the 30-foot speedboat to its maximum speed. The early morning water was glassy smooth and Doc was taking advantage of it. I estimated that only the rear third of the boat was still in the water. I would never be able to drive a boat that fast.

Doc had joined us at Gulfport harbor. Toni and Peggy were both huddled tightly in the cockpit, both because it was slightly chilly in the predawn hours with the wet salt spray, and perhaps even more so because they had bonded on the drive from Virginia back to Gulfport. I wondered how many times they had changed cars. We had changed cars six times and driven all over the southern half of the U.S. before we arrived at our destination. Toni and Peggy were there ahead of us, as was Doc.

Lorne stood beside me in the stern and stared at the wake as well. Both of us were in short-sleeved shirts and both of us refused to acknowledge any discomfort. We were both lost in our own thoughts. I was worried about what I would say to the council. Should I do as they asked, or go my own way to seek revenge for my wife's murder? In either case, I was rebelling against an evil government; one that wanted to kill me—and would kill me on sight. The feds gave me no choice. I didn't think there was anywhere in the world I could go to escape them, nor would I have gone if I could. I could not break my vow to Susan even though I knew that trying to carry it out, alone or with Lorne and Toni's organization, would most likely end with my death.

After we had been underway for about two hours, Lorne turned and pointed to a freighter ahead. "There she is," he said. "That is the worst ship in my entire freight line, but often the most useful."

I looked where he pointed. The ship was small, old, and rustier than I thought it should be. I estimated it would be another twenty minutes before we reached her. To get a better look, I walked forward to the front of the cockpit and stood with my head and shoulders over the windshield. The wind and cold salt spray felt good. Soon, I noticed both Toni and Peggy had risen from their seats and were standing on either side of me. They were both the same height. The top of their heads came almost to my chin. Only their faces were exposed so I was surprised when Toni grabbed my right arm and snuggled close as if for more protection from the wind and spray. Peggy was on the other side of me, but she was holding on to the windshield and not me. She was close enough though, I thought. I noticed Lorne lightly punch Doc in the shoulder and point. Doc smiled. I pretended as if I hadn't seen. Truthfully, Toni and Peggy's closeness made me a bit uncomfortable. In my heart, I was still married to Susan and there was no room for anyone else.

The ship grew larger on the horizon as we approached, but we were still a couple of miles away. Turning my head and speaking to Lorne, I asked, "Satellite photos will show us boarding the ship. Won't that be a problem, especially if they are looking at them in real time?"

"Yes," Lorne said, "that could be a problem."

"As much as they want Peggy, Toni, and me, they could just send a cruse missile and destroy the ship with all of us aboard."

"I admit that did not occur to me," Lorne said, as always giving an honest answer. "What do you suggest?"

"Let me think about it for a bit. I don't know much about ships. Do they have a small boat?"

"Yes," Lorne said. They have a 26-foot launch that is sometimes used in port."

"Have you been around these ships enough to know if they ever use them for fishing?" I asked.

"Yes, and yes, sometimes they do."

"Then, we are going fishing," I said, and laid out my plan. Doc turned the boat slightly away from the ship as if it was never our destination in the first place and we headed toward an oil platform about six or eight miles away. I had heard that there was some good fishing to be had under these production platforms.

The sun was out now. It was warming up. Toni and Peggy both rolled up their pants legs and shirt sleeves, kicked their shoes off, tied their shirt tails up around their midriffs to show more skin to the sun, and lay back in the reclining seats with sun cream smeared over their faces and big dark sunglasses on. Lorne and I dug out a couple of deep-sea rods and sat in the back pretending to fiddle with them.

Doc made a phone call using a satellite phone and passed on a coded message. The code was good. As best I could tell, it was a normal call to a friend.

We had been under the offshore production platform pretending to fish for about an hour when the launch from the ship arrived. We were lucky the production crew was asleep, or otherwise occupied, and they didn't bother us. The ship's launch pulled under the platform and alongside our boat. We were ready.

Five crewmen from the ship boarded our boat as we boarded the launch. As soon as the transfer was made, the crewmen left in our boat, headed off to another rig for more fishing. We had rigged a sun tarp over the cockpit so it would not be obvious who was in the boat in satellite pictures.

In the launch, which already had a sun tarp rigged over the open cockpit, Lorne found the fishing gear and we baited some lines and began fishing for grouper. In an hour we had about 150 pounds of grouper, as well as a few fish I didn't recognize. We put the fish in the large built-in ice chest and Doc swung the boat out from under the rig and set a course to intercept the ship. It took us about two hours to get to the ship with Doc fussing the entire way that we could be there more quickly if he could just open that baby up. I smiled, but insisted he hold about the same speed the ship's launch had used when on the way to the platform. Toni and Peggy both mostly stayed out of sight in the small cabin while we were under way, just in case the government had eyes on the water.

When we were about a mile from the ship, Toni and Peggy came back on deck; Peggy looked out across the water and grabbed my arm tightly and pointed. About a mile away, in the opposite direction from the ship, a mini-predator drone cruised at an altitude of a few hundred feet. Its path was taking it away from us at about a 30-degree angle. As I saw it Peggy's pointing hand grabbed my arm. Toni put her arms around Peggy's shoulders as I studied the drone.

"Lorne, can the drone see us?" I asked.

"I don't think so," he replied. "Our research suggests that the cameras aren't good enough for this range, although the government has a special camera that they can use on the larger drones that can monitor an area of about 20 square miles."

"I hope you are right," I said. "I doubt there are any chaff cannon aboard this launch."

"No, there aren't any," Lorne said. "I think they are more like mortars than cannons though."

I smiled, "My lack of a military background is showing. I should have known that."

"Relax Peggy," Toni said. "We are OK."

I reached across and squeezed Peggy's hand. "It's OK, Kiddo," I said. "We will make it." Peggy grasped my hand and gave me a weak smile. She was terrified. Come to think of it, I was nervous myself. Toni, Doc, and Lorne seemed unfazed by the presence of the drone. I wondered if there was some way to project a picture above us that wouldn't show our presence to the drone—sort of a Romulan cloak of invisibility.

The lift onto the ship was efficient, and the landing was gentle as the crane operator lowered the launch back into its deck berth. I noticed that a tarp was rigged, as per my request, to shield us from spying eyes in the sky. We exited the launch, climbed down the ladder, and a single crewman led us to a door in the superstructure. He couldn't take his eyes off Toni. I don't think that surprised Toni. She ignored him.

We were led into a moderate-sized dining hall and the crewman left. The ship's captain showed us to seats along one of the tables. I chose a seat on the end where I could get up easily. I knew I would have to answer questions and talk about a few things, and I always speak better on my feet. I suspect that is an artifact of having taught college classes for so many years.

In a few minutes, three men, and one woman walked into the dining hall. From the way each of them looked around, I figured none of them were used to being aboard ship either. Lorne, however, seemed to know this ship as well as he knew his own house.

Lorne stood as the others approached. Since there was a lady present, I did as well. Doc did not, but then he was busy talking to Peggy. They were animatedly whispering back and forth.

"John," Lorne said, "this is Nancy Shepard."

I took her proffered hand and shook it. She was about five feet ten had a nice, firm grip and bright, intelligent eyes. "Pleased to meet you," I replied.

"Nancy, this is John," Lorne said.

"I am pleased to meet you too," she said. Her voice was expressive and carried genuine warmth.

"And this is Riley Hashinikarian."

Riley was almost my height and carried a few extra pounds. His handshake was also firm. I instinctively found myself liking him. "Pleased to meet you," I said.

He put his hand on my shoulder and squeezed. "I am pleased to meet you too John."

The next fellow in line was tall, even taller than Myrtle. He was black and that surprised me a bit, but not much. The people I had met in the organization so far had been typical conservative Americans of every race. His hand was huge and swallowed mine in a firm but not painful handshake.

"John, this is Charlie Alsup."

"Pleased to meet you," I said. "You look familiar."

"I used to play pro basketball," Charlie replied.

"I don't watch sports," I said.

"Then, you may have seen me on a television commercial. I used to do quite a few of those as well."

"Could be," I said. Charlie smiled, and his entire face glowed. He also put his hand on my shoulder and squeezed. Unfortunately, he chose the shoulder with the redone stitches. It hurt, but I didn't let the pain show in my face.

The last fellow was of average height and seemed to have a stronger personality than any of the others, although I didn't think it was anywhere near a debilitating feature. He was almost as confident as Lorne. His name was John Pickering. His handshake was firm, and his gaze was straight on.

"John," he said, "I think we need you very much. I hope you agree to lead us." I noticed Peggy's eyes opened a bit wider when he said that, but otherwise there was no reaction that I could see from anyone else in the room.

"Let's talk," Lorne said, and we all sat down around the table.

Washington, D.C.

The president paced back and forth in the oval office while the secretary of the Department of Interior Security fretted. The other cabinet members sitting around the large conference table were all nervous as well. "Where is he?" The president shouted. "Where is that son of a bitch?"

"We don't know, Mr. President," the secretary replied. "He seems to have just vanished."

"That is impossible. We spend almost a trillion dollars a year to keep track of the damn civilians. Are you telling me that money has been wasted?"

"No, Mr. President," the secretary sweated and loosened his collar. "We have only had a small amount of time to find this guy, John..."

"I don't care what the damn target's name is. Just get that son of a bitch for me, and do it fast."

"Yes, Mr. President."

"And what about that target who escaped the drone in Colorado? I was assured that you would have eliminated her by now."

"Mr. President, Sir, apparently she had help."

"What?"

"We sent three more ground hounds after her. They failed."

"Did this woman kill them too?" The president snarled.

"No Mr. President, all three of our ground hounds were sniped from a distance of about 600 yards. Their lapel cams did not pick up the sniper. One was wounded, a 30.06 round shattered his leg, and then he was executed with a single .45 caliber shot to the head. His lapel camera did not pick up his assailant. Apparently, the person was careful to approach out of view of the lapel camera."

"That sounds like an organized para-military group to me," The president said.

"Perhaps Mr. President," the secretary replied. "What you should know is that the first ground hound that was shot was killed with a shot to the back of his head at over 600 yards. He was hit with a single .223 round. Mr. President, Sir, we think it came from a Ruger Mini 14 or Ranch Rifle."

"That is what they used to shoot down the drone, isn't it?"

"Yes, Mr. President. "That is what our analysts believe."

"What is the range of those things, anyway?"

"To hit a head-sized target with any consistency with those rifles, most decent shooters would have to be within 200 yards and use a rifle scope. We had some of our military snipers test these rifles, and that was their conclusion."

"What is it that these rebels have then?"

"We don't know Mr. President, Sir," the secretary looked positively shaken.

"What about the other caliber?"

"We think those bullets were fired from a Garand M1 rifle Mr. President."

"What is that?" The president asked.

"It is a military rifle that our troops used during WWII. They were sold as surplus and purchased by many civilians under the civilian marksmanship program."

"So what you are saying is that we have two snipers with scoped rifles that are taking out our ground hounds?"

"Mr. President, our satellite thermal imaging data shows that there were three in the snipers party, and that one man fired both rifles. We could not identify any of the rebels because our other satellites were not in position.

However, detailed analysis of the thermal data we have suggests that neither rifle was scoped."

"But you just told me that was impossible."

"All but impossible, Mr. President. It happened, so it must somehow be possible."

"So where did these three rebels go?"

"We lost them, Mr. President. We don't know."

"I don't want to hear that. Find them now. Put any resources you need on this immediately."

"Yes Mr. President," the secretary said. "We will find them."

"Good," the president said and started to walk out of the meeting.

"Mr. President, there is one thing that you should know."

The president turned. "And what is that?"

"We think the shooter may have been the same man who escaped the quad-copter drone strike in Indiana and shot down the mini-predator drone in Wyoming."

The president's face contorted in rage, and his fists clenched tightly. He turned his cold stare onto the DIS secretary. "You have one week. Kill that son of a bitch," the president paused. "Or I will have you killed. Do you understand?"

"Yes Mr. President," the secretary said. As the president turned and stomped out of the room, he felt the sweat begin pouring out of his armpits and down his back. He was too shocked to notice the similar shocked looks on the faces of most of the other cabinet members.

Gulf of Mexico

I looked around the table. I instinctively liked these people. Unlike far too many of the faculty and university administrators I had worked alongside for years, they all seemed remarkably human. There was real warmth in each pair of eyes that was all too rare, and a quiet determination on each of their faces. I suspected that every one of them had reasons to hate the government that were as deep for them as Susan's murder was for me. I figured that it was up to me to start the ball rolling.

"Folks, this is apparently a job interview—and for me it may be a job that I don't want and may not even be capable of doing adequately. Before you even decide to offer me the position, there are some things I should tell you." I noticed smiles on every one of the council's faces. Peggy and Doc were listening, but neither smiled.

"First, you should know that I am just a poor boy from the wrong side of the tracks."

"We already know that, John," Nancy Shepard said.

Toni, who was sitting beside me, patted me on the leg. I assumed it was her way of reassuring and encouraging me so I went on. "I have no military training. I was not even a Boy Scout. I have no qualifications to plan and manage an overthrow of a PTA group, let alone the largest and most powerful country in the world."

Lorne spoke up, "John, we know that. We have the military-trained people as well as spies and data analysts, what we lack is visionary leadership. We need your principled creativity."

"What I am trying to tell you folks is that I have no experience at leading anything. I couldn't even get along very well with most of the people I used to work with at the university."

Riley stood, "John, we know that too. We checked all that out, very discretely, I might add. What you should know is that none of us could have gotten along with those unprincipled, and surprisingly dishonest people either. We did notice that you always followed your own principles and were honest and fair in your dealings."

Nancy said, "One of the problems in our society is that nice guys usually finish last. The disingenuous are far too fond of backstabbing, and not just in the upper levels of our government. John, you are among those who think like you. We have all had our problems getting by in the world, and people we trusted have stabbed us all in the back repeatedly in business and in life. Far too often, each of us was unable to even see it coming. You seem to have a real talent for seeing what is coming."

"That is just logic, and critical thinking," I said.

"And a very wide knowledge of how people behave, I suspect." Riley said. "I think you have studied people far more effectively than you may realize, although your formal studies and degrees are in science and engineering."

"You should realize that right now my personal goal is simply to kill those who murdered my wife." I noticed Peggy's head rise a bit and her eyes widen. I thought she might be repulsed by my intentions to kill, but I couldn't let that worry me. "While I would like to see this illegitimate and murderous government fall, that is not my personal goal."

Toni stood and turned to me. She reached out and took both of my hands in hers. "John, the fall of this illegitimate government should be your first goal. It is the only way you can be sure to punish all the people involved in your wife's murder and to make sure that such atrocities stop happening to other American citizens. In reality, our goal, and yours are exactly the same."

Riley sat down and John Pickering stood. Looking around at all of us, he said, "John, our goal is to bring freedom and honest government to America again. Could you tell us how we might do that?"

I thought for a moment and then spoke. "Daniel Webster once said, 'There is nothing so powerful as the truth: and often nothing so strange.' I agree with him. One of the things that I hate about our current government is the lies that they tell us." I noticed several nodding heads around the table, and I noticed a smile on Lorne's face. "I believe that you can win against the current illegitimate government only by being rigorously truthful to each other and to the people of our country."

Riley said, "John, we on the council have always been absolutely honest with each other. We have been able to put personal interests and personalities aside on this council because we have a common goal. We agree with you"

Charlie Alsup raised his huge hand. "John, should we be truthful to the point of telling the government representatives exactly what we are going to do?"

"Yes, Charlie. I think that is exactly what should be done, only not where, when, or how—at least at first. The problem with 'classified' information is that, sooner or later, someone uses the ability to 'classify' information to cover up wrongdoing. The more transparent we can make our efforts, the more people will be on our side. The irony is that our politicians often run on a platform of government transparency, yet never keep those promises."

"Lorne smiled, "That will take some real planning, John."

"That would scare the powers that be for sure," John Pickering said with a smile.

"Yes it will take serious planning," I replied. "And I cannot do all that planning, or perhaps even any of it alone. I think you need someone more talented than I."

"No, John," Nancy said. "We need you for several reasons. First, you are humble and no one who desires power should ever have it. Second, you have an unusual ability to accurately predict how the government is likely to respond to various situations. And perhaps as importantly, you will be the image of the rebellion. We hacked the video of the quad-copter drone strike that killed your wife and wounded you. We have also hacked the video of the drone attack in Wyoming where you, Doc, and Toni thwarted a multi-missile strike. I doubt you realize how powerful those videos will be in waking up the sheeple."

"I am no movie star," I said, "and this isn't a movie."

"No, it isn't a movie," Nancy said. "It is real life and that will be far more convincing to sleeping citizens who are unaware of the harmful machinations of our illegitimate government. No legitimate government kills its own citizens just to cover up illegal acts. The people know that."

"I wonder how many will care?" I said. "As long as many of our citizens get their government handouts, they seem to be able to ignore a lot."

"That is true, John," Charlie said. "But, even among that group are some who are already with us. Some of them are already waking up."

"OK," I said. "For the moment, let's assume that I am with you." I saw Lorne smile. "We will need many principled, loyal, and incredibly talented people working together to accomplish what we need to do."

Lorne nodded, "We have many of those people, and I think we can recruit more."

I smiled at Lorne, "I thought you might have." Then, I paused. "Ladies and gentlemen, this revolt will not be won with rifles alone, although they will be needed as well. It will be won by winning the hearts and minds of the people and by using the government's own technology against them."

"Government, at all levels, is currently a haven for psychopaths. With a government position, the psychopaths have the gun and the freedom, if the people fail to resist, to use guns on the people for their pleasure alone, or so they believe. To displace these psychopaths, at times, guns will be needed."

"Currently, the government is expanding its surveillance of its citizens an incredible pace. Only a government that fears its citizens tries so hard to control them. Therefore, I believe that our government greatly fears the people. After all, we are a country in which the ultimate power, by constitutional right, belongs exclusively to the people."

"Our politicians are, in reality, only employees of the people. They are the usurpers, the terrorists, not the people. Our government has gone rogue, and quite some years ago, I am afraid. They use our taxes to fund technology that they use against us. We can only win by turning this technology against the government. We have to take back that technology, which really belongs to the people, and use government resources to defeat our illegitimate government."

"Perhaps the most important aspect of this revolution will be to win the hearts and minds of the people, the citizens of our great country. To do this, we not only have to be honest with them, we also need to demonstrate by our actions that we are here to not only help people recover their liberty, but also to reverse the current economic downturn and make practical changes that allow people to achieve a better life for themselves and their children."

One by one, everyone at the table stood and clapped. Even Peggy and Doc.

"John, will you lead us then?" Nancy asked.

"Yes," Charlie said. The others around the table, including Doc, nodded their heads in agreement. Peggy just sat there and stared at me. I figured I must somehow have made her mad. I thought for what seemed to me an inordinately long time before answering.

"On one condition," I said. "My condition is, if, at any point, you feel that someone else can do a better job tell me and I will resign. No questions asked." Everyone in the room stood and took turns shaking my hand—except Peggy. Peggy looked like she was deep in thought.

Chapter 11: TONI

"Justice will out." John Debrouillard

Fairfax, Virginia

Toni had just finished cleaning the kitchen when she glanced out of the window and saw a black SUV drive by. The windows were darkened, and she couldn't see through them. She didn't think anything of it, though, because they lived in Fairfax, Virginia and various government vehicles sometimes passed through the neighborhood. She was sure that her husband Bill wasn't the only one who worked for the federal government in their neighborhood. As a matter of fact, she had heard that several of the subdivision residents were fairly high-ranking government employees.

The neighborhood was very nice. In fact, the houses were really McMansions. Sometimes Toni thought that the houses were more similar than they were different, but the other wives in the neighborhood seemed to focus more on the minor differences between the houses and to be content with that. Toni often thought that they were less than observant.

Toni was surprised when her husband Bill came home early. It was only 2:00 PM, and he looked worried. "What's wrong Bill?" Toni asked as she kissed him on the cheek.

"Toni, you are not going to believe this."

"What?"

"I found out today that the current administration is murdering people who oppose them—our own citizens, assassinated right here at home on U.S. soil. Not only that, I have proof that it goes all the way up to the president, himself."

"Bill, you have to be kidding me!" Toni said.

"No Darling, this is real and I am scared. For the first time in my life, I am scared of my own government, and I work for them."

"What are you going to do?" Toni asked.

"I don't know," Bill said. "I don't know what to do. What they are doing is wrong. It needs to be stopped."

"How?" Toni asked.

"I have to let people know what they are doing?"

"Blow the whistle?"

"Yes. I never thought of myself as a whistle blower."

"Bill, you do what is right. I believe in you, always."

"I have to determine who to contact."

"How about the FBI?"

"I am not sure. The upper echelon at the FBI might be in on this."

"Does anyone know that you know this?" Toni asked.

"I think so," Bill said. "However, I don't think they know how much I know."

"Bill, if they are murdering people, what will they do to you if they find out you know?"

"I don't know Toni." Bill hurriedly stepped over to the window and looked outside toward the street. "I felt like I was being followed on the way home, but I didn't see anything. Maybe it's just because I'm nervous."

"You have the right to be nervous Bill."

"Yeah, I suppose so. I have never seen anything remotely like this in my entire career. It has me on edge." Bill walked toward the interior kitchen door, and said, "I'll be right back Toni."

Bill climbed the stairs to their bedroom, and went into the walk-in closet. There, he unlocked the security box, and took out his pistol. Toni didn't like guns, but she tolerated his as long as it was locked away. Bill thought a lot of women were like that. He had been in the Army when he was young, and he knew how to handle firearms. However, Toni didn't like them because they were too loud, and she said they hurt people.

The pistol was a Colt .45, model 1911. Bill dropped the magazine into his hand and assured himself that it was loaded. Then, he inserted the magazine back into the pistol and racked a live round into the chamber and set the safety to on. He took the inside-the-waistband holster from the security box, clipped it inside his pants, and inserted his pistol. He checked to see that the pistol was hidden under his coattail. He then returned to the kitchen where Toni was still puttering around. He could tell from the way she was focused on trivial tasks that she was worried.

"Toni, we need to get out of here," he said.

"But Bill, my sister, and her daughter Ashley are coming over in just a few minutes. Shouldn't we wait for them?"

"No, I don't think that's wise. It may be nothing, but I would rather play it safe."

"Okay Bill, let's be safe."

"Toni, why don't you pack a suitcase, just a small one, and I will leave a note for your sister."

"Okay Bill. I'll be quick." Toni walked quickly to the staircase and trotted up the stairs. Just as she reached the bedroom, she heard a crash, and four quick gunshots. The sound was so loud it hurt her ears.

At first she froze. Then, she ran down the stairs. She found Bill standing in the kitchen with a pistol in his hand. There were two men bleeding on top of her outside kitchen door, which was now flat on the floor. The two men were both dead.

"Oh my God, Bill! Who are they?"

"I don't know, but they broke the door down. I will bet that there are more of them either here, or on the way. We have to move quickly." Bill took Toni's hand and they dashed toward the garage. They got into the car, Toni in the passenger seat, and Bill driving. Bill started the car, and backed out of the garage almost before the door was high enough to clear the car. Toni could hear the scraping sound as the door grazed the roof. Just as a Bill backed into the driveway, Toni's sister pulled up with her daughter in their red Buick. Bill stopped the car. Toni got out quickly ran over to her sister.

"Quick Mary, you two come with me." Surprised, her sister let Toni pull her out of the car and hurry her to the back seat of their car. Mary's daughter, Ashley, followed them. Toni got them both into the back seat as quickly she could, and then got back into the front seat. Bill backed into the street, and then squealed the tires as he drove away.

"What's going on Sis?" Mary asked. It was obvious she was frightened.

"We will tell you later," Bill said. "Just keep your heads down and try to stay out of sight."

Bill drove slightly over the speed limit, watching carefully for anyone who might be following them. He made his way to Interstate 66, and drove steadily. He turned south on Interstate 81 around Strasburg. He had always made a habit of filling the car's gas tank when it got down to the ¾ level. Now, he was very glad of his habit. He had just filled up that morning on the way to work. He thought the Impala would go almost 400 miles before they had to stop for gas.

They drove along in silence. Bill thought that Toni must be in shock. He believed he was as well. He kept watching the rear view mirror, and was just starting to relax when he heard the helicopter approaching them from the rear.

"Toni, do you see that?"

Toni turned her head, ducked lower, and looked out the rear window. "I don't think that looks good Bill," she said.

"Neither do I, Honey." Bill kept driving because there was simply nothing else he could do. When the exit for Raphine Road came up, he took it, and headed toward the town of Steele's Tavern. He knew they were in trouble when the chopper followed. The only thing Bill thought they could do was head for cover. The problem was that he didn't know this area at all.

In his four years in the Army, Bill had never seen combat. In some ways he regretted that, and in some ways he was very pleased he had never had to fire a shot at another human being during his time in the service. When he shot the two men who broke the patio door down, he was acting on instinct alone. His Army training had kicked in, and he fired without even being conscious of what he was doing.

Right now though, he knew what he was doing. He ran through the options over and over again as he drove, and it always came down to the same thing. They would have to try to escape on foot. He thought escaping on foot was a bad bet, but it was the only bet they had.

Bill had always been decisive. He knew that was one of his strong points. When he came to a heavily wooded area, he quickly slowed down and swung the car off the road and under the trees. "Everybody out," he said. "We need to abandon the car and get under cover."

Toni got out of the front seat as soon as the car stopped. She helped Mary out of the car while Bill did the same for Ashley. With Bill leading, they ran for the woods.

The woods were thick enough to hide their progress from the helicopter, as long as it didn't have thermal detection capability. As a minor deputy director with the Department of Interior Security, Bill knew that the state police helicopters were slated to receive that capability later this year, but that it wasn't installed yet. He also knew that it wouldn't take very long for the government to provide a helicopter that had thermal imaging capability, or even a drone, if he were considered a valuable target. Considering what he had discovered, he thought he just might be a valuable target.

It had been accident, not intent, that allowed him to stumble onto a copy of a top-secret report written for the higher ups in his own agency. However, he knew the government well enough to know that would not matter.

He was very worried about Toni, her sister, and niece because the part of the information that had shocked him the most was how witnesses were murdered as well as the intended targets. He knew very well how the government could cover up incidents.

Bill led them into the trees, angling southeast down the slope. Once, they carefully skirted a house set deep into the woods. The house was well kept, and had three cows in a small wooded pasture, and a very large garden. Bill thought it might belong to one of those preppers that this administration kept saying were likely to be terrorists. Bill had never met a prepper and, considering what was usually said about them in is department, didn't want to. At this point, he just wanted to get away with his family intact.

As they moved through the woods as quickly as they could, Bill knew that the cops, or more likely trained agents of the agency he worked for—had worked for he corrected himself—would be after them. It was obvious now that he was no longer a valued employee, just a valued target.

Bill's office in the DIS handled paperwork involved with providing surplus military equipment to the increasingly federalized state and municipal police forces. Even though he was a minor bureaucrat with a moderately impressive title, at least to those outside, he knew almost nothing about the overall operation of the agency. Until he had seen the top-secret report, had not even known that the agency had armed drones or trained killer agents.

He was trying to remember what the killer agents had been called in the report. He remembered only part of a code name, ground hounds, because the alliteration and lack of the use of an acronym had also surprised him. He had glossed over that part because the use of armed drones to kill American citizens had shocked him so badly. It was positively un-American. He was starting to realize that America wasn't the America of his youth anymore.

The name ground hounds suggested they had the ability to track people on the ground. Bill shuddered to think of what technology they had. With the effectively unlimited budget of the Department of Interior Security, he was afraid almost anything was possible

The brand-new, black helicopter landed in the middle of the road. Two men dressed in camouflage jumped out. They were both lean and incredibly fit. They had not said a single word to the pilot, nor to each other.

The taller of the two seemed especially withdrawn, the pilot thought. He had not said a word to either of them either, not because he had been instructed not to, but because there was something about both men that scared him. They were not normal. The cold stare they gave him almost made him sick to his stomach. He was relieved when they left the helicopter.

Once they were far enough away, he lifted the helicopter into the air, and returned to base, as per his orders. As he flew away, he could see where the state police had traffic stopped in both directions. The traffic was starting to really back up. He wondered what the official excuse would be this time? Maybe a training exercise?

Greg led, and the other ground hound followed. It was easy for them to pick up the trail at the car. This time they were under orders to take out the targets as quickly as possible. Intel said that there were three targets, but the tracks showed four. An extra kill would be just fine, Greg thought. He hoped he was able to kill all four, but he knew the other hound was hoping the same. They would probably have to split the kills between them, but Greg could always hope. They followed the trail at a fast jog.

They were on the scene an hour after the car had been abandoned. That meant that the targets were unlikely to be more than four miles ahead of them, and probably much less.

Bill kept pushing them along. Ashley was complaining, although he kept whispering for her to stay quiet. Bill guessed that was typical for a 14-year-old these days. Mary seemed to be in shock and said nothing. Toni was also shocked, but seemed determined. She had always been made of sterner stuff than her sister, Bill thought. Her competence was one of the things that had attracted him to her when they first met.

Bill wondered who would be coming after them. He only had three rounds left in the .45, and he knew they wouldn't be enough.

He also knew for the first time that he wouldn't survive this. The feeling shocked him enough to make him shiver, even though it was warm. He now knew what it was like to be in a combat theater; feeling your impending death as wasted years, and all your future hopes and dreams, flashed before you. Yet, he knew he could not just quit. He was mad now, but it was a cold, thinking madness, one unlike any he had known before.

Bill could think of only one possible way that he could keep Toni and her family alive. He knew how important her sister and niece were to Toni.

He and Toni had never had children. The doctor said Toni was barren. That left her with a deep sadness that had taken years to go away, if it ever had. Bill had always wanted children too, so it was a hurt for him as well; a hurt he never let Toni see.

Mary and Ashley were Toni's only relatives. Her parents had died in an automobile accident when Toni was 15, leaving her and Mary behind. The doctor said that the accident had left Toni unable to conceive, taking away most of both her present and future family in one screeching crash of bending metal and broken glass.

After the accident, Toni had raised Mary, who had only been eight when the accident happened. Mary had been the only one unhurt in the accident, probably because Toni had covered her with her own body when she saw that the crash was inevitable. With no relatives to turn to, Toni quit school, got a job, and petitioned the court for custody of her sister. It was testimony to her competence that the judge granted it.

Bill was an orphan. He had never known his parents. His mother had given him up for adoption at birth. Unfortunately, Bill was never adopted, and had grown up in a series of foster homes, often moving from one to another more than once a year. He joined the army as soon as they would take him, at 18, just to get out of the system. At 22, he left the army and started college on the GI bill. He earned his degree in general business and accounting, and went to work for the federal government right out of college.

He and Toni met at a party and, once they started talking about being orphaned, something just clicked between them. It took Bill about three weeks to realize he was in love with Toni, but then she always was the smarter one. She later told him she had known that first night at the party.

Bill led the women along the creek that ran along the base of the hill. They stayed under cover of the trees as much as possible. After about a mile, they came to a rickety bridge across the creek and a poorly maintained dirt road.

Bill had been hoping for a more traveled road, but beggars couldn't be choosers. They ran across the bridge as quickly as possible and then back into the woods beside the road. Bill watched hopefully for a car.

Bill chose a location where the forest canopy almost covered the road. He stopped. "Toni, Mary, Ashley; please listen to me. We are going to hijack a car and get out of here."

"But Bill, that is illegal," Mary said.

"Mary," Toni said, "just go along with this. It is very important. Do you remember what I told you?"

"Of course," Mary said, "but the government won't really hurt us."

"What about the men who broke our door down?" Bill asked. "I checked. They both had government IDs."

"I don't believe this," Mary said.

"Mom, do what Aunt Toni and Uncle Bill say. We can argue about this later." Bill was surprised. It seemed like Ashley was growing up very suddenly.

Bill heard a vehicle coming and motioned everyone into position. The vehicle was an older pickup truck, and the driver looked like a real country boy. He was maybe 30 years old, unshaven, and just looked rough. Bill thought he might be armed, but he had no choice. Time was short.

Bill stepped into the road in front of the oncoming pickup truck, and leveled his pistol at the driver. The truck quickly braked to a halt in a cloud of dust. Bill could see Toni run towards the back of the truck followed by Ashley who was almost dragging her mother. The driver's eyes were on Bill's gun. Bill didn't think the driver had seen the women. Toni climbed over the tailgate just as the driver suddenly floored the gas pedal and tried to run Bill over. Bill jumped out of the way, and the truck disappeared across the bridge. His plan had not worked completely, but at least he thought Toni might have escaped.

"Mary, you and Ashley stay under cover of the trees and keep going. I will stay here and cover you. Don't come back here for any reason, no matter what you hear."

"Yes, Uncle Bill," Ashley said. She led her still protesting mother away in the direction Bill had indicated.

Bill thought that any pursuers would have to cross the bridge, so he crouched in some bushes where he could watch the bridge. His pistol was in his hand, and he was determined to at least get the three rounds he had left fired at his pursuers. He hoped it would buy the women some time, but, in his heart, he knew he had failed. He never heard the bullet that entered the back of his head and killed him.

"That's one," Greg said as he put his silenced pistol back in its holster.

"Such amateurs," the other hound grinned. "Let's get the others."

"You bet," Greg said.

Both hounds started off at an easy lope in the direction that Mary and Ashley had taken. Reading their tracks was as easy as reading a comic book.

When the truck started moving, Toni instinctively pulled herself over the tailgate and into the bed. At first, she didn't realize that her sister and niece had not made it with her. Since the truck was rapidly accelerating, and she had no choice, Toni lay down in the bed of the truck. She noticed a blue plastic tarp and covered herself with it. The ride was bouncy and rough.

The truck continued along the road for about 15 minutes, then pulled into a driveway, and drove almost a mile into the woods. Toni did not rise up and look because she didn't want the driver of the truck to see her. She waited fearfully until the truck stopped.

After the truck stopped she heard the driver's door open and close, and heard the footsteps of the driver walking away. He was talking on a cell phone as he walked.

"Larry, you're not gonna believe this. Some guy pulled a gun on me and tried to steal my truck. I was almost carjacked."

As the driver walked farther away, Toni could no longer hear what he said into the phone. She waited until she heard the door on the house close. Then, she quickly rose and rolled out of the truck on the side away from the house. She immediately ran behind the barn and made her way into the woods. As she crouched behind some bushes, she realized she was back at the place that they had skirted when they were walking through the woods. Since she didn't know what else to do, Toni sat down and cried as quietly as she could.

Ashley and Mary kept moving. At times Ashley had to almost drag her mother, but they still managed to keep moving. Coming around the bend in the road they ran right into two men dressed in dark camouflage. Each man was carrying a rifle. Both men had holstered pistols on their belt. Mary assumed that they were police, broke free from Ashley, and ran toward them.

"Please save us," she said.

"Yes ma'am," one replied as he drew his pistol and shot her.

Ashley was in shock as one of the men grabbed her arms and said, "You're coming with us, young lady."

Five hours later, Greg looked at the other hound and said. "Well, that's three. That's all they told us to get."

"But the tracks show there were four."

"Yeah, it looks like that one managed to catch a ride with someone."

"The weekend is coming up. I am off duty. I have plans."

"Well, that's fine with me. I have plans too."

"I guess that settles it then," Greg said as they both started toward their pickup point leaving the naked body of Ashley in the woods behind them.

Four days later, Toni was still hiding in the woods near the house. She had been stealing food from the garden at night and water from a horse trough. She was getting tired of eating raw bell peppers, onions, and green beans, but that was the least of her problems. She was worried almost out of her mind about Bill, her sister, and her niece. It took all of her ability just to get through the days. She cried herself to sleep in the woods every night, burrowed into a pile of leaves to stay warm.

It was on her 17th day of hiding that the man found her. He was the owner of the garden she had been stealing food from; the man who had driven the pickup truck that brought her here. She begged him not to turn her over to the government. Much to her surprise, he did not. He and his wife simply took care of her until some of her fear was gone, and her appearance, at least, was normal again.

These were the first preppers Toni had ever met. She began to question the government's story that preppers were terrorists. It was the government doing the terrorism, as she now knew very well.

Then, one day, Lorne Vanders and Doc drove up and took her away to safety. She never figured out how the man knew Lorne, and Lorne never volunteered that information. Most of the fear went away in time as she mourned her loss, but a bright ember of that fear remained deep in her belly, ready to violently explode if she were not careful.

Chapter 12: THE BIG SPLASH

"No man knows the mind of a woman before she knows his." John Debrouillard

<u>Gulf of Mexico</u>

The meeting was over, but everyone stayed around talking for quite some time. After a while, I asked Lorne "How are we going to get off the ship?"

"The other members of the Council will take a small submarine to the Yucatán Peninsula, and then each will return to his or her home from there by different routes. We will take the ship's launch and meet our boat at another oil platform. We will then take our boat back to the Gulfport Harbor."

"That sounds okay," I said. "The sooner the better, I think."

"Let's get going then," Doc said.

Toni, Peggy, Lorne, Doc, and I headed for the ship's launch. Once we were aboard, the crew quickly lowered us to the water, and we started toward the production platform where we were supposed to meet the ship's crew with our boat. It took us about 20 minutes to reach the platform. Our boat was already underneath the platform structure waiting for us. We switched boats and took off in the direction of Gulfport Harbor in our original boat.

After we were well underway, I asked Lorne. "Do we have a backup plan?"

"Well, kind of," Lorne said. "We do have snorkeling gear in case we have to swim."

"I suggest we get it out then," I said.

Doc went below and came back with a large plastic tote containing flippers, snorkels, and masks. We passed those out to everyone.

"Folks, I suggest we keep these very close at hand. Wear the masks around your necks. Does everyone here know how to use flippers and a snorkel?" Everyone nodded so I assumed we were in pretty good shape. I was hoping we would not need the flippers and snorkels, but I knew the government wanted me, and probably Peggy and Toni, very badly. On the water, we were a sitting duck for a drone attack. No matter how many precautions we had taken, I was skeptical that they were enough.

Our trip was uneventful until we were about five miles from shore. Then, Toni saw the drone.

"Look! Over there," Toni pointed. I looked to see what she was pointing at and caught the flash of a white drone silhouetted against the gray storm cloud. Off in the distance, I could see the gray curtain of rain falling from the cloud. Just in case the drone was after us, I asked Doc to take us into the rain. Doc immediately turned the boat and headed for the rainstorm.

"Uh oh, there is another one," Lorne said.

I looked where Lorne pointed and saw another drone, and then another. "I think the jig is up. Doc, get us out of here," I shouted.

Doc thrust the throttle levers forward on the boat, and we took off at maximum speed toward the rainstorm. The twin engines were screaming. I could see lightning flashing in the cloud. We were only a couple of hundred yards away from the rain front when the closest drone fired a missile. "Everybody get your gear and get overboard, now!" I shouted. I handed Toni her flippers, and she quickly went over the side. Doc and Lorne followed quickly. Peggy was still fumbling with her mask so I picked up her flippers in my left hand and, with my right arm around her, forced us both overboard.

The boat continued at top speed toward the storm without us. When the missile struck it was over 100 yards away. The concussion hit me in the face like a board. Toni had her gear on, as did Lorne and Doc. Doc was helping Peggy with her flippers, so I helped her get her mask and snorkel in place. The rain was moving toward us. Soon, I heard the patter of raindrops on the water. The patter soon turned to a roar. We all held hands and swam in a straight line into the storm.

Three times we felt the concussion as drones released missiles blindly onto the storm. The last one was so close that the blast wave threw us almost fifty feet. We were separated. I felt blindly around and touched a hand. It was Peggy's. She grabbed my hand and held on tightly. I could tell she was very afraid. So was I, for that matter. I just didn't have time to think about it. We looked for thirty minutes, but the others were not to be found. Once I thought I heard a boat, but I wasn't sure.

As best I could tell, we were about four miles from the beach. I just didn't know where the beach was. It was almost dark, and the rain seemed to be subsiding. All we could do was tread water and hope we found the others, or they found us.

While we waited, I made sure that Peggy had her flippers on tightly and her mask adjusted properly. I hadn't done any snorkeling since I was a kid, but I still remembered how. We held hands and tread water until dark. I was hoping the others would show up. They didn't. I begin to suspect the worst.

When dark came, I studied the horizon. To my left I could see the glow in the sky above Gulfport. Farther off ahead of me I could see another glow. I thought that was Biloxi. We turned in the water to face the glow that I thought was Gulfport. I reasoned that trying to swim back to Gulfport would be a mistake because they might have people watching for anyone like us. To the left of the Gulfport glow was a smaller glow that was probably Long Beach. I figured we would head for Long Beach.

We begin swimming slowly toward the glow that I thought was Long Beach. For the first time in my life, I was happy for the habit I'd developed of studying the maps of anywhere I visited. As we swam, I showed Peggy how to hold on to my shoulder with one hand and rest her legs. I also showed her how to rest by turning over on her back and floating.

Six hours later we heard the waves breaking on the beach. Fortunately for us the waves were very small. That made reaching the beach much easier. I was surprised when Peggy managed to get to her feet on the beach. I tried but couldn't. The best I could do was crawl.

I wasn't sure of the time, but I estimated it to be about two in the morning. The traffic along the beach highway was sparse. It was a Friday night. Any other weeknight, the traffic would have been sparser still. I managed to sit up and face the water. We had ditched our fins, masks, and snorkels a hundred feet from the beach.

We were sitting on the sand in soaking wet street clothes and bare feet. Peggy was sitting so she could see the highway behind us. From the road, it would look like two people sitting on the beach having a conversation.

"Thank you," Peggy said. "That is the second time you have saved my life. I would never have been able to make that swim without your help."

My legs were starting to ache, and my arms felt as if they were ready to fall off. "We aren't out of here yet," I said.

"What happened to your wife?" Peggy asked. Her question caught me totally by surprise. For a minute, I couldn't speak. After all, it had been less than two weeks since Susan was murdered, although it felt like a lifetime in some ways. The last two weeks had been, by far, the most eventful, and stressful of my entire life.

It took me a while to tell her the story. She had to keep asking questions to keep me going. It was not easy to go over that day again in my mind. Peggy was horrified at what I told her. I could see that in her face.

I was sure Peggy wasn't really interested in the parts that I felt I had to tell about how Susan and I had met, and how happy our lives were together, but I couldn't tell that from her face. I figured turnabout was fair play so I asked her about what happened before we took her from the mountain only three days ago.

She told me about it, and about managing to kill the first ground hound. When she told me about how she did that, my estimation of her, and her abilities, went up a hundred-fold. I could tell she was smart that first time I met her, but only now was I realizing just how smart and how tough this lady was.

"Pretty good for a computer programmer," I smiled.

"Not too bad for a retired professor either," she smiled back at me. We had been sitting on the beach now for over forty minutes. My back, legs and arms were starting to stiffen up and I knew that it was time to get moving. I was just starting to get up when Peggy leaned over and put her arms around my neck. She said, "A police car just stopped. I think the cop is checking us out." Then, she kissed me. It felt like the first time I kissed Susan, and yet it didn't. There was urgency in her lips that demanded a response, yet gentleness at the same time. That struck me as odd. She was a tough and smart woman who had managed to kill a trained and armed government agent with just a rock. I found myself kissing her back without even intending to.

"Hey, you two," the cop hollered from the side of the highway. "Get off the beach. Go home."

Peggy stopped kissing me and turned to face the cop. "He just asked me to marry him," she said.

"That's fine," the cop said. "But go home now."

"Peggy said, "Yes Officer. I can't wait to tell my mother. We are going." The cop seemed satisfied and, shaking his head, turned to go back to his squad car. Peggy and I slowly stood and, as soon as the cop car had pulled back out on the highway, we limped across the beach holding hands.

"That was pretty fast thinking," I said.

"Not really," she said glancing up at me. "That gambit is used in almost every movie and TV show I watch. I am surprised it even worked."

"I think you must be a pretty good actor," I said.

After that neither of us said much. It was as if we were both suddenly shy. I thought that she must be mad at me for kissing her back, just as I was mad at myself for kissing her back. I couldn't believe I had done that, especially so soon after Susan's death. The cop had been far enough away, and the beach was dark enough that he wouldn't have been able to tell the difference.

I found myself looking at Peggy and wondering more about her. She was not classically beautiful. Cute would be more like it, although some folks would just call her plain. For the first time, I found myself wondering if she had a boyfriend or even a husband waiting for her somewhere. I realized that I had never noticed if she wore a wedding ring or not. When she told me her story, she had not mentioned a boyfriend or a husband. I did know she had a cat.

I forced myself to think only about how we could reach safety. The closest safe place that I knew was Lorne's home and that was a hundred miles or so from where we stood. We had no identification, no cell phones, and only about a hundred dollars in soggy cash between us. We had talked about that during the long swim, or the 'Big Splash', as Peggy called it.

Furthermore, there were surveillance cameras and federal police that we needed to dodge. With no shoes, we couldn't even walk very far. It was a dilemma.

We crossed the highway and walked down a side street into a residential neighborhood. Subdivisions like this one usually had fewer surveillance cameras than business districts, which was why I chose to go there.

"Do you know how to hot-wire a car?" I asked.

"No," Peggy said, "do you?"

"No," I replied. "I wish I did right now though."

"Do you think the others made it?" She asked.

"I hope so, but I am not sure. I don't think we can count on them for help right now though. I think we have to figure a way out of this by ourselves."

Washington, D.C.

"Four hellfire missiles and more than eight million dollars, and you are telling me that you didn't even find any bodies."

"Mr. President," the DIS secretary said, "we didn't even find any body parts. However, it is possible that we got them all with a direct hit." The secretary was relieved that the president had not mentioned killing him again, although he was stealthily making plans to resign very soon and disappear.

The president turned his handsome face on the secretary. "Let me tell you a story, Sid. When I was 12 years old, we vacationed in Florida, in a little town east of Panama City called Mexico Beach. My father rented a small cottage right on the beach."

"That must have been nice, Mr. President."

"Not really," the president said. "My mother called the place a dump, and said it was beneath us. My father, the senator, said it was necessary to keep us close to the people."

"But wasn't he a senator from Connecticut, Sir?"

"No, he was a senator from Illinois. He believed that it was important to be close to regular people no matter where we were. My mother always hated that. But that is not the story. Here is what happened. One day that summer a USAF fighter jet crashed in the Gulf, quite a ways offshore. For a week after that there were USAF patrols scouring the beaches for remains of the pilot. What they found were mostly skin fragments. I found some myself. I saved them for years in a jar of alcohol as a reminder of that explosion," the president smiled.

The secretary thought that must have been a good summer for the president. He had no idea that the president's fondest memories from that summer were of finding the pilot's skin fragments floating in the water like soaked pieces of parchment, and imagining the suffering that the pilot must have gone through in the moments before and during the crash.

"Mr. President, what has that..."

The president interrupted, "Now listen to me, you stupid fuck. Either you find the body parts and have them DNA matched to our targets, or they are still alive. There are no two ways about it."

"Yes, Mr. President. I will get our people right on it." The secretary left the room as quickly as he could.

Long Beach, Mississippi

We had been walking in the neighborhood for fifteen minutes, making very slow progress because of our bare feet. I looked back down the street and saw the lights from a federal police car moving slowly on the beach near the water. They were either on to us, or they were looking for some sign of survivors. In any event, Peggy and I needed to get as far away from there as fast as we could, and, if possible, leave no trace behind us. That was a tall order, but the alternative was, at best, unpleasant.

"Do you have any ideas?" Peggy asked.

"Not really," I said. "Let's just keep moving for now." I led her onto a side street so we would not be visible from the beach. The neighborhood was showing a bit of wear under the street lights, but it was a good, middle-class neighborhood, or at least had been before the economic woes started under the current administration. After about five blocks, I saw a light on in the kitchen of one of the houses. The yard was meticulously neat, and I could see a fair-sized garden as well as a shop and a smaller tool shed behind the house. I looked closer and saw what appeared to be fruit trees scattered around the yard. The car in the driveway was about 20 years old and in excellent condition for its age. The windows on the house were barred. They were the only barred windows I had seen in the neighborhood so far.

I took Peggy's hand and led her to the door. I noticed her surprise as I reached out and pushed the doorbell.

Chapter 13: THE RESCUE

"Heroism is caring personified." John Debrouillard

<u>Gulf of Mexico</u>

Lorne was as surprised as the others when the blast wave threw them backwards. He quickly looked around and saw that Doc and Toni were still close to him. Doc was swimming, but Toni was floating face down, unmoving. Lorne swam to her, and raised her head out of the water. Her mask and snorkel were missing, torn loose by the wave.

"Doc. Come here. Quickly!" he shouted.

Doc was still a bit groggy, but got there as fast as he could. He held his head against Toni's chest while Lorne supported her in the water. As indefatigable as ever, Lorne's feet moved rapidly back and forth generating enough lift with his fins to support both he and Toni. Doc raised his head and said, "She's not breathing. Her heart has stopped. We have to perform CPR."

"In the water?" Lorne asked in a tone of voice that showed Doc that Lorne was shaken. "How do we do that?"

"You hold her head above water, pinch her nose closed, and breathe into her mouth every time I say 'breathe', while I do chest compressions." Once they were both in position, Doc said, "Breathe." And using his doubled fists began the chest compressions to keep Toni's heart pumping. With each push they almost went under the water, but Lorne always managed to keep Toni's head above water, even when his own went under. Doc's legs were already sore, but, in spite of that, he managed to work them back and forth quickly, and stay high enough out of the water to do the chest compressions.

They continued CPR for four minutes with no response. In medical school Doc was taught that the cutoff in wilderness situations was 30 minutes of CPR, if no signs of life were observed. He didn't know how they could go on for another 26 minutes, let alone still be able to swim to shore. However, he would rather die than lose Toni. She had been the mom he had never had ever since he had met her a year ago. Doc grew up as an only child raised by his father, a medical doctor. His mom died in childbirth, and his father had never remarried.

Periodically during his childhood, Doc asked his father why he never remarried. He thought it would be very nice to have a mom. His father always said exactly the same thing. "Son, some things and some people are simply irreplaceable."

At twenty minutes, Lorne was still going strong, although Doc was sure, despite the Gulf water on Lorne's face, that he could see tears in Lorne's eyes.

It was becoming all Doc could do just to keep his head above water, but somehow he managed to continue the chest compressions, even when his head periodically sank below the water. Lorne had the rhythm, and now Doc no longer had to give the command for Lorne to breathe into Toni's mouth.

Lorne knew, if he abandoned both Toni and Doc, he could make it to shore by himself. He had once trained to swim in the Olympics, but just barely missed the chance to compete. He also knew that he couldn't leave Doc or Toni behind to die. He could never live with himself if he did. For the first time in his life, he thought he might actually die. Surprisingly, he was fine with that.

Lorne laughed when he thought about the lessons his father had tried to teach him. "Boy, in this world, it is every man for himself. Do whatever it takes to succeed." Until he was sixteen, Lorne had always looked up to his father. At six-feet five, his father was easy to look up to. Most people seemed to admire him.

When Lorne was sixteen, his Mom was dying of cancer. His father went off in search of another business deal, while she was on her deathbed. Her last words to Lorne were, "Son, doing what is right is the only real strength in this world. Sometimes you have to fight for what is right, and sometimes you have to sacrifice for what is right. Son, always do what is right, and you will have no regrets." Lorne thought his mother had been far wiser than his father ever knew. Ever since that day, he had followed her advice, and he had no regrets.

Five minutes later, Lorne thought he heard a noise over the roar of raindrops falling on the water. It was a boat; a boat motor. He didn't see how the feds could have a boat looking for them so quickly, so he opened his mouth, and between breathing into Toni's mouth, shouted. "Help! Help!"

Doc was really struggling now, and Lorne had one hand helping to hold him up too, even as Doc continued the chest compressions. Lorne's legs were starting to fail when the boat found them. He was still shouting for help between breathing into Toni's mouth.

"Damn, what have we here?" The shrimp boat captain said looking out of the pilothouse window towards the deck at the three people that his crew had dragged aboard. The two men just dragged out of the water were still desperately performing CPR on the woman. "This just doesn't look good," the captain said out loud. "There is going to be some damn red tape over this."

In a couple of minutes, before the first mate arrived to take the wheel, Toni sputtered and sat up. She spit water out, choked, and then spit again. Lorne supported her shoulders. Doc collapsed on the deck, unable to even sit up.

Two of the crew wrapped her and Doc in blankets, and then carried them into the cabin. Lorne struggled to his feet, and followed them. The captain greeted him in the cabin. "Yo. What did you guys do? Sink your boat?" The captain motioned toward the galley table and sat down while the crewmembers carried Toni and Doc into the captain's quarters and laid them each down on a bunk. Lorne quickly checked both Toni and Doc over as the crewmembers carried them past. Both Doc and Toni smiled at Lorne, and he relaxed.

"You might say that," Lorne replied taking a seat at the table.

"In this little squall?"

"Yes," Lorne replied.

"I reckon I should call the Coast Guard, then."

"Captain, I would greatly prefer it if you don't."

"Well Lad. It is like that, is it?"

"Yes, Captain. It is like that."

"All right lad. It will be as you wish. I have no liking for the government's red tape anyway."

One of the crewmembers returned to the galley, while the other tended to Toni and Doc. Toni was awake and talking a bit, but Doc was now sound asleep. "I think they are OK, he said."

"Good," the captain said.

"Captain," Lorne said. "We had two more people aboard; a man and a woman. We got separated."

"Aye lad, we'll have a look-see." He motioned to the crewman. "Hey Pete, let Akbar know to go careful and search the area for them. You man the searchlight. I'll be there in a bit."

"Aye Captain," Pete said and was up the ladder to the wheelhouse in a flash.

The search went on until a few hours before dawn. The captain was a careful man. He allowed for the wind and current speed and direction in his search. They found nothing. They were out of the area before the federal search boat showed at first light.

"He was my friend, even though I had not known him very long," Lorne told the captain.

"Aye Lad, I know what you mean. I may not look like much as old as I am now, but I was a river patrol boat captain many years ago in a little country called Vietnam. I lost some friends there. I still miss them, even after all these years. One was my older brother."

Lorne and the captain sat in shared silence as Akbar, the first mate, headed the boat westward towards Corpus Christie, Texas. For many long hours the big, burly, gray-bearded captain and the smaller, trim, and fit Lorne talked while Doc and Toni slept. Finally, only a few hours from Corpus Christie, Lorne fell asleep in his seat. The captain smiled and covered him with a blanket, muttering, "Any man would give his right arm for a son like this one."

Corpus Christie, Texas

Doc got into the driver's seat of the car that was waiting for them at the docks in Corpus Christie. Toni got into the front passenger seat. She was still shaken by her ordeal, but insisted on riding shotgun. Lorne was saying his good byes to the shrimp boat captain. Doc turned to Toni and said, "I am really glad you made it," he hesitated for a second. "Mom."

With no hesitation Toni reached over and hugged Doc. "You are the son I always wanted. Thank you so much for saving me." There were tears in both of their eyes.

"Captain, it has been a pleasure," Lorne said. "I owe you my life, and the lives of my two friends."

"It was nothing lad," the captain said. "I am sorry about your other two friends."

"As am I," Lorne said. "But I must hope they made it somehow. We will keep looking."

"Indeed, you are as determined as any man I have ever met," the captain said. "I admire that greatly."

"And you are an honorable man, Captain; a good American. One I am proud to call my friend."

"Aye, lad. Friends we are. We shall meet again."

"Yes," Lorne smiled, "we shall."

Lorne walked to the car, turned and waved to the captain, and got into the back seat. As he started to settle back into the seat, Toni leaned over the seat and kissed Lorne on the cheek. "Thank you for saving me," Toni said.

"It was Doc," Lorne said. "I was just there." When they were under way and Lorne was sure neither Doc or Toni were looking in the rear view mirror, he touched his cheek where Toni had kissed him. He did that several times before he fell asleep. He slept all the way through Texas. They changed cars in Oklahoma, and Lorne fell asleep again once they were under way. By then Toni was driving, and Doc was catnapping in the front passenger seat.

"Toni glanced at Doc from time to time. She thought her husband Bill would have really liked this young man too. She also glanced in the rear view mirror at Lorne from time to time. She had seen him touch his cheek where she had kissed him before he fell asleep. That left her conflicted. She owed Lorne her life more than once. He was younger than her forty-eight, maybe only a couple of years past thirty. She had not known that he was interested in her. She knew that she didn't look nearly her age, and she knew that she drew male attention wherever she went, but she didn't know what to do about this. She certainly didn't want to hurt Lorne, but she just didn't think of him in that way.

With Doc, it was simpler. They had a mother and son relationship; one that neither had ever had, and each had always wanted. When she thought about John, the tears began quietly flowing down her cheeks. She cried for Peggy too. She liked her as well. Soon, Toni was crying for Bill, her sister, and niece.

Toni wasn't sure she was over losing Bill, but she knew she was very attracted to John. That had surprised her. She remembered that first day she had met John on the ranch. Lorne had arranged for her to take care of a Wyoming ranch that he had a part ownership in. The two ranch hands were also members of the organization, and both were hiding out there as well for some reason or another that neither of them ever spoke of. When John drove up, Toni grabbed a rifle and stepped out to meet him. She had seen the truck coming up the driveway and had been watching it for a while. Her previous dislike of guns was long gone. Lorne had taught her to shoot, and she found she enjoyed it; perhaps because of her fantasy of shooting the murderers of her family.

When the truck door opened and John stepped out, Toni involuntarily relaxed a bit. She didn't feel threatened, even though he was a stranger. He was tall, but not too tall, with wide, muscular shoulders that looked unusually strong. His hair was almost completely gray, yet he looked too young to have gray hair. Then, she noticed the blood on his tee shirt and jeans.

"Hold it right there, Mister," she said, while wondering about this man who she was immediately attracted to. She made sure that attraction didn't show on her face. It was hard for her to even acknowledge the attraction anyway, because she still missed Bill. Being attracted to another man made her feel guilty.

It still made her feel guilty. She drove until the tears were gone, but the memories still hurt. That was the problem with memories of lost loved ones. They don't dry up and go away like surface tears. They remain like a constant pain deep below the surface, sometimes bubbling up at unexpected moments.

"Take the next exit, please," Lorne requested. Toni did as requested. They drove through two small towns and into another one. Lorne gave directions. They ended up in front of a typical, older suburban ranch style house. Lorne said, "Please wait here."

Lorne walked up to the door and rang the doorbell. In a few seconds, the door opened and, after a brief conversation with the man in the door, Lorne turned and waved Toni to drive toward the garage. The door opened, and she maneuvered the car into the garage. The door closed, and they were out of sight.

Toni and Doc got out of the car, and walked to the door into the kitchen where they were greeted by Lorne and his friend. "We will stay here for a while," Lorne said.

"That's good," Toni said. "Where's the bathroom, please?" Lorne's friend motioned down the hallway adjoining the kitchen, so Toni headed in that direction.

"Doc, this is Ray Stringham."

"Pleased to meet you," Doc said.

"Likewise."

"Make yourself comfortable," Lorne said. "Ray has secure communication capability and I want to find out what's going on in the search for John and Peggy." Lorne disappeared with Ray into a back room.

Doc made himself comfortable on a couch in the living room. He knew Lorne would be preoccupied for quite some time. Even though Lorne did his best not to show emotion, Doc knew him well enough to know that he was devastated over the loss of John and Peggy. Soon, Toni joined Doc. They were both tired, so they sat together on the sofa in a comfortable silence.

About an hour later, Lorne came back in the living room, followed by Ray.

"What's happening?" Doc asked.

"Our sources say that there is an ongoing federal police search along the Gulf Coast between Biloxi and Pass

Christian. They have many boats in the water, and an absurd number of observation drones, as well as helicopters flying overhead in the Gulf. There is no indication that the feds have found anything yet. It is possible, however, that they have found John and Peggy's remains and are still looking for us. However, we have no confirmation of that."

"Do you think they got away?" Toni asked.

"I just don't know," Lorne replied. "I hope so."

"I have a feeling that they escaped. John and Peggy are two of the toughest people I know," Doc said.

"I hope you're right," Toni replied.

"Well, there's nothing more we can do here. It is time that we get back to Mississippi," Lorne said. "I have made arrangements for us to take a small plane back to headquarters. Another car will be here soon, and we can use that to drive to the airport."

Chapter 14: REUNION

"When all else fails, just do something." John Debrouillard

<u>Long Beach, Mississippi</u>

A minute after I rang the doorbell, I heard faint footsteps and noticed that the light shining through the peephole darkened briefly.

"Who are you?" A voice said from behind the door. There was no movement of the door or door handle. Just as I suspected, the person in the house—a man from his voice—was cautious.

"My name is not important," I said. "We need refuge. The government is trying to kill us."

"Well, that's a new one," the voice behind the door said. "If you try to come in my house, I may be trying to kill you too." He paused for a bit, "Why did you stop here?" He asked.

"Because you are a prepper," I said. "I am a prepper too."

"Are you armed?" The voice asked.

"No Sir," I said. "Neither of us is armed." I had ditched my Browning in the Gulf because it was hard to swim with. I didn't know how the Navy Seals managed with all their gear.

"OK," the voice said. "Come around to the back door and stand at the far edge of the patio until I tell you different. One word of warning though. If you have friends hiding out there and are lying to me, the front door will still be covered. And we will kill anyone who tries to enter."

"Yes Sir," I said. "That is exactly how I would handle it. We are alone, by the way."

Peggy and I walked through the side yard to the back patio. The patio was about 20 feet wide and 30 feet long. I was willing to bet that the edge of the patio was a bit more than 21 feet from the back door; because that was the distance someone with a knife can cover before a holstered pistol can be drawn. I showed Peggy how to hold her hands over her head with her palms forward. I did the same. We were standing just like that when the patio light switched on. In a few seconds, an older man opened the door and pointed a 12-gauge riot gun at us. He looked us over for a bit. I could tell Peggy was afraid. I wasn't too worried. I might as well be shot by a citizen as by the government.

"OK, you two, come in the house, but keep your hands where I can see them." We complied. We walked through the door into a modest kitchen. I noticed a large pressure canner on a counter and canning jars on the kitchen table.

"OK," the man said, "how did you know I am a prepper? I have maintained excellent OPSEC. Even my neighbors don't know. Hell, I am not sure my family even realizes I am a prepper."

I motioned Peggy to a chair at the kitchen table. The man started to put his shotgun down to move the canning jars out of the way. I said. "Let me move the jars. You keep your shotgun handy." The man looked me in the eye for a few seconds and then leaned the shotgun in the corner.

"Aw hell, I don't want to kill nobody. I just don't particularly want to get killed."

"My name is John," I said, and shook his hand. "This is Peggy." I moved the jars, and he and I sat down at the kitchen table with Peggy.

"My name is Leon," the man said. "How did you know I am a prepper?"

"I wasn't positive but, the garden, the fruit trees, the bars on the windows, and the workshop in the yard were good indicators."

"A lot of folks have those."

"Yes, they do. But I also recognized that almost every plant in the yard and flower beds is edible or useful as well."

"So?"

"So, anyone who is into edible landscaping, security, and self-sufficiency is most likely a prepper."

"You are saying I gave myself away."

"Yes sir," I said. "But, so did I." And I told him my story. It took about fifteen minutes. Leon got all of us some iced tea while I was talking and set a plate of cookies on the table. Peggy ate quite a few cookies.

After I told my story, he said, "I have read your comments on many prepper and anti-government blogs.

Quite a few folks are wondering what happened to the 'RetiredProf'. The rumor on the internet is that it was a drone strike, but the pictures I saw posted of your house on the internet didn't look like an explosion. Now I know why. Many of us have been suspecting that the government was killing people who opposed them for several years now. We have never had proof. I still think that explosion in St. Louis a while back that killed five people and damaged a crap load of houses was a missile strike. Maybe a hellfire missile isn't big enough, but we all know they have other missiles as well. It seems like an awful coincidence to me that the fellow who was killed worked at programing drones."

"I was never sure what it was, but the official explanation of a gas leak didn't seem to fit. Most gas explosions are not accompanied by fire," I said. Peggy looked at the two of us as if we were speaking a foreign language.

"That sort of stuff is on the internet?" She asked.

"Almost everything of any significance that happens is on the internet sooner or later," Leon smiled. "This guy here, the RetiredProf, says that the internet is the first citizen to many citizen interface, and that on the internet, the truth always floats to the surface if you look hard enough for it." Leon smiled. "That is why the government is threatening that we need government-managed cyber security. They want to completely control the internet so citizens can no longer communicate freely, and the truth about government misdeeds doesn't get out."

Peggy said, "Before the drone, I would have never believed any of this."

"You have seen a drone strike?" Leon asked.

"She has seen several," I said. "She was a witness to an assassination by drone, and then they tried to kill her with another one because she saw the first one. I'll bet that is not on the internet." I said.

"Not that I have seen," Leon said. "But I have been busy canning lately and haven't had as much time to read the internet alternative news as I would like."

Peggy thought for a moment. "Well, if it isn't there, it is going to be. I am sure there is a way to hack into the government system and retrieve the video filmed by the drones. They must have cameras on them, just like the drones our government uses to assassinate people overseas. The bastards just can't be allowed to get away with this."

"So far, no one has been able to hack the drones camera feeds that I am aware of," I said.

"None of them are as mad as I am!" Peggy scowled.

"Tell me your story, if you want," Leon said. So Peggy told him her story while I ate some of the cookies. I was still trying to stay off wheat, but those cookies looked so good I couldn't resist. Peggy talked for almost 30 minutes. I could tell she was mad. Leon listened quietly. When she was done, he said. "There is going to be a revolution in this country. Folks have just been talking it up before because they are mad at the fools in Washington, D.C. for messing up the economy and taking away so many of our liberties. Once the people find out about this, the true patriots are going to go ballistic."

"I agree," I said. "The challenge is to destroy the government's power in such a way as to keep them from slaughtering large numbers of American citizens who rebel. Freedom of speech is almost dead in this country already.

As soon as the government seizes control of the internet, the people will be effectively silenced."

"I think things are coming to a head," Leon said.

"I concur," I replied. "I don't think we have very long before the government becomes so oppressive that they openly kill American citizens who disagree with them."

"They stole the election this time. From what I have read, there was so much voter fraud that there's no way they didn't steal the election. We were all expecting it to be close, however, the polls showed the other candidate should have won by a significant margin. Yet, the election results showed that, time after time, in the swing states, voting was not what the polls predicted it would be."

"Yes," I agreed. "Did you see where in some of the counties as many as 149% of the registered voters voted for the current president."

"Yes, I did." Leon slowly shook his head. "I'm worried about the future of this country. I am 76 years old, and I grew up in a different country. It was called the United States of America, but it's not the United States of America I live in today. When I was young, people worked. People took care of their own. Charity was local. Importantly, anyone who wanted to work—which was nearly everyone—could work. Now, our foolish leaders conspire with international corporations and greedy bankers, and export our jobs overseas. Any fool could have told them that the result would ultimately be a failed state here at home."

"You are right," I replied. "We started to go wrong when we began to elect lawyers to political office. I realize that lawyers believe that they are excellent critical thinkers. However, very few are. This is because they are taught in law school that facts are pliable. That the loudest expert is right."

"What do you mean?" Peggy asked.

"Well," I said, "let's start by examining the education that most lawyers receive. To be accepted into law school, you first need to earn a four-year degree. Very few lawyers earn their bachelor's degree in science, engineering, or mathematics. Most, especially those who are interested in entering politics, usually earn bachelor's degrees in political science, or some allied field. What you should know is that political science is not really science. It is just a non-quantitative way of looking at human relations. I must admit, the study of people and how they behave is of primary importance in more than just politics. However, without an understanding of mathematics, the science of physical resources, and economics based on physical quantities, accurate decisions concerning the course of the country are difficult to make."

"Also, lawyers are trained to be advocates for those who pay them. If you are accused of a crime, you need an advocate. However, if we send someone to Washington to represent us, we need someone who understands the issues and does not simply act as an advocate for the lobbyists who give him the most money."

"I hadn't thought of it quite like that," Leon said. "I can see your point though. I think part of the problem was when the federal government legalized lobbying. It is just legalized bribery, nothing more. If you or I did a fraction of what our congressmen do, we would go to jail."

"You are correct again," I replied. "Our elected representatives, our employees if you will, have used our money to remove themselves from our control. What's worse, the Department of Interior Security has purchased several billion hollow point bullets. The United States of America has not been invaded on their watch; nor have terrorists attacked in any manner that requires the use of firearms by the DIS. The only thing that most of us can figure is that they plan on using all those bullets, and all the firearms they recently purchased, on Americans who disagree with the current administration."

"I hadn't heard about that before," Peggy said.

"I'm afraid there will be a revolution upon us, and we will not even be required to fire the first shot," Leon said.

"There are preparations underway by a significant number of people in this country for just such an eventuality," I said. "The problem right now is the people have little organization."

"I look for the first overt moves against people who openly disagree with the current administration's policies to begin within a few weeks of the government seizing complete control of the Internet. I don't think this administration will be content to use only secret assassinations. I think they want complete tyranny."

"That makes sense," Leon said. "Without the ability to communicate, developing an organized resistance will be difficult. If the government manages to take our guns, the people who oppose the current regime, the majority of the working citizens of this country, will be massacred."

"What I don't understand," Peggy said, "is why the American people are not already up in arms about the drone strikes by our government in countries like Pakistan? These strikes don't just kill enemies of the state; they kill innocent civilians, men, women, and children. If it were our children being killed, I think we, as Americans, would march on Washington, D.C. and hang the people who killed our children."

Peggy looked at me, "John, I have been thinking about this for some time now. I understand why you want to kill the people that murdered your wife. What I am having trouble understanding is why, before all this happened, I was able to put most of what I read about the overseas drone strikes completely out of my mind. I guess I thought it was just someone else's problem. Now, I realize that it's everyone's problem."

"Evil is every decent person's problem no matter where they live, no matter in which country they reside. If evil wins, the good people of the world lose. Our government is evil. No matter how many times we have been told what they do is for the good of our country, no matter how many times we've been told that they know best what is good for us, no matter how many times they tell us that they're looking out for us, we should never believe their lies."

"I believe that she has woken up," Leon said.

"Yes," I said, "waking up for most of us has been much slower process than what Peggy was forced to go through. The problem that we currently face in this country is, even if we, as individuals, are awake, we are not well enough organized to remove the evil from our government."

"I hope that will change soon," Leon said.

"Some of us are working on it right now," I replied. "We have suffered a bit of a setback. That's why we knocked on your door. But, I believe that we will ultimately be successful at removing the evil from our country, or die trying."

"You have my support," Leon said. "What can I do to help?"

"We don't want to put you in any danger," I replied.

"Let me worry about that, John. Like I said, I'm 76 years old. My wife passed away five years ago, and we don't have much in the way of family. I haven't heard from our son for 11 years. He lives out in California somewhere."

"Okay, Leon," I said, "We need some help getting back to a safe location. I am afraid that if you simply drive us to that location, that the federal surveillance analysts will, sooner or later, identify you. That will put you in danger. I think the feds want Peggy and me so badly that they would torture you to find out anything that you might know."

Peggy said, "It would not be fair if anything happens to you, Leon."

"You said there will be people searching for you and Peggy. You think they will expand their search from the beach."

"Yes, I do."

"Then, we are wasting time," Leon said. "Let's get out of here."

Leon quickly packed a small suitcase, mostly with pictures, and we went to his car. Leon carefully checked the street for observers and the sky for drones before we got in the car. Peggy got into the drivers seat. Leon got in the front passenger seat. I lay down on the back seat with the shotgun. Apparently, the shotgun was the only firearm Leon had. He said his prepping budget was not big enough for an arsenal.

Peggy backed out of the driveway, and we headed deeper into the neighborhood. Leon showed her the way. He said he knew a back way that would take us all the way to Highway 49 and keep us out of Gulfport. Highway 49 ran north through Hattiesburg close to where we needed to go. Leon also said that there were unlikely to be many surveillance cameras along the route because of the low population. Leon had lived in the area all of his life and told interesting stories of how the landscape had changed since he was a boy hunting in the local fields and swamps that were now covered by subdivisions.

Once we were on Highway 49, we made good time. Peggy kept the car about five miles an hour below the speed limit. There was almost no traffic. It wasn't quite daylight yet. I was worried about possible roadblocks, since Highway 49 was a major route in the area. I asked Peggy to be alert for anything like that ahead. I was particularly worried because Highway 49 N. passes right past a large National Guard training site, Camp Shelby, just south of Hattiesburg. I thought that would be a good place to set up a roadblock. It turned out I was right.

We topped the hill and saw the flashing lights in the road ahead of us. It appeared to be just two police cars. I figured that meant that the feds had no idea where we really were, and this was a just in case roadblock.

"Should we try to go through the roadblock?" Peggy asked.

"Leon, is there a way around the roadblock?" I asked.

"I don't think so, John," Leon said. "I don't think there's any way for us to get off the highway now without them seeing us turn off."

"I guess we go through them," I said. "Here is what we are going to do."

We stopped briefly alongside the road. I took the shotgun and got into the trunk. We left the trunk lid open, and I held it down with one hand. Then, we drove toward the roadblock again. Peggy stopped the car and leaned out as one of the officers approached. "What's the problem, officers?" She asked. When the officers got close to the car, Leon started coughing very loudly and choking. That drew both officers' attention and I slipped out of the trunk as Peggy said, "Dad, what's wrong?"

That's when I pointed the shotgun at the officers who were standing about two feet apart on Peggy's side of the car. They were both Mississippi State Highway Patrol. They were not feds. "Just who are you boys looking for?" I asked as I raised the shotgun and pointed it at their heads.

The one on the right started to reach for his pistol. I said, "Please don't do that. I will kill both of you if you do."

"You can't get away," The other officer said as they both raised their hands above their heads.

"Don't you worry about that," I smiled.

Leon stopped coughing and got out of the car. He walked behind the two officers and, one by one, took their pistols.

"Please check for backup pieces." I said. Leon smiled and put the pistols in his back pockets. Then, Leon frisked both officers. Neither was carrying a backup piece.

Leon walked around the car and stood beside me. He now had a gun in each hand. They were pointed at the highway patrol officers.

Peggy slid over, and got out on the passenger side of Leon's car and walked towards the patrol cars. She got into each one in turn and turned off the radios and the cameras. She then walked around beside the two officers, out of the line of fire, and said. "Hand me your lapel cams, please boys, one at a time." They did as she asked. Peggy then turned the lapel cams off and tossed them onto the seat of one of the patrol cars.

"There's more cars headed our way," Leon said, pointing to the lights flashing in the distance along the highway to the south.

"OK, Officers," I said gesturing at the officers. "Please get into our car." They both got into the back seat. Peggy got behind the wheel, and Leon got in the front seat after handing me one of the pistols and turned and pointed a pistol at the officers. I squeezed in the back with the officers after putting the shotgun in the trunk. Peggy then drove us out of there. We made it past Camp Shelby and then took a side road out into the woods just south of Hattiesburg. Peggy stopped the car, and I asked the two officers to get out. They got out with their hands in the air. Leon was already out of the car and covering them. I got out and did the same.

"Do you know who you were looking for?" I asked.

"The feds said we are supposed to be on the lookout for five people. Two of you fit the descriptions we were given."

"What did the feds tell you about why we are wanted?" I asked.

"They said you were terrorists who are plotting to kill the president," the taller of the two said.

"Well, I'll be," I said. "They got that right about wanting to kill the president, in my case anyway."

"Then you guys are terrorists?" The other officer asked.

"Only to the evil bastards in our government," I said. "We do not want to harm any citizens."

"Why?" The taller of the two asked. I was surprised by these two. They were more intelligent than most of the cops I knew, especially the taller one.

Leon spoke up, "I was 16 when my father let me enlist in the military. I fought in Korea. I was wounded and awarded a Purple Heart. I was promoted to Captain before I retired. I swore to uphold the United States Constitution against all enemies, foreign and domestic. That is what I am doing now. The current administration is decimating our Constitution and our civil rights. They are also murdering American citizens right here on U.S. soil."

"No way," the shorter of the two highway patrol officers said. "There is no way our government would kill Americans here at home."

"Yes they are," Peggy said. She quickly summarized her story, and mine, and described how the feds tried to kill us with hellfire missiles just yesterday afternoon out on the Gulf.

"Gentlemen," I said when Peggy had finished, "we are going to leave you here. We have no beef against you, and I hope you hold no hard feelings."

"I don't know how we will explain this," the shorter one said. "It might get us fired."

"If you want to stay safe," I suggested, "don't repeat any of what we told you to the feds. Other than that, feel free to tell it any way you like."

The taller officer said, "We heard reports of explosions out in the Gulf yesterday afternoon. No one seems to know what caused them. The feds have the entire area cordoned off right now." He looked at me, "Do you give me your word that what you have told me is true?"

"Yes, I do," I said.

"I believe you," he said. "I don't want to, but I do."

"I don't," the other officer said.

"I wouldn't have believed it either just a week ago," Peggy said. "Then, the feds tried to kill me with a drone and ground hounds."

"I have heard rumors of those ground hounds. I thought it was just conspiracy theory bullshit," the taller cop said.

"They were news to me just this morning," Leon said.

The shorter officer looked at the other officer, "Fred, do you really believe these folks?" He asked.

"I am afraid I do," Fred said, "and that scares me."

"It scares me too," I said. "More than you could know."

Fred stepped forward and offered me his hand. I shifted the pistol to my left hand and shook his hand. He had a strong, honest grip. "Good luck," he said. "And I can't believe I said that. I feel like I am being disloyal to my country."

"No, Son," Leon said. "You are a loyal American. It is the evil men and women in Washington who are not loyal to America."

"This is crazy, just fucking crazy," The other officer said.

"I agree," Peggy replied. "You have no idea how much I wish everything was back to normal."

We left them standing there beside the road as dawn began to break over the trees. Fred waved. Leon waved back. Peggy was driving and didn't notice. I tossed their pistols out of the rear window about fifty yards from them. We were out of sight around a bend in the road before they got to them.

"Leon," I said, "I am afraid it will be too dangerous for you to go home now.

"That's OK, John. This is the most fun I have had in years. Besides, the doctor diagnosed me with colon cancer a while back and he said I don't have very much time left. It is stage III, and I don't want chemo or an operation. I guess I am still prepping just from habit."

Peggy looked shocked.

"Well then, I will enjoy your company," I said.

"Me too," Peggy agreed. "And we will look after you, too."

"Aw, I don't need no lookin' after. I am a tough old codger, you know."

I could see the tears start flowing down Peggy's cheek. For some reason I was delighted that she cared. Far too few people did these days.

We made our way back to Hattiesburg by back roads and guess. We found Hattiesburg as much by luck, as by good direction. I knew we needed another vehicle, but I had no way of arranging one. It was too dangerous to drive the one we were in, and it was too far to walk, especially since Peggy and I were still barefoot. It made me think about ways to avoid this problem in the future—at least, if we could get to safety without being caught.

For once we were lucky. We stopped at a big box store on the south side of town, and Leon bought some spray paint. He said that he didn't think anyone would be looking for him because he didn't think the two highway patrol officers would identify us to the feds. Outside of town, we sprayed Leon's old car with rust preventing paint, the dirty-looking red kind. When we were done, it looked like a ratty old car instead of a well-maintained classic. Once the paint job was done, Leon took a tire iron out of the trunk and started smashing in one of the fenders. I caught his hand after the first blow.

"Leon, we can get your car repainted. This isn't necessary."

"Yes, it is, John," he replied. "This old car needs to look completely different." I backed off and let him continue. Soon, at Leon's request, Peggy took over. When they were done, the car looked nothing like it had before. We even covered the tag and much of the car with mud.

"Leon," I said, "you kept that car like it was your pride and joy."

"Yes, it was," Leon said, "but liberty is far more important. I am an old man who most likely won't live to see this battle through. Please let me do what I can."

Peggy hugged Leon, and I shook his hand.

"Yes Sir," I said.

We drove back to Lorne's place with no problems. When we got there, I drove the car into one of the sheds and shut the shed door behind us as we walked to the house. Myrtle was there and he looked worried. He perked up considerably when he saw us.

"John, Peggy," Myrtle almost shouted. "It is good to see you. We thought you were killed by the drones offshore."

"What about Lorne, Toni and Doc?" I asked.

"They are on their way. I expect them in about ten hours or so."

I was relieved. I had worried about Lorne, Toni, and Doc since we had been separated. I was afraid to think about what might have happened to them. I had grown closer to those three, and Myrtle and Peggy as well, more quickly than anyone I had ever known, except Susan. For Susan and I, it had been love at first touch, if not first sight. I remembered shaking her hand when we were first introduced all those years ago. Her touch was electric. The surprise in my eyes was reflected by the surprise in hers.

"Myrtle," I said, "this is Leon."

"Pleased to meet you," Myrtle smiled. "Welcome!" Myrtle led Leon away as they both talked. I think Myrtle could tell that Leon was tired, and was most likely taking him for some refreshments before showing him to a room to rest. I wasn't sure how many bedrooms Lorne's place had in that basement, but I suspected there were quite a few.

I fell asleep in an overstuffed chair in the living room. Peggy fell asleep in another chair. I woke when Lorne came into the room, followed by Toni and Doc. Lorne strode over to me and shook my hand before I could even get out of the chair. Toni hugged me and kissed my cheek and then hugged Peggy. Doc said, that unlike Toni, he would be satisfied to just shake my hand, and did so as Lorne shook Peggy's hand. Doc then shook Peggy's hand too. Myrtle appeared and said, "OK, folks, there is a meal on the table in the kitchen. It is time to eat.

We all filed into the kitchen. Leon was there and apparently had been helping Myrtle. I introduced him to Lorne, Doc, and Toni. We all spent the next two hours around the table catching up. When I heard about how Lorne and Doc had saved Toni, I was even more impressed with these two guys.

I also felt confused. I knew I would have been very upset if Toni had not survived, but I couldn't figure out what was going on. I knew I was starting to like both Toni and Peggy more than I should. I felt like I was being disloyal to Susan, who had passed away less than two weeks ago. All the years I had been married to Susan, the thought of another woman never even entered my mind. Oh, I had 'opportunities' tossed my way from time to time, but I never even thought about taking advantage of any of them, no matter how insistent the hints were. Yet, now there were two women on my mind. I wasn't used to that. It made me feel guilty.

Once the conversation died down, I took Lorne aside and said, "Lorne, we need to talk." We spent the next 14 hours in private conversation."

Chapter 15: PLANNING

"Planning is necessary even though no plan survives unscathed." John Debrouillard

<u>Near Kansas City, Missouri</u>

I looked around my new office. It was far larger than anything I had ever had as a professor, even larger than my home office before I retired, and Susan and I moved from our politically correct McMansion to our little house in the country. Again, I was amazed at the resources that Lorne and the other members of the council had.

The room was about twenty by thirty feet and filled with WWII surplus desks and filing cabinets, the least expensive functional office furniture to be had. Contrasting the old furniture, were five of the newest and most modern computers scattered around the room. Two were Macs, two were PCs running sanitized versions of Windows, and one as a PC running Linux. I had used PC's all of my working life, and had switched to Mac when I retired. I now much preferred Mac's for my personal use. I would have been content with a single iMac, but Peggy insisted that more computers were needed. I wasn't sure why more computers were necessary, but I trusted her judgment.

My desk was bare wood. There was an iMac on a table next to it, but I preferred to work without the distraction of a computer as much as possible. My colleagues at the university had laughed at this habit, yet my publication record was better, both in number and quality of peer-reviewed publications, than theirs. I found the computer to be nothing more than a distraction when I was thinking, and only of use in writing, recording ideas, or looking up specific information on the internet.

One wall was bare unpainted sheetrock. Lorne was going to have it painted, but I told him the resources were better used elsewhere. Besides, Toni and Doc were busy covering that entire twenty-foot long wall with maps, including a very large map of the United States that showed not only major roads and cities, but topography as well. There was no time to paint anything.

Peggy was busy directing a couple of guys on how to mount the biggest flat screen TV, which she insisted was a computer monitor, I had even seen on the opposite wall. Lorne had agreed that this was necessary. I didn't even know what it was for yet.

Someone had also recovered Peggy's cat, Loco. It was a large white Ragdoll with long hair and a majestic visage. The cat kept watch over all of us and accepted the many pats and caresses that came her way with a deep dignity that only cats possess. At present Loco was supervising from the corner of my desk. For some reason, Loco's eyes always followed Lorne as he moved around the room.

Lorne had also mounted three gun racks around the room so that they were only a step of two away from any of the workstations. Each rack held a couple of selective fire M16s and about 20 loaded magazines in shoulder bags, as well as a couple of 1911 model Colt .45s. I wasn't sure they were needed, but Lorne insisted. He had acquiesced though to finding me another Browning to replace the one I had dropped into the Gulf of Mexico, even though he strongly preferred pistols in calibers larger than 9mm. The new Browning now rested in an inside the pants holster butt forward on my left side. Of everyone in the room, Doc was the only one not carrying a holstered pistol.

What amazed me the most was the location of the new office. It was over 300 feet underground, and located on the outskirts of Kansas City, Missouri in what had been an old underground limestone mine. Nancy bought this old mine, and a dozen others, a few years ago. She developed a number of the mines as cold storage facilities, and others as document storage facilities. While not as large as the Hunt Subtropolis in the same area, she still had a sizable operation.

She had several government contracts to store documents that needed to be kept safe. One of her mines was even rented to the DIS and was where DIS stored their own important documents. DIS had their own armed guards on that one and no one else was allowed in. When I asked her about that, Nancy laughed and said there was a back door that they didn't know about when we needed it.

Our new headquarters was excavated even deeper than the original mine, and there was no public record of the new excavation. All the work was done by patriots and oathkeepers loyal to the Constitution and the organization. Electricity was generated onsite by solar panels on the ground above, and the electric and communication lines were carefully hidden. Heat came from a series of old fashioned steam radiators powered by a small coal plant on the surface. The coal plant was a part of Nancy's surface limestone mining operation. There were also half a dozen well-hidden escape hatches, just in case. I still didn't know the entire layout, and doubted I ever would.

There were also a number of other offices and a very large workshop in the same tunnel complex. Lorne said that we were going to expand into the rest of the open space underground very soon and build small factories to make any special items and weapons that were needed for the resistance.

Lorne was convinced that soon the administration would institute complete gun control, and not long after that country-wide gun confiscation, in an attempt to disarm the people so that they could be more easily controlled. He believed that we should make weapons available to any patriots who needed them; weapons that were the equal of anything used by our military. While I had no desire to carry a grenade launcher around, at least under normal circumstances, the Second Amendment to the Constitution does not forbid it. Our founders fully expected, and wanted, the citizenry to always be at least as well armed as the military so that the citizens could overthrow our government if, and when, it went rogue. Actually, most of our founders thought in terms of when, not if. Well, it had certainly gone rogue now, I thought.

Lorne also believed that our government was likely to use genocide to readjust the population mix to where they wanted it—more sheeple and fewer patriots. Lorne said that the government would especially be interested in getting rid of preppers because people who depended on themselves more than the government scared the powers that be shitless. He also said that they would love to get rid of old white men because they were too conservative for the current administration. Military veterans had to go because, according to the feds, it was possible that veterans, who were mostly conservatives, might use their military skills against them. And Christians had to go because they ultimately answered to God, not the federal government. I agreed with Lorne that all this was possible, although I didn't think it was as likely as he believed. After all, that would mean getting rid of half the population of the USA, and the productive half at that.

Our quarters were also underground near the office complex. Lorne, Doc, Toni, Peggy, Myrtle, Leon, and I, as well as a dozen technician and ex-military security guys and gals, each had our own quarters. They were identical and each comprised a small bedroom, bathroom, and sitting room. Each was equipped with an intercom and an old-fashioned dial telephone that was wired into an internal telephone system with no outside access.

The galley was run by Myrtle, who had Leon and a couple of others as helpers.

There was also a very large conference room that looked like it would hold almost a hundred people, though there weren't nearly that many chairs. The big conference table was made from plywood and 2x4s and seating was a menagerie of folding chairs of various types. A video camera and tripod were set up in one corner.

At the end of the hall, there was a darn good gym with treadmills, elliptical machines, and a couple of weight machines and some free weights. I was looking forward to slamming some weights around. It seemed like a good way to vent—until I could kill Susan's murderers, anyway.

My first act as the new leader of the revolution was to have a long talk with Myrtle. After all, any army is only as good as its ability to feed the troops, even though I wasn't sure yet if we even had any troops.

Myrtle and I found a small, empty room and set up a couple of folding chairs. Myrtle carefully lowered himself into the chair as if he expected it to collapse underneath him. I made a mental note to request some stronger chairs.

"What's up John?" Myrtle asked, "Or should I call you general, or something?" Myrtle smiled.

"Dumb Ass, will do nicely," I smiled. "I am not sure how I got myself into this."

"The same way we all did, John," Myrtle replied more seriously. "We just ran out of patience for tyranny."

"Anyway, Myrtle," I said. "I want to know more about the food and water situation here. This is not a critique, just me learning enough to plan effectively. I know Lorne, and the committee, have already done a lot of planning, and put a tremendous effort into building this facility, but I need to come up to speed on all of this, as well as what our capabilities are around the country.

"I thought we would just write reports like we used to in the military," Myrtle stated.

"I thought about that," I replied. "However, I don't think we need to commit very much information to paper, or digital files, for that matter."

"You must have a good memory, John," Myrtle said.

"No, just a trained memory," I said. "It is a useful tool, especially when one is trying to make sense of an ever increasing flood of information."

"Did you take a memory course?" Myrtle asked.

"You might say that," I replied. "I read and studied *The Memory Book* by Harry Lorayne and Jerry Lucas. It is a very good memory system."

"Do you think we all need to use it to reduce paper trails?" Myrtle asked.

"I am not sure yet," I answered. "On one hand, no paper or digital trail leaves no trace, but—and this could be a big but—if someone is captured who knows a lot, torture might let the government get at that information. I still need to think about it."

"Yeah," Myrtle said. "I thought about that too. Why would a government that kills our citizens at home not torture them for information?"

"I think they will," I said. "That is why no one should get caught."

"Tell me about the food and water supply 'down under', as it seems to be called lately," I requested.

"Well," Myrtle said, "water is the most important. We have three wells that are drilled into a deep aquifer below. The wellheads are all underground. Two of those wells have electric pumps, and one has a deep well hand pump. That one is just a backup.

"How much water do you think we will use?" I asked.

"I am guessing about 200 gallons a day per person, everything included," Myrtle replied.

"That sounds close," I said. "I suspect it may run a bit higher." "As I understand it, we have room for about 30 people at present down here. That would make our daily water use about 6,000 gallons."

"The wells seem to produce that and more, as best I can tell." Myrtle said.

"I will ask Lorne for the well tests. That will tell me more. Then I need to do some computer modeling to see if the drawdown from our wells will affect any of the wells on adjacent properties. If any of water levels in surrounding wells are affected, then it will be possible for a hydrogeologist to infer the existence of our wells. That information might end up in government hands. That would be bad for us," I said.

"I don't know much about water wells," Myrtle said. "Could they actually tell that?"

"If water levels in surrounding wells are affected, and I had that data, I could tell," I said. "Remember, I am a hydrogeologist."

"That's lucky for us," Myrtle said.

"We have to be that through about everything," I smiled. "Success is in the details. We are up against the most thorough data collection and surveillance system the world has ever known."

Myrtle nodded, "You are the right guy for the job. But I already knew that."

"Thanks for the vote of confidence," I said. "I wish I felt that way myself. Can you tell me about our food supply?"

"That's the easy one," Myrtle said. "We have enough freeze-dried emergency food for three years, or a bit more, at eventual full capacity of over 100 people. I am inventorying it now."

"OK," I said. "Please let me know what you find out."

I spent the next three days asking questions about rock stability during potential bunker-buster strikes, how we received our electricity (a combination of generators, surface mounted solar panels with battery back up), and our outside communication system, as well as facility security. Once I had the answers to most of my questions, I realized that our electrical power might be our weakest point. Our generators ran on diesel, and though the ventilation system was excellent, and exceptionally well hidden, the volume of fuel we used was great. I needed to talk to Nancy about how the fuel purchases were hidden and what fraction of her operation they were.

Lorne and I also went to the surface to inspect the solar array. It was truly impressive—too impressive. I was worried that the size of the array, clearly visible by satellite, might arouse government suspicions. That was something else I needed to talk to Nancy about. Lorne said she was due to arrive in about three days. I figured I had no choice but to wait, so I moved on to other things.

I had always heard that "revenge is a dish best served cold." I was beginning to think that the old saying was wise indeed. I was determined to kill Susan's murderers, but the more I thought about it, I realized that I agreed completely with the committee that the entire government had to fall and be replaced with one that honored our Constitution. Otherwise, the psychopaths in charge would murder many more innocent citizens, like Susan. I did not want that to happen.

Lorne and I spent the next three days discussing what we should do and in what order we should do it.

"I think we should put together an army and take the White House and Congress," Lorne said.

"Lorne, in many ways I agree with you," I replied. "However, how would that make us look to the sheeple?"

"Should we care about what the sheeple think?" Lorne asked.

"They are citizens too. Their lack of knowledge would work against us and many might stand with the government out of habit."

"Except the supporters," Lorne said. "They will stand with the government out of meanness."

"Lorne," I said, "many supporters are well-meaning people who are simply not cognizant of the way the world really works. They are often critically thinking challenged; programmed by our politically correct education system, if you will. I don't want any citizens hurt, if at all possible, no matter what their ideology. In the end, it will be our efforts to prevent collateral damage that will rally the citizenry to our cause and cause massive desertion among the ranks of federal workers and police. We can't be the ones leaving dying and dead innocent children and citizens from our attacks on the government. Leave that to the government— and we need to prevent as many government caused civilian casualties as possible."

"I see your point," Lorne said. "I get so mad though, that sometimes I just want to shoot the government bastards."

"As do I," I smiled. "It is perhaps the greatest temptation of my life to just take a gun and start searching out and shooting the drone operators who murdered my wife. However, in the bigger scheme of things, that would be pointless. This revolution will ultimately be won with technology, not with guns."

"You have said that before," Lorne said. "I have been thinking about that, but I don't understand how we can beat the system since they have most of the technology."

"Paid for with U.S. citizen dollars," I reminded Lorne. "We will simply take back the technology we need and disable the rest. We will need some talented programmers, hackers, hardware, and internet technology folks to do it, as well as some very good electronic engineers. I don't have the knowledge, nor can one person do all that needs to be done along those lines."

"Make me a list of the skills you need and we will start recruiting," Lorne said.

"It might be possible to get a government contract to facilitate much of the work and not even have the people solving the problem know why they are solving the problem or for who," I said. "I will have a list to you this evening."

Lorne grinned. "Now, that sounds like a plan. Let me see what I can stir up."

After I spoke with Lorne, I went in search of Peggy. She was a computer programmer, and I needed her input. I found her sitting with Toni in the cafeteria dining room. They were drinking coffee and chatting. It appeared to me as if they were becoming good friends. I walked over and sat down at the table. They were sitting across from each other near the end where I sat down. They both stopped talking as I got closer. I was too lost in thought to hear anything I might otherwise have. That was starting to be my normal mode again, much like it had when I had been doing research at the university.

"What's up, John?" Toni asked.

"Yeah," Peggy said, "what's up Doc?" She looked at Toni, "After all, he is a retired professor."

"John is plenty good enough," I said.

"You look stressed," Peggy said. The smile on her face faded a bit, but it was still peeking out. I liked that.

"Peggy," I said, "I need some advice about computers, and such."

"OK," Peggy replied.

"I'll go and let you guys talk," Toni said.

"No," I smiled. "Please stay. I can use your input as well."

"OK," Toni said, "I was hoping you might say that."

"Let me set up the conversation by saying this," I said. "Our first task is to understand what the government is doing, and how they are doing it. We need to know what they are doing before we can counter it."

Toni nodded. "This I want to hear."

"There are three things that every tyranny has done to control a free people. First, they remove the peoples' ability to reason."

Toni said, "That would be the dumbing down of the school curriculums over the last 20 years."

"Longer," I agreed. "Although I doubt it started as a deliberate attempt, it has certainly morphed into one. Also, the democrats have been breeding a less than clear-thinking population by continually increasing the number of people drawing welfare. Even those citizens among them capable of thinking clearly are constrained from thinking clearly at election time because the welfare has become their only option for survival. They have no jobs available."

"That was done by our government simply by signing NAFTA," Peggy said.

"That's right in part," I agreed. Toni was nodding her head.

"The second thing that is done is to constrain the citizen's ability to access and exchange information. That's where the recent attacks on the first amendment and the attempts to get the entire internet under government control are directed. The internet is part of what I want to talk to you about, Peggy," I said.

"OK," Peggy said.

"The last thing is to remove the ability of the citizens to defend themselves and to protect their property. In this country, that is the current gun control push which will lead to gun confiscation."

"The first thing after the election was a ban of semi-automatic weapons," Toni said. "That is clearly unconstitutional."

"Yes, it is," I replied. "Also on the horizon is the UN treaty on small arms control that will ban all firearms in private possession here in the US. That is also unconstitutional, but I believe it will be signed by our traitorous president and ratified by the senate."

"Tyranny is getting close," Peggy said.

"I think it may already be here. Most folks just don't yet know it," Toni said.

"OK," I said. "We have to fight on all three fronts. We need to reeducate people in constitutional law and in critical-thinking skills. We need to design and implement a method of communication beyond government control and detection that both we, and the citizenry, can use. I think we need a secret internet, or something."

Peggy nodded, "I have some ideas on that."

Toni said, "I checked into your idea of piggybacking signals on the current internet. The experts I spoke to think it might just work."

"Can we get them on our side?" I asked.

"They are already on our side and are working on it." Toni looked at Peggy, "I will put you in touch with them."

"Great," Peggy smiled.

"The third thing we need to do is keep guns in the hands of the citizenry."

"And the 3D printing gun factory that Lorne wants to develop may allow us to keep the citizenry armed," Toni said.

"We also need to manufacture ammunition." I said. "The government will crack down on the availability of that as well. They are already demanding that records are kept of all ammunition sales."

"We also, if possible, need to find ways to block the state surveillance system and even turn it around so we can use it but the government can't."

"I have a contact who might be able to help us with that," Peggy smiled.

Peggy, Toni, and I talked for about three hours. By then we had several good ideas that we considered implementing. Peggy may have had the best one. She said that since television and the movies had contributed to the dumbing down of the populace, that we should use the same medium to brighten them up again. I wasn't sure if we had the resources to do that or how long it would take, but I thought that, given time, it could work quite well.

Nancy, Lorne, and I sat in one of the small conference rooms discussing the solar arrays and facility security.

"We need to be able to move operations quickly," I said. "Until we control the government data stream, they will be able to find us fairly quickly."

"You think they might drop a bunker buster on us if they find us?" Lorne asked.

"Yes I do," I replied. The three of us talked for a couple of hours before Lorne excused himself to see about a previous engagement. When he left, Nancy turned to me and said. "Lorne is quite a guy, isn't he?"

"Yes, he is. I think he is the backbone of this revolution. I am proud to call him my friend."

Chapter 16: FIRST STRIKE

"Those who make peaceful revolution impossible, make violent revolution inevitable!" John F. Kennedy

Alabama, Highway 17 near Chatom, North of Mobile

"It just ain't right," Larry said. "Those Federal Transportation Security Police thugs set up a checkpoint on the highway, and now we have to get groped every time we go to Mobile to go shopping. I thought those dumb asses were just supposed to be at the airports."

"I know," Lowboy replied. "They groped my five-year-old grand-niece just last week. She is still upset over that. And so am I."

"I flew to Houston to visit my son last Christmas," Larry said, "The FTSP bastards felt up my junk and the bitches left my wife in tears. I think that was part of what contributed to her death last month; that and the breast cancer."

"I am truly sorry about Mildred, Larry," Lowboy said. "You guys were married how long?"

"41 years," Larry answered. "I just want to kill some of those FTSP bastards. They have to be evil people just to be able to do what they do. Where does the government find these retards, anyway?"

"I think they hire them right out of prisons, gay bars, or the psych ward or something," Lowboy laughed.

"I want to get rid of that damn checkpoint on highway 17." Larry said.

"They will put you in jail," Lowboy said.

"And at my age I should give a damn about that? I ain't got so long left, you know."

"Me either," Lowboy said. "I miss the America we grew up in. Where did it go? Where did these bastards come from who believe they have the right to tell everyone how to live their lives? Hell, 70 percent of what the feds do now is unconstitutional. That checkpoint and their forced, warrantless searches are unconstitutional. Highway 17 is a state-maintained road, for Pete's sake—it ain't even a federal highway. I think I am ready to do something to get even myself."

"What can we do? Those baby feeler-uppers have an armored checkpoint and full-auto M-16s."

"Don't you still have one of those M-16s?" Lowboy asked.

"I sure do, and the Government ain't getting it either. I brung it back from Nam, and that baby is mine. It won't do much good against that armored checkpoint though."

Lowboy grinned, "I think I know how to do this. Are you in?"

"You bet your sweet ass," Larry smiled. "What have you got in mind?"

Washington, D.C.

The president paced around the oval office, stopping occasionally to admire himself in the full-length mirror he had ordered mounted on the rear of the door to the oval office. He was tall, fit, and often wore lifts to make himself seem even taller, especially when he had to appear in public. After all, being president was as much about looking good as anything else.

As long as he looked good, he found it easy to win the confidence of most of the useless eaters. As long as he spoke well, and he certainly had remarkable skill in translating the teleprompter into well-received words on the stage, he felt he could sway public opinion in any direction he wanted with his oratory. It would be so much easier when he had no opposition to his plans, though. "Soon," he said to himself. "Soon."

There was a soft knock at the door. The president checked his appearance carefully in the mirror and slightly adjusted his coat before saying, "Enter," In his best regal voice.

The door opened, and the Secretary of the Department of Interior Security walked in. "Mr. President," the secretary said. "We still have not located the missing targets. We do, however, know that target number one, the man who escaped the quad-copter drones and shot down our mini-predator drone, was with target number two, the woman who escaped our ground hounds in Colorado. They were seen in Mississippi."

"Why did we not get them?" The president asked. "I told you people to kill these targets. If word gets out about what these people have seen, people may start to believe those damn rebels instead of us. That cannot be allowed to happen!"

"Yes Sir, Mr. President," the secretary wrung his hands. "We are working on it, and we have a line on their headquarters in Mississippi. We think we have it located. We are planning a coordinated air and ground strike. We have also identified the primary owner, Mr. Lorne Vanders. This man is a wealthy and influential member of the opposition, we believe."

"Do you have any solid evidence of this?" The president asked.

"Not exactly, Mr. President," the secretary stuttered. "The evidence we have is all circumstantial at this point."

"That's good enough for me. Blast the bastard!" the president said waving the secretary out of the Oval Office. The president smiled, "And be sure to send me the videos when you're done."

<u>Alabama</u>

Larry and Lowboy lay flat on their stomachs in the grass and fallen leaves under a small scrub oak on a hill about 300 yards from the FTSP checkpoint. The area was heavily wooded, covered mostly with pine trees and scattered scrub oak. Consequently, when they scouted the area the previous day, they had some difficulty finding a spot with a clear view far enough away from the checkpoint.

The scouting was easy because Larry and Lowboy had been on many, many deer, turkey, squirrel, and other hunts together over the last 43 years. They seldom had to say a word. Long familiarity let them anticipate the other's moves with ease. Many years before, Larry had taught Lowboy the hand signals he had used as a U.S. Marine Force Recon team member in Nam; signals Lowboy had never used as a grunt. Since then, they had added to those signals so that now they could almost speak to each other with just their hands. It had been years since they had even spoken a word on a hunt.

Larry wanted even more distance than the 300 yards they managed, but he also said that any .223 fire from the FTSP agents would probably not be accurate at that range. Larry was also fairly sure that the FTSP agents did not have any high-powered rifles. Even so, he suggested that they had best keep their heads down.

Larry and Lowboy each held their best hunting rifle, which, in Lowboy's case, was his only hunting rifle, and his only rifle, for that matter, just like his Winchester Model 12 pump shotgun was his only shotgun.

Both hunting rifles were 30-06 Remington model 700s with 6 to 9X variable Leopold scopes. Lowboy wondered if they favored the same rifle because they were such long time friends, or because the Remington 700 was the best rifle either of them could afford.

Larry and Lowboy had spent part of the previous day being certain that their rifles were sighted in for exactly 300 yards. Lowboy was an excellent shot and managed to put five out of five into a 1.7" group at 300 yards. Perhaps that came from only having the one rifle. His father had always said to beware of the man with only one gun, because it was likely that man would know how to shoot it very well. Larry's group was 3.3". They both figured that would be good enough.

Taking careful aim, Larry and Lowboy each chose an FTSP agent. Both of their rifles were carefully stabilized on small homemade sandbag rests and a ground cloth lay under the muzzles of their rifles to prevent leaves and dirt from being kicked up when the guns were fired. Larry said, "I'll take the bitch. She might just be the one who made my wife cry." That suited Lowboy fine since he wasn't sure he could shoot a woman, no matter how much she needed shooting.

Both shots rang out within a fraction of a second of one another, and the two FTSP agents dropped limply to the ground. Both were shot through the head. Through his scope, Lowboy could see the blood and brains spray out of their skulls before they fell. He felt momentarily sick before his hatred of the feds kicked in and the feeling went away.

The other FTSP agents immediately, and quite unprofessionally, retreated to the portable, armored checkpoint building without firing a return shot. Through his riflescope, Larry could see two FTSP agents frantically calling for assistance on their cell phones. Larry thought about bouncing a bullet off the checkpoint's bulletproof glass just to make those bullies shit in their pants, but decided he would wait for a valid shot instead.

Lowboy rose from the ground, brushed off a few of last winter's leaves stuck to his shirt, and began working his way through the woods toward the other side of the checkpoint where they had chosen a second vantage point. Larry remained in place. Their plan was to try to get off a few more shots and then leave the area.

Larry laid his rifle down and began watching the checkpoint through a small pair of binoculars. He could see one of the agents on the radio. His best guess was that there were at least three agents in the tiny building. Larry couldn't see them very well, and couldn't tell what they were doing. He hoped Lowboy would be able to see something from his new vantage point. They had a pair of small walkie-talkies for communication.

Larry did not see the quad-copter drone that rose with a whirr from the back of one of the FTSP 4WD trucks parked a short distance from the checkpoint. He was too busy watching the checkpoint through his binoculars. He did however hear the drone when it got close to him. He rolled over. The last thing he heard was the roar of full auto .40 caliber rounds as they tore through him.

Lowboy by then had found his new vantage point, gone prone, and had just focused his binoculars on Larry's position. He witnessed the quad-copter drone shoot Larry to pieces. "Oh shit!" Lowboy rose and started to run. "It is time to leave," he muttered out loud.

Washington, D.C.

The secretary of the Department of Interior Security had just returned from his meeting with the president when his assistant secretary caught him in the hall and said "We have a problem, Sir."

"What is it?" The secretary asked.

"There has been an attack on one of our FTSP checkpoints in Alabama. There were snipers involved. They killed two of our agents."

"Did we get the snipers?" The secretary asked.

"Yes sir, the agents at the checkpoint got one with the quad-copter drone that was assigned to the checkpoint. Fortunately, the drone pilot was not hit. If they had hit the drone pilot first, our people would have been unable to respond."

"So what you are saying is that one got away?"

"Yes Sir, but we will get him. We have a ground hound mobilized."

"Should we assign more than one quad-copter drone and pilot to each FTSP checkpoint?"

"Yes Sir, I believe we should," the assistant secretary said. "I also believe we should assign a mini-predator drone to each FTSP checkpoint."

"I don't think we have the manpower or the drone power to do that," the secretary mused. "However, what we can do from now is set up multiple checkpoints in the same area. Then, we can keep a mini-predator drone in flight in the general area of our checkpoints and on alert so that the response time to an incident at any checkpoint would be minimal."

"Yes Sir," the assistant secretary said. "I will see to it."

Alabama

Lowboy ran as far, and as fast, as he could into the woods. At his age, that was neither very far nor very fast. However, he was a good old Alabama country boy, and he knew these woods like the back of his hand. He did not know a lot about technology, but he had good common sense, and common sense told him that the government probably had nearly every technology he had ever seen used in the movies. That meant that the government would be able to locate him using thermal imaging devices, even when he was deep in the woods. Lowboy knew of a small cave in a hillside not too far from where he was and that was where he went. He figured that they wouldn't be able to find him as easily in the cave.

Lowboy crawled deep into the cave. He now had more than 30 feet of solid rock above him, but could still watch the entrance. He knew that no one ever went to the cave anymore. When he was a boy the cave had been a popular place, but now all the kids did was play games on their computers and iPhones, or post senseless tidbits of non-information such as, I just ate a sandwich, on Facebook or Twitter.

Lowboy knew that anyone he saw coming into the cave would be a government agent. He laid his rifle down and pulled his .44 out of its holster and checked the loads. His revolver was a huge old Walker Colt that he had inherited from his grandfather. It was a black powder piece that his grandfather had converted to use .44 caliber metal cartridges.

Lowboy favored this revolver above all other handguns. He always carried it in the woods, or in his truck, even though he knew he could sell it for a big pile of money. He hand-loaded the cartridges himself; using bullets he cast from lead tire weights, and black power he bought at the local hardware store.

Lowboy settled himself in for a wait. He only had to wait five hours. He was getting stiff, cold, and sore when he saw the shadow cross the light at the front of the cave. The hammer was already cocked on his revolver. He waited patiently.

Reston, Virginia

"Sir, I have bad news," the assistant secretary told the secretary. "The ground hound that we sent after the second sniper in Alabama has disappeared."

"What the hell is going on here?   After four years of not losing a single ground hound, how have we now lost five in the course of a few months?"

"I don't know Sir, but we are on it."

"You better be. The president is on our ass about this."

Alabama, just off Highway 17

Lowboy tossed the dead government agent over his shoulder like he was a sack of grain. Standing six feet six and, even at age 68, built like a tank, tossing the body over his shoulder was effortless. Lowboy then started walking toward a friend's house. He took the government agent's rifle and his pistol and studied them as he walked. The stupid government agent had been no match for his old Walker Colt and had not even got off a shot before that big hunk of lead had drilled him right between the eyes.

Lowboy had been shooting the old Colt since he was five years old, before he could even lift the heavy old piece by himself. Now he never missed. He figured folks could have these newfangled pistols. He just wanted one he could hit something with. That old gun had saved his life today.

Sam stared in amazement as Lowboy walked out of the woods carrying what Sam at first thought was a deer over his shoulder. As Lowboy got closer, Sam realized that Lowboy was carrying a man. From the way the body hung, Sam was fairly sure the man was dead.

"What the fuck?" Sam shouted.

"You gotta see this," Lowboy shouted back at him. "I have a lot to tell you." Sam followed Lowboy into the barn where Lowboy unconcernedly dumped the body on the floor.

"Who is that?" Sam asked.

"It's a long story," Lowboy said.

Sam leaned down and fiddled with the dead man. "That there is a government man, ain't he?"

"Yeah, the son of a bitch was gonna kill me."

"Why?" Sam asked.

"Well it might have some to do with the fact that Larry and I shot two of those granny-fondling FTSP agents at the checkpoint."

"What did you do that for?" Sam asked.

"Aw, the bastards deserved it. They been grannie-groping and junk-fondling everybody that goes up and down Highway 17 for about a week now. Larry and I just thought we'd let them know how we felt."

"Where's Larry?" Sam asked.

"The bastards killed him with a drone."

"With a drone?" Sam shook his head. "I thought the government just used those overseas."

"Apparently not," Lowboy replied.

"What are you gonna do?" Sam asked.

"Well, I have a plan," Lowboy said. "And I could use some help."

FTSP Checkpoint, Highway 17, Alabama

The two dead agents had been removed and replaced. The FTSP checkpoint was back to normal operation. "Step out of the car!" The FTSP agent shouted. You don't have a choice, you're gonna be searched."

"What for?" The lady driver asked.

"Because I said so, that's why," the surly FTSP agent said. He was enjoying his job immensely that day. The lady was white-haired, slight, and obviously past 70. He just loved abusing old people—and this one would be special to him. She reminded him of his grandmother. He had hated old people ever since he had gone to live with his grandmother after his parents had died when he was eight. She had been a strict disciplinarian and had never liked or tolerated his lying and stealing. He could sometimes still feel the pain from the belt she wielded at his all too frequent whippings.

Just about then he heard a rumble and looked up to see two dump trucks quickly approaching the checkpoint from opposite directions. Both trucks were blasting their horns and forcing everyone to move through the checkpoint ahead of them. When the old lady in the car beside the FTSP agent saw the big truck coming up fast in her mirror, she stepped on the gas and left too. There was nothing the FTSP agent could do to stop her so he drew his pistol and fired three .40 caliber rounds at her car before turning and shooting at the approaching dump truck. His rounds had no effect on the dump truck. The bullets were bouncing off the dump truck window. The agent didn't notice that the car at which he had fired had now stopped. The lady who had been driving it spryly stepped out of her car and leveled a .380 auto at the FTSP agent and screamed.

"You shot at me, you stupid son of a bitch!" The FTSP agent turned, and the old lady put four rounds into him while screaming "That will teach you not to shoot at me, you son of a bitch!" The agent staggered to the portable checkpoint building without firing another shot and dropped his pistol on the ground along the way.

"Stupid moron!" The lady shouted after him before putting her pistol back in her purse, getting back in her car, and driving away.

"That there bulletproof glass is pretty good, ain't it."

"Yeah, you're right about that Lowboy," Sam smiled. "Look at those little shits run, will you?"

"Yeah, Sam. They are running right where we want them to."

All four FTSP agents ran back into the armored checkpoint as they saw the trucks coming. They asked the pilot to use his quad-copter drone, but he said he had been refueling it when the trucks came upon them, and it wasn't ready. Not that it would matter, he said, because it wasn't of any use against armored trucks.

Lowboy drove the dump truck a little bit past the portable armored FTSP checkpoint. Then, he backed up and dumped a full load of gravel on top of the tiny building. The other dump truck did the same from the other direction. The portable checkpoint was almost covered. That wasn't a problem, Lowboy thought, because the other two dump trucks were almost there. When the first two dump trucks were out of the way, the last two dump trucks pulled up and finished burying the checkpoint.

"That'll fix those sons of bitches," Sam said. "Let's get out of here."

"You bet," Lowboy said. "Let's go." All seven men in the four dump trucks left the cabs and ran into the woods. In less than five minutes, they had all piled into an old pickup truck on a nearby dirt road and were rapidly leaving the area.

"I bet those sons of bitches will really be mad when they figure out that those were genuine U.S. government dump trucks that we used."

"Yeah, I wonder if those idiots at the fed center in Mobile even realize they are missing yet?"

"Well, it wasn't on the news this morning, so I doubt it," Lowboy chuckled.

The pickup truck was only two miles away when they heard the explosion. "Damn, would you look at that?"

"That was a big un, all right," Sam said.

"Do you think they blew up their own people?" One of the men asked.

"I think they did. I think they did," Lowboy said. "We had better make ourselves scarce for a while Gentlemen."

Washington, D.C.

"I think we got the bastards this time," the assistant secretary said to the secretary. "I called in a hellfire missile strike on the trucks that sealed our agents into that mobile FTSP checkpoint in Alabama. We lost some agents in the blast, though."

"That was the same checkpoint that was sniped last week?" The secretary asked. "Right?"

"Yes Sir, Mr. Secretary."

"Oh, well. Agents are cheap. Blame the explosion on the damn constitutionalists, or whatever they are, when you talk to the news media."

"Yes Sir."

"Have we had a problem at any of the other checkpoints?"

"No Sir. We have not."

"I hope this does not mean that other people will get the same idea and start attacking our checkpoints."

"Sir, I doubt that. This appears to have been an isolated case."

"Why do you think this particular checkpoint was attacked?"

"Sir, perhaps our agents have been a little too aggressive?"

"Nonsense. We cannot be too aggressive. We have to show the people we are in charge. Send out an order to all of our agents to ramp up the intensity of searches and interrogations. Pull the stops out. Let's show the people that we are in charge."

"Yes Sir, Mr. Secretary, I will do so. You are right." The assistant secretary left the secretary's office. He had a fleeting thought that maybe this was a mistake, but it was only a fleeting thought. He was soon lost in his plans on how to make searches and interrogations even tougher on citizens everywhere."

Chapter 17: UNDERGROUND

"We are not to expect to be translated from despotism to liberty in a featherbed." Thomas Jefferson

<u>Near Kansas City, Missouri</u>

Lorne strode into my office. "John, you have to see this." He went over to the computer attached to the huge screen mounted on the wall, and slid a DVD into the slot. In a minute, he had a news clip playing.

I got up from my desk, and walked over to the big screen. On the screen, a news announcer for one of the major networks was shuffling papers at his desk. He looked up at the camera with his flawless makeup and perfectly coiffed hair and said, "Today in Alabama, two hard working FTSP agents were murdered at a highway checkpoint by snipers. The snipers used assault rifles, illegal guns no citizen should be allowed to have, to murder these innocent federal workers. One of the snipers was killed in an exchange of gunfire, but the other managed to get away. Everywhere in America, we will mourn the loss of these two innocent federal agents."

"The president said today that he will soon issue an executive order banning sales and possession of absolutely all firearms by civilians. He said there will most-likely be a 30-day grace period for everyone to turn in their guns to the local police, and that there will be severe penalties for non-compliance. This announcer feels that this law is long overdue..."

Lorne paused the DVD. "They didn't use what the press is calling assault rifles, John. Our intel says that the agents were each simultaneously shot once though the head from about 300 yards. Witnesses also said that the other FTSP agents ran to their armored checkpoint without firing a single return shot. One even dropped his weapon on the way. The FTSP retaliated with a quad-copter drone. Apparently, it was already on site, and one of the FTSP agents was trained as a drone pilot. This one was full-auto, by the way. One witness saw the feds loading the body of one of the snipers into a truck. He also saw a scoped, bolt-action rifle loaded into the truck with the body. We think these agents were shot with plain old deer rifles."

"Well," I said, "the government never lets a good crisis go to waste. I have been expecting a false flag attack by the federal government, probably a huge attack on children, which they would use to force a gun confiscation bill like this through Congress. I guess the president couldn't wait. Apparently, this was too good of an opportunity for him."

"Executive orders do not have force of law," Lorne said. "My legal people tell me they are unconstitutional."

"Like the bastard-in-chief and his ilk care about that," I said. "Murdering citizens with drones is unconstitutional as well, yet they are doing it. Laws don't stop them."

"Apparently bullets can," Lorne smiled. "I don't think the attack on the checkpoint was a false flag attack."

"I agree, but how many patriotic citizens, and innocent citizens as well, will die like that sniper if we encourage an all-out civil war? I think we will still be better off to turn the government's own technology on them, and deprive them of its use before we let too many citizens attack the government."

"I agree, John. But, we don't have that capability yet. Until then, we need to implement the 'Doctrine of 100 Heads.'"

"Do you think it is time for that?" I asked. "Before we have the capability to eliminate the feds drone attacks as retaliation against innocent citizens."

"I don't think we have any choice, John," Lorne said.

"Do you really think that killing 100 feds for every citizen killed is possible?"

"Yes John. We already have a database of the name, job title, description, photo, workplace location, and home address of every single person who works for the federal government, except workers at some of the hush hush agencies. We also have a complete list of all of their relatives and their information as well. If we implement the Doctrine of 100 Heads against the feds, it will cause a mass exodus of people from government jobs."

"Lorne, I can't condone killing innocents for any reason. That is immoral, and will turn the population against us. If you deliberately target innocents, then I will be against you as well."

"I understand that," Lorne said. "However, we can search through the database and put together a list of drone pilots and..."

"Lorne," I interrupted, "I doubt that the names of the drone operators killing civilians or the names of the ground hounds, etc. will be a matter of public record. Even the feds are unlikely to be that stupid."

"OK," Lorne replied. "I just get carried away sometimes when I think about how crooked the feds are. These bastards make me so mad."

"I hate them with deep passion, myself," I replied. "However, this war will be won by those with the coolest heads. Remember, we are up against psychopaths who have no emotions. They are coldly calculating monsters. It is this lack of emotion that will ultimately defeat them, but not if we act like hotheads and let them manipulate us to their advantage. This, in so many ways, is a game of chess with the lives and future of all the citizens of our country at stake. Only a few percent of the people, even among the feds, are actually monsters. Most are just being manipulated by their psychopathic masters," I paused.

"As much as I hate the government for killing my Susan and all the other citizens they have killed, I know that, in reality, only a very small portion of people who work for the government are bad people. Stanley Milgram said:

'Ordinary people, simply doing their jobs, and without any particular hostility on their part, can become agents in a terrible destructive process. Moreover, even when the destructive effects of their work become patently clear, and they are asked to carry out actions incompatible with fundamental standards of morality, relatively few people have the resources needed to resist authority.'"

"Darn, John," Lorne said. "How do you remember that stuff."

"I usually say it is just the professor in me, but actually I use a memory system. I have been using that system since I was a child."

"Seems as if it works well," Lorne said.

"It does, and we should teach all of our key people the memory system so we can reduce paper and digital trails."

"Ok, I hope we can all learn the system. I hope we have time. The conflict seems to be escalating out of our control."

"In war, control is only an illusion." I paused. "I think everyone can learn the memory system. It isn't difficult."

"OK," Lorne said. "What about the idea that if someone does evil following orders, they are still guilty of that evil?"

"That has merit," I said. "I guess it will have to be figured out on a case by case basis."

"Only with the survivors," Lorne muttered. "Only with the survivors."

"Take it one step at a time, Lorne," I said putting my hand on his shoulder and giving it a squeeze. "You are the bravest man I have ever met. I don't want to lose you just because you are in too much of a hurry to fight."

Lorne nodded, "That's why we need you John. You think things through."

"Can we identify just the psychopaths?" I asked.

Lorne grinned, "We may have enough information, or can get it, to identify some, maybe even most, of the monsters."

"That is excellent. Do we have any psychologists on our side?"

"A very few, I suspect," Lorne said. "Most psychologists support the government."

"And, thus easily manipulated by their psychopathic masters," I nodded.

"Exactly."

"Can we find enough people to put together a task force to identify the psychopaths in federal service?"

"Yes, and on the federal police force as well." I will get this started. I know just the person to head this up."

"Great," I said. "I just hope we can bring everything together before we lose any more civilians."

"Me too," Lorne agreed.

"I need to ask Peggy how the drone hacking program is doing."

"I spoke with Peggy this morning about it," Lorne said. "She said that they have now assembled a team of over twenty experts, and they are negotiating with the premier hacker group to help us. Peggy said they are the best and brightest of the hackers."

"Unknown?" I asked.

"No, apparently these guys are so secretive that they won't even allow a nickname for their organization. Peggy said they consider Unknown to be amateurs."

"Wow," I said. "I have always considered Unknown to be the very best and the brightest. I think those folks in Unknown are absolutely incredible. I wish they were on our side."

Lorne shrugged, "Those hacker folks can out-spook the spooks. We may never know just who is actually on our side."

"Well," I said, "I guess you can say that average citizens beat us to the first strike."

"Pretty cool, Huh?" Lorne replied.

"Yes," I said. "But, if the president pushes through that executive order on gun confiscation, the people in this country will rebel, maybe sooner than we would like. I don't think we have very much time to get ready. We need to be able to strike hard against the government and disable their ability to extract revenge against regular citizens just as soon as we can. We need to do all we can to minimize civilian casualties."

"You think they will strike against regular citizens as a result of this FTSP attack?" Lorne asked.

"I know they will, and they will use extreme violence. Remember Waco and Ruby Ridge? Those were nothing compared to what this false government will do against patriotic citizens who defend the Constitution," I said. "These government psychopaths are in love with violence. They are remorseless control freaks and actually get off on harming people. It is a game to them. The good news is that this administration is run by amateurs."

"You really think so?"

"Yes," I said. "Sun Tzu says that 'The supreme art of war is to subdue the enemy without fighting.' If the president issues that executive order and attempts to confiscate guns, he will get massive resistance from the citizenry. In effect, it will soon be a full-blown civil war. He will have single-handedly created a fight that will most likely end in him being hung from a tree for treason to the USA and our Constitution."

"I want to see that," Lorne smiled.

"So do I," I replied. "But, I don't want to see the bloodshed and loss of loyal patriot lives that will result."

"Thomas Jefferson said, 'The tree of liberty must be refreshed from time to time with the blood of patriots and tyrants,' I agree."

"Yes, so do I. Let's just work toward the majority of that blood being from the tyrants. Lorne, why are you against the government? I never asked you."

Lorne paused a bit and said, "It all started with something my mother told me. She said. 'Son, doing what is right is the only real strength in this world. Sometimes you have to fight for what is right, and sometimes you have to sacrifice for what is right. Son, always do what is right, and you will have no regrets.' I remember what she said word for word."

"She was wise," I said.

"Yes, she was," Lorne nodded. "She had a quiet wisdom that I have always admired. Anyway, over the years I saw bad things done by our government. The thing that put me over the top was when they started killing children with drone strikes in Pakistan and Afghanistan. That is something that just makes me sick."

"Me too," I said. "Even before they killed Susan, many actions of our government made me sick to my stomach. Did you know that they simply claim that any adult male killed is a terrorist just because they are of military age?"

"I have heard that."

"Have you heard that the government is coming right out now and saying that it is OK for them to kill children, as long as they are hostile, of course?"

"No," Lorne shook his head. "I had not heard that. No wonder so many countries hate the U.S."

"If it gets out to the populace that they are killing children here in the U.S. as well, we may have an extremely violent revolution on our hands."

"I know that there have been several children in the U.S. killed by drone strikes already. All murders of children have been covered up by the government so far. Several have also been killed by ground hounds, including Toni's niece."

"I didn't realize that Toni's niece wasn't an adult."

"She was only 14," Lorne said.

I felt sick to my stomach. It just firmed my resolve to kill every one of the bastards that killed innocent American citizens. I also thought it would not hurt my feelings the least little bit if I also killed the politicians responsible for the deaths of innocent children overseas. I have never understood how some people can do things like that. Although I had studied psychopaths and their behavior, I did not think I would ever be capable of truly understanding them.

Things went well for the next four days. I got a lot of planning done. I would have much rather been out there with a rifle shooting the drone pilots who murdered Susan, but that might mean I only got a few of them. This way, I hoped to get them all. Lorne had taken a team to see if they could recover the sniper who got away from the FTSP in Alabama. This time Myrtle went with him.

Toni quietly walked up behind me. I was lost in thought at my desk with the cat Loco perched on top of the printer next to me. I assumed the cat was a self-appointed desk monitor. Toni put her hands on my shoulders and said. "John, there has been a development concerning the FTSP attack in Georgia. We managed to get several partial videos of the event from organization members who got them from witnesses. Peggy spliced them together. I think you need to see this."

"Have you heard from Lorne yet?" I asked. "Is he still in Alabama?"

"No we have not heard anything yet. We think he is still in Alabama."

"Was he involved in this?"

"Not that we can tell. You have to see this for yourself."

"OK," I replied and followed Toni over to the big screen where Peggy was holding a DVD. After an odd, but subtle, glance at Toni, she put the DVD in the slot and played the video clip.

I watched as the images flashed across the screen. The first video clip showed what was obviously an armored FTSP checkpoint.

"Is this the same checkpoint where the snipers shot the two agents?" I asked. Toni nodded. I continued watching.

There was a male FTSP agent standing beside a typical four-door sedan. Although the video had no sound, the agent was obviously berating the driver of the car. I could see that a large dump truck was crowding the cars ahead of it through the other lane of the checkpoint, much to the consternation of the FTSP agents. The FTSP agent next to the sedan looked over his shoulder at approaching dump truck as the car beside him drove away. The FTSP agent turned, drew his pistol, fired three shots toward the escaping car, turned again, and, with his back to the car that drove away, begin firing his pistol in the opposite direction.

I was surprised when the sedan that pulled away from the roadblock stopped, and the driver got out. The driver was a tiny, older, white-haired woman of maybe 70 or 80 who pulled what looked like a 380 automatic from her purse. She leveled the pistol at the FTSP agent and shouted something. I couldn't read her lips for sure, but I thought she said, "This will teach you to shoot at me, you son of a bitch." The FTSP agent turned toward her just as four rounds from her tiny pistol struck him in the chest and neck. The FTSP agent staggered, dropped his pistol, and moved toward the armored checkpoint. Obviously, he was not wearing body armor.

By now I could see that there was yet another dump truck driving up in the opposite lane. Before the dump trucks got close, all the FTSP agents retreated to the inside of the armored checkpoint. I watched as two dump trucks pulled past the FTSP armored checkpoint, and then carefully backed up, and dumped their loads of gravel on top of the small mobile checkpoint building. The gravel nearly covered the checkpoint. I noticed with amusement that both of the dump trucks belonged to the Department of Interior Security.

In the next scene, two more large dump trucks backed up to the armored checkpoint and dumped their loads of gravel. These were also DIS trucks. By now, the checkpoint was entirely covered by gravel.

I saw the drivers, and three passengers, get out of the four dump trucks and head for the surrounding woods on foot. As best I could tell there had been seven people involved in this incident, not counting the woman who shot the FTSP agent for shooting at her.

The viewpoint changed again to a camera obviously much farther away from the site. This time there was not much activity except for a few citizens standing around. After a couple minutes I was astonished to see a flash coming in from the left hand side of the screen. Then the gravel-covered checkpoint blew up. Obviously some of the citizens nearby had been killed or hurt. I could see a couple of people lying unmoving as the dust and smoke cleared and was starting to have that all too familiar sick feeling in my stomach. "Was that what I think it was?" I asked.

"Yes, it was," Peggy said. "That was a drone missile strike." I noticed that the footage had affected Peggy as well. She looked a little green around the gills.

"It looked like a hellfire missile," Toni said. "It may have been from one of the full-sized reaper drones."

"They blew up their own people trying to get the citizens who did this?" I asked.

"It appears that way," Toni said.

"Are they so desperate to get whoever did this that they kill innocent civilians as well as their own agents?"

"I think these people will stop at nothing to get what they want," Peggy said. "They are monsters."

"I agree, they are indeed monsters," I replied. "I wonder if they realize that we have this on film, and what the impact will be of this footage on the Internet. They have given us perhaps the best film footage that we can use to wake up more of the citizenry. Can we put this on the Internet?"

"Yes," Peggy said. "That is easy. I can have it on several video sharing sites in ten minutes. I think it would help if you can give me a bit of a write-up so that I can annotate the video with text to show people what was going on. I can keep putting it up again and again after the government figures out where it is and takes it down."

"That makes sense," I said. "To do that though, we need to know more about why this occurred and who was involved. Can you get word Lorne about this? Maybe it would be best for us to wait until we hear more from him."

"I agree," Toni said.

"OK," Peggy nodded. "I will let you know when I hear from Lorne."

"Thank you," I said.

I returned to my desk and sat down; still sick at the pit of my stomach from the images I had just seen. Again, I doubted my ability to lead the people to victory against the oppressive government, and create a return to individual freedom. I wasn't sure I was made of stern enough stuff. It seemed to me that the people needed a leader who was hardened to death and destruction. Yet, at the same time, I understood that someone who was too hardened to battle and loss of life might not take the same care to avoid losing innocents that I was trying to do. My greatest fear was that what I had been through, and what I was sure was coming, might leave me too callused and unfeeling to still be human.

Two days later we heard from Lorne. His coded message said that he had safely secured all of the participants in the checkpoint incident, as well as family members, and was headed with them to Mississippi. All in all, Lorne had 27 people with him, not counting Doc and Myrtle.

The next three days passed without incident. Peggy told me that the hackers were able to jam some drone signals, and they had managed to capture a small, surveillance drone, much like Iran had done. They still were not able to take control of the drones in the air and repurpose them for our use, but they felt like once they had captured a mini-predator, or other attack drone, they would easily be able to reverse engineer this capability. Peggy had also told me that three top notch electrical engineers had been added to the team, and that one of them had designed control circuits for the federal government's tactical nukes before he awoke and quit his job.

Lorne sent us the details of the checkpoint incident, and we got the annotated video online along with interviews with the guy who had initiated the whole thing, and the older lady who had shot the FTSP agent with her pistol. Both interviews were good. The video went viral in less than two days and had over five million views before the government had it taken down. Peggy just put it back up again using another account and in three more days it had another eight million views. Some movie producer in Hollywood said on Twitter that he was going to make a movie of the incident.

Chapter 18: MISSISSIPPI

"Never underestimate a woman of years." John Debrouillard

<u>Alabama</u>

Myrtle looked Lowboy eye to eye. They were exactly the same height. They both grinned simultaneously.

"Well, who have we here?" Lowboy asked. He was still holding his Remington model 700. He prized that rifle, and didn't want to give it up.

"Just what I was wondering?" Myrtle replied.

"You two lummoxes get your asses in gear and get on the bus," Lorne said while scanning the small crowd to make sure that everyone was accounted for. Doc was at the back end of the bus doing the same. The crowd was varied in age. There were six children from 14 or so down to the age of two, and several wives and grandmothers. The age of the men ranged from 20 to over 70. All were surprisingly cheerful considering the situation. Lorne didn't hear a single recrimination from the families of the men who had done the deed.

The bus was sitting under the roof of a big hay barn. It was a retired Greyhound that had been painted to look like a band bus. 'The Lymphocytes' was painted in big letters on the side of the bus, and the windows were blacked out. From the paint job, and decorative art, the band appeared to be a cross between punk and rock. Too bad there was no such band, Doc mused. They might be fun to listen to.

After everyone was loaded on the big old bus, Myrtle and Lowboy still stood talking by the door. It was obvious that they had instantly hit it off. Lorne walked up to them and pushed them both towards the bus door. They got the hint, and got on the bus. Doc and Lorne then opened one of the luggage compartments and began passing AR-15s to each of the men on the bus and several of the women. Two of the boys, 10 and 11, and one nine-year-old girl wanted rifles too, but Lorne suggested that they just hold extra magazines for their parents. They acquiesced, although the oldest boy seemed very disappointed. Lowboy declined an AR-15 and said, "I'll stick with my Remington, Thanks."

Doc got into the driver's seat and closed the door. Lorne stood beside him, with his rifle out of sight on the floor. Lorne was glad the bus had been available. The bus was heavily modified by a friend of Lorne's who had bought it used and made the alterations. Lorne supplied the money on the odd chance that something like that might be needed. It had taken about six hours to get the bus to location. Its owner was now headed home to buy a few more old buses, and modify them as well. Naturally, the bus was not registered to the owner. It was, instead, registered to a federal judge in Washington, D.C. It was amazing what a good patriotic lawyer could accomplish.

The bus was armored, and would stop a big fifty round. The tires were custom-made run-flats capable of high-speed operation. The bus's engine and drive train were modified as well, and the bus had over twice the horsepower of a standard model. The diesel tank held enough fuel for a thousand miles. There were also a dozen chaff mortars mounted in the rear that could shoot through camouflaged ports in the roof. Despite that defense capability, Lorne wanted to reach Mississippi without having to fight off any feds. It was only 178 miles. He thought they had an excellent chance.

They had only been in Mississippi for ten miles on highway 42 when a Mississippi Highway Patrol car pulled up behind them and turned on the lights and siren.

"This sucks," Doc complained. "I was only doing eight over."

"I guess we better pull over," Lorne said. He turned to the folks sitting in the bus and said, "Keep your rifles out of sight, but handy. You will know if you need them."

Doc signaled a right turn, and pulled the bus to the side of the highway. He chose a spot where the shoulder of the road was wider than normal to pull over. Lorne handed his rifle to one of the men in the bus, and it was quickly hidden. Lorne then motioned for Doc to open the door to the bus. They waited.

After a minute or so, the Mississippi Highway Patrol officer got out of his vehicle and walked around to the open bus door. He stepped up onto the first step and asked Doc for his driver's license. Doc reached into his wallet, took his drivers license out, and held it so that the officer had to step further into the bus to grasp it. The officer took the bait and stepped all the way up into the bus. Knowing that it would not do for Doc's driver's license to be run, Lorne gestured to the guys sitting in the back of the bus. As if of one accord, almost 20 rifles rose and were pointed at the Mississippi Highway Patrolman.

"Oh shit! Not again." The officer said.

"Does this happen to you with any regularity?" Lorne asked.

"Well it never used to," the officer replied keeping his hands far away from his pistol, "but not too long ago a fellow pulled a shotgun on me. He was hidden in the trunk of a car."

"Who was he with?" Lorne asked.

"A blonde woman and an old man," The officer replied.

"How tall are you?" Lorne asked.

"What has that got to do with anything?" The officer asked.

"Just answer the question."

"I am 6 feet 2." The officer replied.

Lorne smiled, "You must be Fred."

"How the hell would you know that?" The officer asked. "Unless..."

"Yes, they are friends of ours," Lorne replied. "Don't do anything stupid with a pistol of yours now."

"With that many rifles pointed at me. You must think I'm crazy."

"No, not crazy. We just don't want an accident. Please hand your pistol to Doc, very carefully." Lorne motioned toward Doc with his hand. The officer, very carefully, handed Doc his pistol, butt first.

"What are you going to do with me?" The officer asked.

"I am hoping to get you to join us," Lorne responded.

"Now I know who you guys are—sort of," the highway patrolman said.

"John spoke highly of you."

"So John must be the guy with the shotgun?"

"Yes, that was John."

"What if I don't want to join you?" The patrolman asked.

"Don't worry, we're not going to hurt you, or any member of your family for that matter."

"Somehow I didn't think you were," the patrolman said. "Even though, with that many rifles pointed at me, that might be a stretch." Lorne motioned and the rifles disappeared.

"How about you come along with us and you and I talk for a while," Lorne said.

"It appears as if I don't have a choice," Fred replied. "However, I must admit that I am quite intrigued by you guys and not unsympathetic to your goals."

"Okay then, let's get this done," Lorne then turned to Myrtle and Lowboy and said, "How about you two drive the cruiser and follow us?"

"Sounds like a plan to me," Lowboy said. He and Myrtle rose, exited the bus, and walked back to the police cruiser. They got in, and the cruiser noticeably sank down on its shocks. Lorne motioned for Fred to have a seat on the bench that Myrtle and Lowboy had vacated. Lorne sat down beside the officer. Doc closed the door, put the bus in gear, and started back down the highway. The cruiser followed.

Two days later, everyone was comfortably quartered in Lorne's Mississippi headquarters. Lorne looked around and thought it was good to be home. For him, the Mississippi ranch was home. He had lived, at various times, in most of the states, but there was just something about Mississippi that called out to him. Perhaps it was the freedom-mindedness and independence of the citizens? Lorne observed that the people of rural Mississippi, in spite of being opinionated and hardheaded at times, were invariably far more self-sufficient then the people in most of the other places he had lived. He also noticed that, despite their often-cantankerous words, these folks tended to help their neighbors more than elsewhere. Lorne liked that. He thought his mom would've also liked Mississippi.

Lorne knew that he had to get most of these people away from the Mississippi Ranch as soon as he could. So far, he had managed to send five people to another ranch that he had part ownership of in Wyoming, and three more to a ranch in Utah owned by a friend. He was still looking for safe havens for the rest of the people they had brought to the Mississippi ranch.

Fred, the Highway Patrol officer, decided to throw his lot in with the rebels, as he called them, especially after he and Lorne watched the viral video of the missile strike on the FTSP checkpoint in Alabama. Lorne suggested to Fred that he could be the most useful if he remained in his position as a Mississippi Highway Patrol officer. After some discussion, Fred agreed. Lorne and several of the others waved goodbye to Fred as he drove away. Arrangements had been made to teach Fred what he needed to know about the organization, and what he needed to know to be useful to the organization. Fred was also given a half-dozen prearranged escape plans in case he needed them, as well as ways of getting additional help, should he need it.

"I have a bad feeling about this," Doc said.
"What do you mean?" Lorne asked.
"I don't think we should stay here."

"I think we're safe here," Lorne replied.

"I hope you're right. But there's something that's making me nervous."

"What do you think it is?"

"I don't know," Doc replied. "It just seems to me that by now, the feds will have managed to figure out that we used the bus and track it to here."

"I hope you're wrong," Lorne replied. "I would hate to lose this place. I like it very much."

"Let's go take a look at the radar," Doc suggested. "That may set my mind at ease."

Washington, D.C.

"Mr. Secretary, we have a development."

"What is it?"

"Our surveillance of the Mississippi property suggests that we should strike there now. There seems to be movement on the property, and an unusually large number of people are present. I think this may be our chance to strike hard at the core of the resistance movement."

"I think you're right," the secretary responded. "The president is anxious for this to occur."

"Yes sir."

"Everything is ready for the strike?" The secretary asked.

"Yes sir we are ready to go."

"Then set loose the dogs," the secretary said.

"The dogs Sir?"

"Destroy the place, you idiot."

"Yes sir. It will be done."

"And make sure the president gets a copy of the video."

"Yes, sir. Our video editors will prepare a film for him as usual."

"Remember to have them digitally enhance any bloody parts."

"Yes Sir," the assistant secretary said. "We always do."

Mississippi

The first hit came as they sat down at the computer to call up the output of the small radar that Lorne had installed at the ranch. The explosion was huge and the ground roll threw Doc and Lorne out of their chairs onto the floor. They were both up in a few seconds. The ground roll lasted less than two seconds.

"Let's get out of here," Doc shouted.

"Follow me," Lorne said.

Myrtle, Lowboy, and Gwen, the lady who had shot the FTSP agent at the checkpoint in Alabama, were sitting in the kitchen playing cards when the first missile struck. They were playing five-card draw, and Gwen was up 23 dollars. She thought these two huge guys were letting her win, but she wasn't sure. The blast threw them all to the floor, and the ceiling fell on them. Gwen was surprised to find herself covered, but not crushed, by two huge bodies. Not one bit of the sheetrock collapsing from the ceiling above hit her.

Myrtle pushed himself to his feet and grabbed Lowboy's arm and helped him up. They both helped Gwen to her feet. Myrtle said, "Follow me," and started for the trap door in the kitchen that covered the entrance to a small tunnel that exited in the nearby woods. The tunnel was a very tight fit for Myrtle and Lowboy, but they squeezed through. Gwen, who was about the same height as Lorne, but much thinner and lighter, had no trouble.

In less than three minutes, they were in the woods, running away from the ranch buildings. They heard another explosion behind them as they ran. Gwen was the fastest of the three. Myrtle and Lowboy both struggled to keep up. They made it nearly to the top of a nearby hill where Myrtle showed them a small, cave-like dugout that contained a few escape supplies and gear.

They were sitting in the dugout, looking back at the ranch, when the bunker buster hit dead center on the ranch house. The concussion left them deaf for almost 30 seconds. The ground roll collapsed the dugout. It would have buried all of them if Lowboy had not pushed Gwen and Myrtle out of the dugout as soon as he saw the streak of the missile headed for the ranch house. The collapsed dirt covered him from his toes to the middle of his back. Without saying a word, Myrtle and Gwen started digging him out using just their hands. It took them twenty minutes, but they finally pulled Lowboy free of the dirt.

"Nice retirement, huh guys?" Lowboy said as they sat wheezing on the hillside. They all laughed until they couldn't breathe.

"It beats Social Security," Gwen said, and they all started laughing again. After a few more minutes, they managed to get to their feet.

"Do you think anyone else got out?" Lowboy asked.

"I hope so, but after that big one I doubt it. I sure hope I am wrong," Myrtle hung his head. "I had good friends in there."

"Who did that?" Gwen asked. "The government?"

"I am afraid so," Myrtle replied. "I am afraid so."

"Mean bastards, aren't they," Gwen muttered.

"You have no idea," Myrtle said. "They have killed a lot of citizens whose only crime was opposing the current administration's policies."

"You mean like people who cause violence?" Gwen asked.

"No, mostly influential people who speak up publicly against them, and any witnesses who happen to be in the way."

"That is horrible," Gwen frowned.

"I agree," Lowboy responded.

"To think I snapped and shot that FTSP asshole," Gwen said. "I wonder what my grandchildren are saying?"

"If they are loyal to the Constitution, they will be applauding," Lowboy said. "After all, he shot at you first."

"Well, after going through this, I don't feel so bad about shooting that lowlife FTSP guy. He was a jerk, you know."

"I know I don't feel bad about killing the one I shot. I sure miss Larry, though. They killed him with a damn drone. I saw it through my field glasses." Lowboy hung his head a bit.

"Well, heck. You guys each managed to shoot a fed. All I have done is avoid them," Myrtle lamented. "I feel ashamed."

"Don't worry," Lowboy said. "I think we are all going to have a chance to shoot as many of those rascals as we want, and pretty darn soon."

"Yeah," Myrtle grinned. "It sure looks like you guys really got the ball rolling."

"Boys," Gwen said, tugging at both of their sleeves at the same time. "Don't you think we should get out of here?"

"Ma'am, you are right as always. Let's go," Lowboy laughed. The three started walking away from the ranch with Myrtle leading the way. They had not managed to recover any supplies from the dugout, nor any weapons from those cached there. Myrtle had no weapon at all, but Lowboy had his old Walker Colt tucked in his waistband and a pocket full of cartridges. Gwen had left her purse behind, but her .380 had been stowed in the pocket of the apron that Myrtle gave her while they were preparing lunch. She only had the bullets in the magazine, which had been thoughtfully reloaded by Lorne.

"How did you know that the blast would cave in the dugout?" Gwen asked Lowboy.

"Ma'am, I was just a kid when I went to Vietnam. I didn't know much then, and I doubt I know much now. But, I had a buddy who was in a spider hole when the stupid Air Force dropped a 1000 pounder a mite too close. That spider hole swallowed him like he was never even there."

"Tough on your buddy?" Myrtle asked.

"Yeah, his name is on the wall," Lowboy said.

"Army?" Myrtle questioned.

"No, Marines. I was just a grunt."

"Army for me, but I never saw combat," Myrtle said. "I was a cook."

"Well you have seen combat now," Lowboy smiled. He looked at Gwen, "You too ma'am...twice now. Were you ever in the military, Ma'am?"

"No," Gwen answered. "I was a store clerk for fifty years. That's all."

"What kind of store?" Myrtle asked.

"A gun store," Gwen replied. Both men fell over laughing.

Lorne led Doc to a small door in the wall. Beyond the door, a staircase led down to another level. Lorne led the way, jumping down four steps at a time. Doc followed, but got his feet tangled at the bottom of the stairs and fell. Lorne pulled him to his feet and pointed down the tunnel at the foot of the stairs, "Run, Doc. As fast as you can." Lorne ran down the brightly lit tunnel and Doc followed. They had run about 500 feet down the tunnel when the ground shook and the tunnel collapsed behind them. The air pressure from the blast and tunnel collapse blew them off their feet and left them choking in a cloud of dust almost too thick to see through.

"Whoa," Doc yelled. "That was a big one." Then the lights in the tunnel went out.

Lorne pulled a small, bright LED flashlight from his pocket, and turned it on. "They may not quit with that one. Keep moving," Lorne said and started off holding his flashlight so they could see a few feet ahead through the dust. In about another hundred yards, they came to the end of the tunnel. Lorne climbed the ladder and opened the hatch above. They had both just climbed out when the bunker buster hit. The shock threw them both to the ground.

"Holy shit," Doc shouted as he got up. "That was huge. What was that?"

"I think that was a Tomahawk missile with a bunker buster," Lorne said.

"I hope everyone else got out."

"I doubt it," Lorne said. "I hope so though."

"Could anyone be left alive in there?" Doc asked.

"Unlikely," Lorne responded. "The complex was only three stories deep. That bunker buster most likely destroyed the entire complex."

"So the first strike was to drive us underground, and the second and third were to finish us off?" Doc asked.

"Yes," Lorne replied. "I am willing to bet that they also have ground hounds and federal police on the ground to get any of us who escaped the destruction of the ranch," Lorne said.

"What are we going to do?" Doc asked.

"I thought it might come to this someday. Follow me." Lorne took off at a run. It was a pace that Doc, a marathoner, could maintain only with serious effort. By the time they reached a hidden bunker, Doc was gasping for breath. Lorne wasn't even breathing hard. Lorne opened the combination lock on the door and they went inside. The lights came on when the door opened. Doc stood in amazement looking into the 16 by 32 foot bunker dug into the hillside and stocked with all manner of useful items.

Doc went to a set of shelves in the back and came back with two uniforms.

"Those are federal police uniforms," Doc said in amazement.

"You bet," Lorne grinned. "Put this one on." Soon, they were both dressed as federal police, right down to the black tactical boots. Lorne handed Doc a duty belt and various bits of tactical gear. Lorne had to show Doc how to put some of the gear on, but soon they were dressed and armed just like members of a federal police swat team, including helmets and face shields.

"Wow," Doc said. "You think of everything.

"No," Lorne said, "if I thought of everything, we wouldn't have lost anyone today. I will try to do better after this, much better."

"How many of these bunkers are there on the ranch?"

"There are 14 of these bunkers on the ranch, as well as a few others with a different design and contents. I should have showed the escape tunnels and bunkers to everyone. I was pushing OPSEC a bit too hard, I think. Myrtle knows—knew—about the escape tunnels, though."

"Maybe Myrtle got out with some of the others? I am glad John wasn't here; or Toni or any of the others."

"I hope Myrtle did get some folks out," Lorne said. "John was right about moving operations headquarters from here. I thought he was wrong, but this shows he was right. He is the right man for the job."

"I agree," Doc said. "Can we get out of here now?"

"You bet," Lorne started off at a fast walk with his rifle held at port arms. Doc followed.

"Are there any escape vehicles hidden?" Doc asked.

"Yes, there are," Lorne smiled. "But I have a better idea."

Lowboy snuck up to the top of the hill and peered over it. Myrtle was right behind him. Gwen watched with amusement as the two behemoths tried to move quietly. The wind was really picking up and she could feel it on her face as they neared the top of the hill.

"What do you see?" Myrtle whispered.

"Nothing," Lowboy whispered. "Let's go." The three of them stood and crossed the hilltop. In four steps, they came face to face with two ground hounds. Both groups were surprised. Gwen calmly shot both ground hounds through the head with her .380, while Lowboy struggled to get his Walker Colt out of his belt. Gwen had been carrying the little .380 in her hand since they left the collapsed dugout, so it was easy for her to fire first. Both ground hounds collapsed and didn't move.

Lowboy finally got his pistol out of his belt. "That was some fine shooting, Ma'am." He said.

"Well, I was the Women's National Pistol Champion for eight years running back in the 70s," Gwen said. "Besides, I am starting to get mad at these feds. They seem to think they have the right to kill anyone. Just because a bunch of ball-less wonders signed an unconstitutional law in Washington does not mean that they can kill American citizens with impunity."

"I see that you mean what you say, Ma'am," Myrtle smiled. "Thank you for saving our lives."

"No problem," she pointed to Lowboy. "Boy, you better carry that monster of a pistol ready in your hand from now on."

"Yes Ma'am. I will," Lowboy said, exchanging glances with Myrtle. In spite of themselves, they both smiled. Myrtle stooped and stripped the weapons and ammunition from both the ground hounds. He took a pair of pistols for himself, and handed the rifles to Gwen and Lowboy.

"I suspect you guys are both better shots than me," He smiled. "Besides, I have never fired a bullet in anger. I better start with these little guys first, gesturing with the pistols."

Lorne and Doc crouched in the bushes. At the base of the hill, on the road, there were six federal vehicles and a helicopter. Lorne leaned over and whispered in Doc's ear, "That is our way out of here," he said, pointing to the helicopter.

"You've got to be kidding me?" Doc whispered back.

"Nope, we're gonna steal that baby."

"OK, I'm in," Doc whispered. "Let's go."

After taking inventory of the federal police scattered around the vehicles and a helicopter, Lorne said, "I count eight."

"That's how many I see too," Doc said.

"We will take them out one at a time."

"How?" Doc asked.

"With this," Lorne said, pulling a large knife out of his pocket.

"Yours is bigger than mine," Doc said, also pulling a folding knife out of his pocket.

"We had best wait for good dark," Lorne said. "That should be in about 15 minutes. Doc nodded his head in agreement.

Following Lorne as quietly as he could, Doc held his open pocketknife in his right hand. His knife was a medium-size Case stockman, made in the U.S.A. The big blade was less than three inches long. Doc wasn't worried, however, because, he knew enough about anatomy to make his small knife very effective. Coincidently, Lorne's knife was also a Case. It was the single bladed folding hunter model with a four-inch blade.

Lorne crept up behind the federal policeman. The fed was well over six-feet in height. Lorne jumped up, put his hand over the fed's mouth and pulled his head back while slicing his throat. The fed did not make a sound. Doc helped Lorne ease the body to the ground. It seemed to Doc that it was much messier in real life than it had ever seemed in the movies.

The next three federal officers were just as easily taken. In each case, Lorne used his knife. Doc didn't have a chance to try his. For that, he was very grateful. In less than ten minutes, Lorne and Doc reached the helicopter. Lorne got into the pilot's seat, and Doc crawled into the front passenger seat. Lorne fired up the helicopter and hurled it into the air before the turbine was even up to full speed. Doc had picked up another M-16 and a few extra magazines from the federal police officers that they had eliminated. He wasn't sure how he would fire a weapon from the helicopter, but he figured if the time came, he would figure it out.

Lorne flew the helicopter straight for the ranch building.

"Don't you think we ought to just get out of here?" Doc asked.

"No," Lorne replied. "If anyone else got away I want to see if we can get them out."

"That makes sense," Doc replied. "But how are we going to see them. It's pretty dark out there."

"Look at the screen to your left on the control panel," Lorne replied. "That is a thermal imaging detector."

"So we can detect people on the ground in the dark by their body heat signature?" Doc asked.

"Yes," Lorne replied. "The feds have the best equipment our money can buy."

"Okay, I'll watch the screen," Doc said.

Lorne began circling the helicopter around the smoking remains of the ranch headquarters. The bunker buster had blown a hole almost 60 feet deep and 80 feet across where the ranch house used to be. They could see the hole because the federal police on the ground had a number of spotlights set up and were searching through the wreckage. Not one of the feds even looked up as the helicopter circled overhead.

"That's what I was counting on," Lorne said. "These guys are so used to having their own helicopters overhead that they don't pay them any attention anymore."

"What if somebody's keeping track of the number of helicopters?" Doc asked.

"I think this is the only helicopter on site right now," Lorne replied. "I doubt they will send any other helicopters until daylight."

"That's at least seven hours away."

"That's right," Lorne replied. "That gives us a nice window of opportunity to see if we can find some of our people who may have survived."

They flew a spiral search pattern outward from the crater. They had been flying for about 20 minutes when Doc noticed three heat signatures on the infrared screen. "That looks like that might be three of our guys. They are deep in the woods and separated from any of the federal police that we saw on the ground. All the feds we have seen are located much closer to the ranch headquarters."

"I think you may be right," Lorne replied. "I doubt the federal police will venture into the woods until daylight." I do suspect that they will have some ground hounds out. I doubt the hounds would operate in groups as big as three. Keep your rifle ready. I will put the searchlight on them. If they are not our people, I will get us out of here as fast as I can."

"Okay, that sounds good," Doc replied.

Lorne flew the helicopter toward the three figures on the ground. He waited to turn on the searchlight until he was close. If they were some of the folks who escaped from the ranch house, they would try to hide as fast as they could when the searchlight came on.

When Lorne flipped on the searchlight, he immediately saw that one of the figures was Myrtle and there was another man and a woman with him. "Doc, pick up the microphone and let Myrtle know that it's us."

"You bet," Doc replied.

It took them about 20 minutes to rendezvous with Myrtle and his friends at a location where the chopper could be set down. When everyone was loaded, five people— two of whom each weighed as much as two people—in a four-passenger helicopter. Lorne turned in the pilot's seat and said "you guys better lose weight real fast because I don't think this baby will get all this weight off the ground."

"Well hell, then I'll just get out of this son of a bitch right now!" Lowboy said. Before Lowboy could unfasten his seat belt and open the door, Lorne wound up the turbine as high as it would go, and managed to get the chopper airborne. It was obviously a struggle. Altitude gain was very slow. Once he got the chopper to an altitude of 200 feet, Lorne flew the helicopter slowly across the landscape.

"I was hoping to fly this thing all the way to Missouri. However, I think we'll have to find some other transportation," Lorne said.

Doc reached into his pocket and pulled out his cell phone. "Can you get us to Tupelo by daylight?" Doc asked.

"I think so," Lorne replied.

"Good, I will arrange to have a car waiting for us."

"Maybe you better make it into a two and a half ton truck." Lorne laughed.

"A heavy-duty, half-ton, crew cab pickup truck will do just fine," Lowboy chimed in.

Chapter 19: KANSAS CITY, MISSOURI

"Man's best weapon is not a rifle; it is his mind." John Debrouillard

<u>Near Kansas City, Missouri</u>

I met with Toni and Peggy in the conference room. We had heard from Lorne that the Mississippi ranch was destroyed, and he was returning with only four other survivors. We lost 18 people, men, women, and children, at the Mississippi ranch. I felt sick. Our purpose in having Lorne and the others go to Alabama was to get those folks and their families to safety. In that, we had failed. I knew that in any war, there were always casualties. I didn't like that fact one bit. I didn't think I ever would.

"Peggy. Toni," I said, nodding in their direction where they sat across from me along the narrow table in the conference room. I had suggested to Lorne that we use a narrower table than normal because it gave a more intimate feel to meetings. I would have suggested a round table like King Author used, if the room had itself not been long and relatively narrow. Myrtle had responded to my suggestion by taking a circular saw and slicing the overhanging sides off of the conference table. Lorne shrugged and sanded the edges while he teased Myrtle about not being able to saw a straight line. I thought Myrtle did an excellent job. No attempt was made to stain the cuts. Apparently the organization was more about expedience than appearance. I liked that.

"You two are the best organizers that we have," I said. "Both of you have developed far more connections within the organization than I have.

"That's just because you have a hermit-like nature," Toni said, while Peggy nodded agreement.

I have been thinking about using low-tech methods to defeat some of the high-tech that the government is using against us," I said. "I think our best chance to develop usable low-tech techniques is to first study the inherent weaknesses of the surveillance methods and weapons used by the feds so that we can counter them with as little expense and effort as possible. Let the feds spend as much money as possible. The more they spend, the more they damage the federal budget, and the sooner, and with fewer patriot casualties, they fall."

"A war of economic attrition?" Toni asked.

"Exactly," I replied. "At least much of it, I hope."

"Inexpensive methods like the low-power LEDs that we have been using in caps and hats to keep closed circuit television cameras from being able to identify us?" Toni asked.

"Yes," I said. "I have been doing more reading on this, and many other topics, and I have some thoughts, although neither the knowledge or talent to do very much with any of my ideas. For that we need talented, creative, and knowledgeable patriots to work on each problem and devise inexpensive and practical solutions, as well as come up with even better ideas. I put forth my ideas only to get things started."

"For example, I don't think it's enough to just be able to hide our faces from the closed-circuit television cameras. That may be working for now, but I doubt it will work for very long. I suspect the government will soon begin to use biometric information taken from airport body scanners, and similar scanners from other locations, such as post offices, along with the data from the ubiquitous closed circuit television cameras to identify people from other body measurements."

"I've been wondering about that," Peggy said.

"Do you have any ideas?" I asked.

"Well, we could use makeup, hairstyles where some hair drape is across the upper face. Perhaps prosthetics inside clothes to enhance shoulder and/or hip width, or even just shoe lifts to help hide bone structure measurements might work. Something as simple as a knee brace might change a person's gait so that they would not be recognized."

"I agree," I said. "However, when they start putting thermal filters on some of these cameras, if not all of them, they will be able to see the heat of blood flow through facial arteries, even when the LEDs are in place I suspect. The distribution of your facial arteries is as unique as a fingerprint. I can't think of any low-tech ways to falsify this."

"Maybe we can get some of our doctors and biologists to work on this?" Toni asked.

"That sounds like a good idea," I replied. "Can you find a couple of researchers to look into this for us?"

"Let me see what I can do," Toni replied.

"Toni," I asked. "Can you get someone to obtain some infrared LEDs and see how they work for fooling the thermal abilities of the security cameras?"

"Yes, I can do that," Toni said as she took some notes. I told myself again that I needed to get everyone trained in the memory system, but right now I didn't feel that we had time.

"I can see that we will probably need access to various federal facilities at some point," I said. "It is my understanding that many of these facilities have entry points controlled by fingerprint scanners. Can we find someone who can prepare kits for making molds from latent fingerprints so that we can fool these systems?"

"I will look into it," Peggy said. I noticed Peggy was not taking notes. She seemed to remember everything quite well, so I assumed she had a great memory, perhaps even a trained memory.

"The next technology we need to be able to circumvent is RFID chips. The government is putting these chips in nearly everything. That allows them to track the movement of many items, as well as people. It is my understanding that the feds have already started placing RFID chips in driver's licenses."

"I have heard that too," Peggy said. "Some people say that when they put these chips in people, it will be the Mark of the Beast."

"Can we find some electronics technicians who can build, or manufacture, RFID emulator/cloners for us? We will most likely need thousands, if not tens of thousands of these units." I paused. "These RFID cloners need the ability to read RFID chips from a distance, and then counterfeit the RFID chip's unique signal. That means that we can read a chip from a distance, and then the code from that RFID chip can be implanted into a card, or some other item containing another programmable RFID chip. With that we can fool the system using RFID emulator cloners and appear to be where we are not, or simply disappear from RFID tracking."

"We will see about setting up a small factory to manufacture these units," Toni replied.

"It might be better to scatter the production across a number of locations, each unknown to the others," Peggy said.

"OK," Toni said, "that sounds safer."

"Another problem that we will commonly encounter is the government's propensity to record GPS readings on newer vehicles everywhere they go. We can't always drive old cars and trucks. They will be far too obvious. We need to be invisible."

"Recently, the government has mandated that all vehicles be equipped with a black box. These black boxes have GPS capability and record the location of the vehicle and periodically send that data to the big government spy centers, as do many of the Government Motors vehicles with their navigation system. We need to be able to fool, or shut down GPS tracking at will."

"Can we use GPS jamming systems?" Toni asked.

"Yes, we can," I said. "However, there are several types of GPS systems in addition, to the one used by civilian GPS instruments. We need to be able to block all of these systems using the same unit."

"GPS blockers are available, or were until recently when the government shutdown sales of these items. However, as far as I know these units only block civilian GPS," Peggy said.

"We need to get our electronics boys working on developing GPS blockers that work on all known systems, including the encrypted system that the feds are now developing, I pointed out."

"We will get some people working on that," Peggy said. "We also need to incorporate GPS emulators into these devices so we can tell the government that we are somewhere else.

"Good idea," I said. "That will be a neat and extremely useful trick."

"What about EMP devices?" Peggy asked.

"If these can be used in a directed fashion, they would be invaluable to us," I replied. "We could probably take drones, helicopters, cars, trucks, etc. out at will. I doubt all federal equipment is as armored against EMP as military equipment.

"We will get the electronics boys working on this as well," Peggy replied. "I know there are several companies that work on small-scale EMP devices for the federal government. We will see if we can hack into their systems and find out what they have."

"So how are the negotiations with the hackers coming?" I asked.

"Much better than I thought they would," Peggy replied. "It turns out that the majority of these hackers are just as anti-government as we are, although usually less violent. The hackers are proving to be a tremendous resource."

"I have heard of other devices that the government is beginning to deploy," I said. "One of these is the sound canon. I don't know anything about these, so I have no idea how to counter them."

"I will have the electronics techs work on that as well," Peggy replied.

"What about the silence gun the Japanese have developed? I hear that the U.S. government is beginning to use that as well."

"How does that work?" Toni asked.

"I think it works by reflecting what you say back at you with a slight delay. This is supposed to confuse people so much that they are no longer able to speak."

"That's an easy fix," Peggy laughed. "Just wear earplugs."

"But we need to be able to make the earplugs available in large numbers to the patriots if the feds start using this device."

"I will find a way to get that done," Toni replied.

"What about being able to avoid thermal imaging from drones and airplanes when our people are in the field?" Peggy asked. "Lorne told me that the ground hounds—she shivered a bit when she said ground hounds—even have thermal visual capability implanted in one of their eyes. We need some way of avoiding detection from thermal imaging systems."

"The best way that I can think of to avoid being detected is to make a cloak lined with the reflective Mylar from space blankets. The cloak should have a hood that closes tightly around the face."

"Maybe we should even make a pair of pants that are lined with the space blanket material as well," Peggy suggested.

"That's a good idea, Peggy," I replied. "Maybe the pants should have spats that also cover the shoes."

"That would be good," Peggy said. "How about if we put tie strings on these garments that allow you to tie on local vegetation to further camouflage the outfit."

"That would also help match the emissivity of the outfit to the emissivity of the surrounding area, making it more difficult to detect with thermal imaging," I said.

"I can see about having these made," Toni said. "How many do you think we will need?"

"I think we can start with a few dozen for testing and then work our way towards being able to provide the suits to any patriot who wants one."

"Another method that will work if we have a situation in which we have a number of people on the ground, is to scatter heat sources in the area. That should confuse the drone cameras and prevent them from easily homing in on our people," Peggy said.

"That's a great idea, Peggy," I said. "Are you sure you are just a computer programmer?"

"I don't know," Peggy replied. "Are you sure you were just a professor?"

"I guess we are all having to develop skills and learn things that we never thought we would need," I said.

"That's a fact," Toni replied. "We could just use light sticks. They are cheap. We could issue them to everyone in large numbers. Then, all they have to do is break them and scatter them on the ground."

"That's a great idea too," I smiled.

"Road flares would work too," Peggy said.

"For that matter, camera flashes would work as well," I said. "Could we design battery-powered strobes that could be tossed out of vehicles, and always landed an upright position like a caltrop?"

"We can manufacture those as well," Peggy said. "We can get the electronics folks and machinists working on this."

"We also need to know more about the capability of the various government drones," I said.

"I have been researching drone capabilities," Peggy replied. I will put together a small pamphlet that we can pass out to patriots that delineates the capabilities and weak spots of each drone used by the government."

"I gather you have taken a personal interest in this?" I asked.

"You might say that," Peggy said. "I don't like those damn drones."

"Neither do I," I said. "There are a number of other things we should examine as well."

"Go on," Toni said.

"I anticipate that the government will retaliate against rebel strikes by withholding food supplies, gasoline, medicine, etc., just like the Russians did in the Ukraine. Unless the people in the restricted area turn the rebels in to the government, they will not be able to get food. The government would just starve them until someone cracked."

"That means we need to have ways of getting food and supplies into any affected regions," Peggy said.

"Not only ways of getting food into affected regions," I replied. "We need to, as much as possible, anticipate where those regions might be, and make sure that there are stores of food and water already stockpiled to supply as much of the citizenry as possible."

"That sounds like we need to get all of the local preppers involved in this?" Toni asked.

"Yes, that is exactly correct," I said. "Preppers are the people who know best how to store and hide food. I think we need to contact influential preppers in various strategic areas, and arrange for them to have the funds needed to begin major stockpiling of food, and securing of water supplies."

"Do you want me to contact the council for the funds?" Toni asked.

"Yes," I said, "please do."

"Another thing that the government would be likely to do," I said, "is shut down the electrical grid as retaliation for rebel activity in the area. They are especially likely to do this in the heat of summer, or the coldest part of winter."

"How about we have the preppers distribute information to patriots that tell who to contact if the grid goes down?" Toni asked. "We may be able to make arrangements for a number of wood stoves and wood heaters, or at least plans on how to make them, to be available for citizens in need. I don't think this will be inexpensive, but it would help."

"If these wood heaters or wood stoves are installed for free during grid down, I think that would go a long way towards winning people over to our side. I suspect our preppers could organize the installation of these heaters on as needed basis."

"So basically we are replacing FEMA with our own organization," Peggy said.

"That won't be hard. They don't do anything right anyway," Toni chuckled.

"The logistics will be very difficult," I said. "That means that we have to be the ones to initiate action against the government in the areas that we think are best prepared for any possible consequences. That will take a lot of planning. Toni, can you set up a series of meetings with influential preppers once we establish the most likely key areas for action against the feds?"

"I will get some people on identifying influential preppers all across the country right away."

"When Lorne gets back, we will decide where, and how, we can take action most effectively. What I worry about is the government continuing to piss off citizens, like they did in Alabama, so much so that the citizens take action independently. A conflagration like that will make our efforts to protect citizen's lives much more difficult."

"There is also a high probability of a preemptive strike by the feds against the people," I said. "A shock and awe tactic intended to break the people's will to resist."

"This rebellion stuff is more difficult than I ever thought it would be," Peggy mused.

"Actually, what we are doing is not rebellion," I said. "What we want is to keep the Constitution and the constitutional structure of our government, the executive branch, the legislative branch, and the judicial branch. We simply want to remove all traitors to the Constitution from office, and rid the country of the bogus laws that have been passed by these traitors to limit constitutional freedoms for the people. The problem is that almost all 545 members of the current government, 546 counting the vice president, and many federal workers as well, are traitors to the Constitution, and the country," I paused. "Our founders knew this day would come. That is the purpose of the second amendment; to make sure the people have the power, not only to resist, but to depose a tyrannical government."

"Well, those bastards in D.C. sure think that what we are doing is a rebellion," Toni said. "It kind of feels like it to me too," She paused. "Those idiots brought it on themselves though. They think so little of the American citizens that they feel they can kill us at will."

Peggy nodded, "It feels like a rebellion to me too."

"I agree that it feels like that, but we need to always remember that we are the patriots and oath keepers. The people who are in charge of the country at the moment are the traitors," I said.

"I think we need to have everyone we recruit, as well as the rest of us, swear an oath to uphold and protect the Constitution, much like the oath sworn to by our military and many police officers," I paused. "Perhaps it should go something like this. I swear to protect the Constitution of the United States of America, and the principles on which it stands, from all enemies, both foreign and domestic," I paused. "We should talk about this with Lorne and the council."

"We should also make this part of our publicity campaign, which we need to kick off very soon now—especially since that incident in Alabama," Peggy said.

"Yes," Toni agreed. "We also need to put some good writers to work in stating our principles and position to the public. They need to understand that it is we are fighting for."

"And we need to make videos stating our position available online. I think the hackers can help us there too," Peggy said. "And, John. You need to make some videos so people know who you are. You, like it or not, are the symbol of our fight for freedom. The public has to know that the government is not all powerful."

"I think you should also make videos, Peggy. And so should you, Toni. Your stories need to get out to the people as well. We also need to get the lady who shot the FTSP agent in Alabama on video again, if she survived the Mississippi attack."

"I will set this up," Peggy said. "One of our people is a former advertising executive. I think he will be better at planning our 'advertising' campaign than the rest of us."

"Good," I said. "I think this will come together well, if we can move quickly enough."

"I also think we need a military person to plan the overt action against those who need to be deposed," I said. "However, military training may often produce plans that are quite predictable by the other side. Right now, we have major plans being made by a retired professor, a computer programmer, and a former housewife. I doubt that our plans will be as predictable as the feds would like them to be. We do need an experienced military advisor though, probably more than one."

"I will see who I can find," Peggy said.

"I hope we have the time to accomplish what we need to accomplish," Toni worried. "It seems like all of this is moving exceptionally fast."

"I agree," I said. "And not only does it seem exceptionally fast to the three of us, it has also resulted in extreme changes in each of our lives. I suspect that means, even if the feds profile each of us, as I am sure they have done, their profile may not accurately predict our actions or plans now."

"I know I have done things recently that I never thought I was capable of doing," Peggy said.

"The same for me," Toni said.

"And me as well," I agreed. "I never thought I would be able to take a human life." Peggy reached out and gasped my wrist with her hand and looked me in the eye.

"Neither did I," she said.

"I just hope that we come out of all of this still human,"
I replied. "I don't want this revolution to turn any of us into
the kind of monsters that run our government."

"I don't think that's possible," Toni said, "but I'm
worried too."

We spent two more hours discussing various things
that we needed to do to prevent both patriot and civilian
casualties in the upcoming fight. Both Peggy and Toni each
had several more great ideas. The more I was around them,
the more I liked them both, and the more I thought about,
and missed Susan. I knew I had to keep my wits about me,
and not become distracted by either Toni or Peggy if we
were to win this fight. It was hard for me to admit to myself
that I was attracted to both of them. The feel of Peggy's kiss
was often on my mind, as were the touches from Toni. They
both made me feel guilty. Strangely, the killing of the
ground hounds did not.

Chapter 20: CHALLENGE

"You often get exactly what you ask for, whether you want it or not." John Debrouillard

<u>Washington, D.C., The White House</u>

"Mr. President," the secretary of the Department of Interior Security said, "I think we have a problem." The secretary put a DVD into the player attached to the giant screen TV on one wall of the president's working office, his study, located close to the oval office. The oval office was mostly for show. The study was where the real work occurred.

The secretary, who had been in the federal government his entire career, and who had seen several presidents come and go, reflected to himself that, under this president, the study saw relatively little actual use.

The president stood, approached the television, and, immaculate as ever, gracefully sat in an overstuffed chair that faced the screen. "OK," he said. "Roll it."

The DVD started and a well-dressed man sitting at a desk appeared. He looked like any other news announcer; however, there was no identifying station logo. The man shuffled several papers, and then set the stack on the desk. "Ladies and gentlemen, citizens of our once great country, we have a problem. That problem is that our government has gone rogue. Our Founding Fathers warned us that this might happen and laid out the steps that we have a moral responsibility to take if and when it did. Well folks, it has finally happened."

The president pushed the pause button built into the arm of his chair, "Who is this clown?" He asked, standing so he could tower over the shorter secretary.

"We don't know yet sir. We have run facial recognition and biometric identification programs and he is not in our database. He speaks with a Midwestern accent, but we have no idea who he is."

"Well, find out and have him killed," the president said.

"Yes Mr. President. We will do so as soon as possible." The secretary paused and nervously stated, "Sir, you should watch the rest of this."

"Very well," the president said and once more seated himself—with the innate grace of royalty he thought as he settled into the chair and pushed the play button. The video resumed.

"It has been a slow decline," the man at the desk said. "Hardly noticeable day to day for many of us who have been occupied earning a living and paying taxes, but a decline nonetheless. It started with small inroads on our constitutional rights as citizens and it has advanced to the point that our government now feels that it has the right to kill our very own citizens, here at home on American soil, in secrecy and with no due process, just because these citizens may oppose the actions and/or agenda of the current administration, or even simply be witnesses to what the this administration did not want them to see."

The president hit the pause button again. This time he had lost much of his composure and he failed to stand. "This is outrageous!" He shouted. "How did they find out about this?"

"Mr. President, surely you remember the advisor who told you this was inevitable."

"And I had that SOB killed. No one questions my decisions. No one. Do you understand that?"

"Yes Mr. President," the secretary cringed. "I understand that very well."

The president cursed under his breath and finally hit the play button once more.

"Ladies and Gentlemen, in my lifetime we have gone from a nation founded on, and respectful of, our constitution and the rule of law, to a nation where rich and powerful men make laws only to protect their own interests and positions."

"Many of these laws are written and passed in secret, and often not even using our basic constitutional procedures. The public knows nothing of these illegal laws until they are forced at the point of the federal gun to comply with them. This, ladies and gentlemen, is nothing less than tyranny; a tyranny born of evil, and in place right here today in the United States of America."

"That's enough," the president stood in anger and shouted. "Kill these bastards, every damn one of them. I will not be impugned nor disobeyed!"

"Yes Sir, Mr. President," the secretary said to the president's back as he stalked from the room.

Socorro, New Mexico

"And what may be even worse, is that so many of our high-ranking federal employees are basically on the take. Under the guidance of our elected officials, our country has descended from the place of honor that it once held in the world to the role of hated hegemony. No longer are our employees; and yes, all federal employees are our employees, our employees. They are supposed to work for us, the citizens. Our taxes pay their salaries. The way our government was originally set up was for these people to answer to the citizens and obey the Constitution. However, so many of these high-ranking federal officials today feel like they do not need answer to the people or the Constitution. The Constitution is to them only an old document that keeps them from taking what they wish from the people. They believe that the people are so many sheep, to provide money for the government to use as it sees fit, to be herded into whatever belief paradigm they wish us to have, or to be killed for their pleasure, or simply when we inconvenience them."

"Many of these high-ranking federal employees are sucking at the teat of large corporations whose only goal is profit. While some CEOs do care about people, there are an increasingly large number of them who do not. Like many of our elected representatives, too many of these people are psychopaths. They have no feeling for the rest of humanity."

"Perhaps, like myself not too long ago, you don't believe that what I'm saying is true? Perhaps you have seen some signs of the disintegration that our country is going through? Perhaps you've seen isolated cases were you believe high-ranking federal employees are indeed either not following the laws of the nation, or are corrupt?"

"Boy howdy, do I agree with that!" Bill hit the pause button on the video. Then he downloaded the video in its entirety onto his computer, and transferred the video to a blank DVD. "Let's see what the boys at the Longhorn have to say about this?"

Bill took the DVD, got into his old pickup truck, and drove the mile to the Longhorn Bar in downtown Socorro, New Mexico. The bar was the local hangout for the college crowd and usually included not only students, but also staff and occasionally faculty of the New Mexico Institute of Technology, as well as a few ranchers. Fifteen minutes later, Bill inserted the DVD into the DVD player in the bar and cued up the video for everyone to see. The TV was mounted on the wall and was big enough to be seen from anywhere in the room. It was Friday night and the Longhorn was full, as usual. Bill recognized most of the people he saw. They were regulars.

The patrons watched the beginning of the video in silence, concentrating on what the announcer had to say while occasionally sipping their beers. Other than the occasional remark that that 'son of a bitch of a president was not going to confiscate their guns', not much was said.

The man on the video said, "I am now going to show you a video that shows what it is like when the government decides that you are persona non-grata. Pay close attention to this video. It was hacked from government files. So, you are seeing the events through the cameras, the eyes, of the government drones that were involved."

The picture faded from the announcer and showed a man hoeing a garden. The video had sound and everyone in the room could hear the swish of the hoe as the man chopped weeds. Suddenly, the man turned and began to run. There was also an unfamiliar roar in the background.

"Well shit." Someone said. "Those are bullets. Somebody is shooting at that guy."

"No, that's not someone. That's a drone," someone else said.

They all watched as the fellow dodged bullets in a run all the way across the yard and into a small building.

"He's toast," a random voice shouted. "That building won't stop those bullets." The crowd in the Longhorn Bar watched as bullets continued to punch holes in the metal walls of the building. It was obvious the bullets were often passing all the way through the small building. After a bit, the bullet impacts ceased. In just a few seconds the man appeared in the doorway of the building with a shotgun. He pointed the shotgun at the camera. A few people in the bar ducked involuntarily, but most cheered when the shotgun fired. On the fifth shot the image careened away from the door of the building and went black. At that point someone in the bar shouted.

"He got the damn drone with a shotgun!" At that everyone in the bar stood and cheered.

The view cut to another camera farther away. By now the man was at the back door of the house where a woman had just stepped outside. Dropping the shotgun, the man grabbed the woman and they started through the doorway into the house. Everyone could clearly see three bullets strike the woman. She shook at the impact and they could see the bloodstains grow as the pair disappeared into the house. At this point there was complete silence in the bar;

something that had not happened at the Longhorn before in anyone's memory.

The audience was horrified to see that now, in the view of another drone camera; many other drones were converging on the house. They each had four, or six, helicopter blades and seemed to be about five or six feet across, and there were pistols with drum magazines mounted underneath each drone. The patrons of the bar watched in horror as the house was completely shredded by bullets. The roar of gunfire on the video sounded like a continuous boom of thunder. Not one word was said as the house collapsed onto its foundation.

The camera now switched back to the announcer. "What you have seen, ladies and gentlemen, is shocking. You have witnessed actual footage taken by video cameras on government drones of the assassination of an innocent United States civilian by our current administration, with no due process, right here in the United States. This happened in mid-Indiana only a few weeks ago. However, the man they were after escaped. The drones, and their cowardly operators, killed his wife.

"How the fuck could anybody get out of that?" Somebody asked.

"Beats the hell out of me," Bill said. "This is unbelievable!"

The camera shifted to another room where a man stood. It took most of the patrons a second or so to recognize the man who had downed the drone with a shotgun. Then everyone in the bar rose and cheered. The only liberal in the room was Hector Garcia. He rose and cheered with everyone else.

"Hello, my name is John. If you have watched the first part of this video, you know that my wife, Susan, was killed—murdered—by the U.S. government. They were trying to murder me.

Apparently, my crime against the current administration was simply posting comments on various internet blogs. At no time then did I, either verbally or in print, advocate overthrow of the U.S. government. I only predicted what I thought the government might do next. Apparently I predicted too well.

I have since been told that this administration found my predictions of their clandestine activities troubling. For that reason, and that reason alone, they decided to murder me. My wife and I were attacked at home by over 40 copter drones, each carrying a .40 caliber gun capable of firing 100 rounds. As you can see from the video, our house was completely destroyed. At this point I'm sure most of you are wondering how I managed to survive," the man paused.

"My wife and I were preppers. If you know anything at all about prepper movement, you know that the vast majority of preppers are not violent people. They are simply people who are looking at the way things are going in this country and are preparing their families and friends for what they believe are possible future hard times.

Preppers stock extra food in case of hard times. Most of us strive to have about a year's supply of food put away. This is no different than our grandparents did, especially those that lived on farms. This is no different than the Mormon Church encourages all of its members to do. Storing food in case of hard times is an American tradition that our ancestors understood and universally practiced."

"For some time now though, the government has been hell-bent on making preppers seem like irresponsible citizens. I believe that is because their communist approach to ruling the U.S. is to exert the maximum control over every citizen. They feel that anyone who thinks for themselves, as our founders did, is a threat to their power."

"For example, recently, in some of the major cities, there have been vapid laws passed that make organic foods illegal—most likely because the corporate backers of this communistic fascist regime want higher profits from sales of the genetically-modified, slow poison that they wish to force feed each and every American citizen."

"Many preppers also have an emphasis on organic food, and we tend to grow and raise much of our own food. In the minds of the anti-constitutional terrorists who inhabit our government, this must not be allowed because people who do not depend on the government to feed them, or tell them what to eat, cut into corporate profits, and therefore decrease political contributions to the rogue politicians."

"In addition to stockpiling food, most preppers also prepare for times when the electric grid might be down, such as during a hurricane, or perhaps after an EMP event. We make sure that we have a good supply of water that can be accessed if the grid is down. We also have medicines and other supplies on hand just in case we may need them, and, of course, we typically have guns to defend our families and friends if needed. That too is an American tradition and is our irrevocable birthright as Americans.

Preparing—being a prepper—is a lifestyle. Many of us try to anticipate situations that might occur and act accordingly. With that in mind my wife and I wondered if we might ever have to escape our house without detection. For that reason we hand-dug a root cellar under the house and then dug a tunnel from that root cellar to the edge of our property. In order to maintain operational security, we told no one of our root cellar or tunnel and we did not file for permits before we built them.

"My wife died in my arms in our root cellar, killed by bullets fired remotely by the cowards in our rogue government. I escaped through the tunnel."

"I am now, at the request of many American patriots, leading the effort to remove our rogue government from power. We are not trying to overthrow the United States. We are, each and every one, loyal American citizens. But, we are loyal to the Constitution of the United States, and not the tyrants, imbeciles, and fools who occupy the positions of highest power in the current administration."

"The president is currently building an army of DIS agents who swear loyalty to him, and not to the United States of America, or to our Constitution. The president is simply an employee of the people. We pay his salary. If you owned a business, would you swear fealty to your janitor and then follow his orders on how to run your business and live your life while letting him spend almost all of your money?"

"I do not believe that any president of the United States who would murder American citizens with no due process deserves the office." The man paused for almost ten seconds.

"That's a fact," one of the bar patrons said.

"Yeah, we should kill the POTUS son of a bitch," another patron said holding his beer up to toast the crowd. There was much clinking of glassware and reaffirmation that that son of a bitch in the White House needed to be killed.

The bar grew quiet again when the man on the video said, "We are leading the effort to replace all of the corrupt lawmakers, justices, and members of the executive offices in Washington, D.C. with honest people who love America and Americans. It is also our intention to remove any high-ranking federal officials who have blatantly disobeyed constitutional law. This is not a coup. We are not seeking power. We wish only to return the power to the people as our Founding Fathers wished."

"Thomas Jefferson said, 'when the people fear their government, there is tyranny; when the government fears the people, there is liberty.' It is time for the people to stop fearing our corrupt and evil government. Rather, it is time that the government fears us."

"I used the word we in describing the people I work with and for. By now you're probably asking just who we are? At present, we are a loose organization of patriots, a militia in the original sense of the word. We have no name. That is because we are you; Americans throughout our land who are loyal to America and her Constitution."

"Some of you may have heard of Tench Coxe, and some of you may have not. Tench Coxe was one of our Founding Fathers here in America. Listen to his words from 1778:"

"Who are the militia? Are they not ourselves? Is it feared, then, that we shall turn our arms each man gainst his own bosom. Congress have no power to disarm the militia. Their swords, and every other terrible implement of the soldier, are the birthright of an American.... The unlimited power of the sword is not in the hands of either the federal or state governments, but, where I trust in God it will ever remain, in the hands of the people."

"Look around you. There may be one of us sitting beside you. We are legion. No one of us knows everyone else. However, I know that there are very many of us patriots, and only a few of the evil ones occupying offices, both appointed and elected, in our corrupt government. Therefore, this video is a warning to those members of our rogue government. We, the People, are coming for you. You cannot stop us. The best thing you can do is resign your position or office and leave the country, if you are able. Do it now, or face hanging for your crimes of treason."

A loud cheer rang through the bar as everyone stood. "It's about time somebody got rid of these government sons of bitches," Bill said. "What I want to know is where do I join up with these guys?"

The video ran on for a few seconds and then ended. Everyone in the bar was disappointed. They wanted to hear more. They re-watched the video half a dozen times throughout the night, and animated conversations continued until dawn.

Near Kansas City

"How did the video do?" I asked Peggy.

"It has only been out four days now and we have had over five million internet views. The feds managed to take it down three times, but I put it back up using different accounts and different video hosting sites. I also posted comments to a number of conservative and liberal blogs, using fake IDs and IP addresses with the help of our hacker friends. Those comments drove a lot of traffic to our video. If we can keep it online for another week or so, I expect the views to top 20 million."

"I expect the feds are countering this video somehow?" I asked.

"In addition to removing our video from the internet when they can, they are erasing all of the evidence of you and your wife's existence in every data base they have access too, which, of course, is essentially all of them."

"Does that mean I don't have to pay taxes any more?" I joked.

"Well, since our hacker friends are hacking you back into the databases as soon as the feds remove you, I don't think you will be that lucky," Peggy smiled. "At least once we win this thing."

"At that point, I will be glad to pay taxes," I said.

Chapter 21: NORTH CAROLINA

"A blind and deaf person is better informed than those who ingest only mainstream news." John Debrouillard

<u>Tupelo, Mississippi</u>

They split up in Tupelo. Lorne and Doc drove off in a flashy red sports car headed for Kansas City, Missouri. Myrtle and Lowboy watched them drive away. Gwen was already in the back seat of the crew cab pickup truck. The three of them were going to a safe location in North Carolina. Lorne set it up for them to work as support for a group of 'rebellious nerds' who were designing a shotgun-fired, short range, remote-controlled missile that carried enough high explosives to destroy a small tank. The first prototype was ready to be tested. Myrtle called it a modern grenade launcher, but apparently the term mini-missile was more popular among the nerds.

On the road, Gwen slept in the back seat with her .380 in her hand. Myrtle and Lowboy carried on a conversation as easily as if they had known each other all of their lives. When asked how he got his name, Myrtle told the story to Lowboy.

"Ok then," Myrtle asked when he finished. "How did you get the name Lowboy?"

"My real name is Marion Wilcox," Lowboy said. "How I got the name Lowboy isn't something I want to tell in front of Miss Gwen."

"I think she is asleep," Myrtle said.

Lowboy glanced into the backseat and rubbed his beard. "Well, it came about in the Marine Corps. The guys in my platoon gave me the nickname."

"Was it because you could carry heavy stuff like a lowboy trailer used to move heavy equipment?" Myrtle asked.

Lowboy hung his head, "No, it was because my balls hang down almost halfway to my knees."

Myrtle said, "Hey, that's not so bad. I have heard much worse nicknames," Myrtle reached over and shook Lowboy's hand. "I won't tell," he promised.

"Well I just might," Gwen piped up from the back seat.

Lowboy put his huge head in his hands. "You wouldn't do that to me, now would you Miss Gwen?"

Gwen laughed, "No, I reckon not. A man's balls are his own business. When do we get to our destination, Myrtle?"

"In about an hour Ma'am," Myrtle chuckled and glanced at Lowboy.

Washington, D.C.

The president signed the paper with a flourish. "Well, this ought to take care of it," he said. "I just love executive orders. The people of America are just plain stupid. They should just do what I say. Fortunately, the power to write executive orders allows me to force them to do exactly as I say."

"Yes Sir, Mr. President," the secretary of the Department of Interior Security said.

"Congress is a bunch of imbeciles. It would take them 100 years to pass the legislation I want passed. The executive order that I just signed bans all guns in the United States, except, of course, in the hands of federal police and military on station outside U.S. borders. It wouldn't be wise to let military personal have easy access to weapons here in the U.S., especially since so many voted against me in the last election. We will go out and take the guns from anyone who will not turn them into us. These weak-minded fools will give them to us while they are shaking in fear and shitting in their pants. We have drones, we have a one-million-man federal police force, and we have digital surveillance, visual surveillance, satellite surveillance, and many, many other tools to control the population. There is no way that the people can resist me."

"I think some of them may try, Mr. President," the secretary of the Department of Interior Security said. "Remember our experiences in Afghanistan and the Russian experience in Afghanistan, Sir? The population there was never unarmed by either of two superpowers. The Afghans even made rifles and ammunition from scratch using nothing but hand tools. I don't see Americans being any less difficult than the Afghan people."

"I disagree," the president scowled at the secretary, tempted to fire him for his impertinence. "Only a few people will resist," the president laughed. "And we will make an example of them."

"Yes Sir, Mr. President."

"Get notification out to the press on this executive order. Especially, let them know that there is a 30-day grace period for citizens to turn in their firearms."

"Yes Sir Mr. President, I will get right on it."

"Good. Now listen closely. I have something else I want you to do as well."

"Yes Mr. President."

"I want you to pick out a small town, preferably fairly rural, where gun ownership is moderate. Look for a town in which less than 15% of the people own firearms. That will probably make it on the East Coast or the West Coast. Once you have identified a likely town and checked with me on it, I want you to take 5000 federal police and take that town apart door by door. Each and every time you find a firearm in a house, kill every occupant of the house–man, woman, and child."

"Mr. President, that sounds overly harsh," the secretary said.

"It will get the people's attention," the president smiled. "After that, we will have no problem collecting all the weapons from the people."

"Yes Sir, Mr. President. I will make arrangements for that to be carried out after the 30-day waiting period is over."

"No," the president laughed. "Do it 10 days from today."

"Yes Mr. President," the secretary said. "I will get right on it."

The president watched the secretary leave his office. It made the president feel good to see that the secretary of the Department of Interior Security was afraid of him and that the secretary's knees were slightly shaking. The president liked the feeling he got when people feared him. Yes, he could see this was going to be a good day.

The Farm, North Carolina

Jonas Talisman was putting the finishing touches on the second prototype of the shotgun mini-missile. Jonas enjoyed his work, always. He reflected that he was a nerd, and had always been a nerd. He didn't mind a bit.

Jonas was tall, almost 6 feet 4, six feet three and five eighths inches, to be exact, and he weighed 138 pounds. His idol was Nikola Tesla, the man who invented the alternating current transmission system and the alternating current electric motor and generator. Jonas had done his best to emulate Tesla since he was a small boy. He thought he had succeeded rather well in some ways, yet not nearly as well as he would've liked and others. He mused that he was almost two inches taller than Nikola Tesla and weighed four pounds less. He wasn't sure if he would ever match Tesla's brainpower though, even though sometimes he felt he might come close.

Jonas was 25 years old, held a PhD in electronics and another PhD in physics with a minor in rocket science, as well as Master's degrees in both mechanical and chemical engineering. He was a genius, profoundly gifted, with a personality that made it extremely difficult for him to get along with anyone, including himself. Jonas had no illusions about his lack of people skills.

He was, however, dedicated to the Constitution of the United States of America. Jonas had first read the Constitution of the United States when he was two years old. It made an indelible impression on him, then and now.

Jonas regarded the drafters of the Constitution as being some of the most politically intelligent people in the history of the world. Most perhaps not as intelligent as Nikola Tesla, who was a genius of first magnitude, but certainly true geniuses of the practical. Except, of course, Thomas Jefferson, who was absolutely brilliant.

Once John F. Kennedy held a dinner for the brightest people in the country. Looking over all of the geniuses in the room Kennedy said:

"This is perhaps the assembly of the most intelligence ever to gather at one time in the White House with the exception of when Thomas Jefferson dined here alone."

The United States was a successful experiment unlike any other in the history of mankind. It was a government of the people, by the people, and for the people. As described in the Constitution, it was the most effective approach to peaceful coexistence mankind had ever evolved. Jonas did not believe that he could exist under any other type of government.

Jonas was not a joiner, nor was he a follower, nor was he a leader. Jonas was unique. Jonas was simply Jonas. All Jonas wanted to do was what Jonas wanted to do. That was mostly research and creating things that had never existed before.

Jonas had no urge to hurt anyone, nor did he have any urge to let anyone hurt him. In truth, he was most content when no one else was near him and he was alone. However, a few years ago when he had realized that the United States of America was rapidly changing toward a communist form of government that had no respect for the Constitution, Jonas quietly, deliberately, and determinedly became a resistor. After doing about six months of very hush-hush part-time research, he identified Lorne Vanders as someone who was highly likely to believe that the current government had gone rogue, and who had the influence and money to do something about it.

That was why Jonas quit his job at the university, where he had been a tenured professor since the age of 17, and showed up on Lorne's doorstep. A week later, he had his own laboratory and staff in an isolated location in the mountains of North Carolina.

He informed Lorne that, because he had essentially no people skills, it would not do for him to be in charge of his own staff. Lorne laughed and made arrangements for Jonas to have a chief of staff who would remove the responsibility of dealing with people and finances from him. It was a situation that worked very well for Jonas, if not Porter, his chief of staff.

Now, three years later, Jonas was working on a project that was not even his own idea, a shotgun-fired, drone mini-missile. That was a first for him. However, the concept was tactically brilliant and fit the potential needs of his patriots, as Jonas liked to think of the constitutional supporters he was working so hard to support.

Jonas doubted anyone else in the world could put this project together as well as he could, or as quickly. He had been working on the project for almost two weeks now, and was now on his second prototype, which he was sure would work quite well, although there were a few tweaks he still wanted to include.

He laughed again because, while he knew how the single barrel shotgun on the bench before him worked in theory, he had never fired a gun in his life. His one irrational fear in life was of guns. Intellectually, he knew there was nothing to be afraid of, nor was he opposed to them, but his fear of guns was so intense that he often got sick to his stomach when he even looked at one.

He was hoping that at least with the second prototype, he would be able to pick up the single barrel shotgun and fire the test missile. He had tried to do that with the first prototype, but had gotten sick to his stomach and puked before he could touch the shotgun. To their credit, none of the staff laughed at him. That made him happy—after he cleaned up anyway. All of his life other people made fun of him, even at the university. He had grown to expect it; therefore it surprised him greatly when the staff did not.

Lowboy drove the truck up the winding, tree-lined road that climbed beside the small, rapidly rushing mountain stream. Myrtle was asleep in the back seat and Gwen sat in the front passenger seat, her .380 still clasped in her hand. They turned into a small farm lane that looked seldom used and, for 20 minutes, the truck bounced over ruts and rocks until an old farmstead came into view. The house was small and unpainted and the small barn backed up into a steep hillside in the style of some of the older Smokey Mountain, high-country barns.

As they pulled into the yard a man dressed in ragged overalls came out of the house and opened the barn door. He gestured for Lowboy to drive the truck into the barn and so Lowboy did.

Outside, the barn was sided with weathered boards that only occasionally carried traces of the original red paint. Even though the barn had a new metal roof, the overall milieu was that of a never quite prosperous farm that was now rundown to the point of being unprofitable, if not uninhabitable.

Inside the barn, the difference was astonishing. The inside opened up into a cavernous section excavated into the hill behind. There was a new concrete floor, newly finished walls, and electric lights, and several quite large bays where numerous vehicles were parked. The man in overalls directed Lowboy into an empty space.

Lowboy parked and then stepped out of the truck and closed the door. The man in the overalls opened the passenger door for Gwen and helped her out of the truck. Myrtle was still asleep in the backseat so Lowboy opened the rear door and shook Myrtle's shoulder. Myrtle awoke and groggily crawled out of the truck. The fellow in the ragged overalls introduced himself.

"My name is Porter, Lyle Porter," he said. "I am sort of in charge here."

"My name is Myrtle," Myrtle stuck his hand out and shook hands with the fellow in overalls. "Don't laugh. I'll tell you the story of how I got my name later." The fellow in the overalls grinned and shook hands with Myrtle.

"My name is Lowboy," Lowboy said. "And I ain't gonna tell you how I got the name, so don't even ask." Gwen laughed quietly and then introduced herself.

"My name is Gwen, Mr. Porter," she said. "I'm pleased to meet you."

"I'm pleased to meet you too Ma'am. If you folks will follow me I will get you settled." The three of them followed Porter to a small room in the older part of the barn that looked like a feed room. Porter opened the door and, instead of feed, there was a stairwell leading downward. "Follow me folks." Porter said and started down the stairs.

"Looks like this one's underground too," Lowboy said.

"I hope it's deeper than a missile can penetrate." Gwen said.

"Actually, it is," Porter replied. "This facility was finished very recently and, in this location, we had the advantage of being able to tunnel deep into solid granite. We also have blast doors installed. This facility is designed to be able to withstand a strike from as many as four bunker buster missiles or a tactical nuke and remain intact. In fact, it is more secure than the bunker under the White House."

"How much did this cost?" Gwen asked.

"I am not sure," Porter said. "However, I suspect it was upwards of $400 million. Most of the materials and labor were donated by patriots, and some of the material was liberated from certain government contracts."

"Man, that's still a lot of money," Lowboy said. "I doubt that I've ever made even a few hundred thousand in my entire lifetime."

"Neither have I," Porter laughed. "I think you folks are going to like it here. We have a good crew."

Jonas stepped up to the table at the firing line. Carefully controlling the queasiness in his belly, he picked up the single barrel shotgun. It was a commonly available model that was still made in the USA. Jonas thought that this model would be simple to copy and put into production in any modern machine shop. He had plans to do just that, with a few improvements. Of course, he thought, any type of shotgun could be used to launch his remote controlled mini-missile bombs. Jonas was planning on testing the system with a pump shotgun later. The advantage of a pump shotgun would be that the patriot had the option of quickly firing several normal shotgun rounds if he or she needed to defend himself or herself immediately after firing the missile. Or, the special rounds could be loaded into the magazine and several mini-missiles fired very quickly.

He inserted a specially modified 12 gauge round into the chamber and snapped the gun closed. The round he dropped into the chamber acted like the first stage of a two stage rocket. Its entire purpose was to launch the mini-missile into the air so that the built in rocket could then take it toward the target. Once in the air, it could be guided by remote control using the built-in camera, or encrypted GPS coordinate signals sent back to the controller.

Next Jonas picked up the mini-missile and carefully slid it down the barrel. There was a small magnet at the base of the missile and another on the end of the cartridge that held the missile inside the barrel until it was fired. That way, any patriots using the system wouldn't have to worry about dropping the missile out of the barrel. However, Jonas still needed to replace the small permanent magnets he had used with electro-magnets and put a battery system and controller into the stock of the shotgun. The electro-magnets would make the missile easier to unload. For now, once loaded, the missile had to be fired. It could not be unloaded. The mini-missile controller was just a joystick device sitting on the table in front of him.

Taking a moderately careful aim at the target almost a mile away, Jonas pulled the trigger. The shock against his shoulder surprised him and hurt much more than he thought it would. This was the first time he had ever fired a gun in his life. The missile streaked toward the target as the built-in rocket engine fired some 200 feet from where Jonas was standing. Jonas quickly handed the shotgun to Porter and picked up the controller. On the video screen Jonas could see what the miniature camera in the missile saw as it approached the target. The missile could be guided with the joystick and Jonas now used the joystick to put the missile right on target. The explosion as the missile struck the target was huge. The sound would have damaged everyone's ears if they were not wearing hearing protection. The ground roll from the explosion was noticeable under their feet, but not quite enough to disturb their balance.

Jonas smiled. The super-high-explosives in the mini-missile were of his own design. A few grams of his new explosive had the explosive force of ten sticks of dynamite and was safer to carry than anything presently on the market. The mini-missiles could each carry 276 grams of the new explosives, although, depending on intended use, it was unlikely every missile would need to carry the maximum payload of explosives.

"That was a success," Myrtle said from the sidelines. I got it all on film too." He said holding a video camera up in the air. "We can splice the video from the missile with that and send it to John and Lorne."

"Now that is a shotgun," Lowboy said. "That will fix those FTSP goons for sure."

Jonas was lost in thought and didn't hear a word that any of the others said. He was already designing in his head the modifications he would make before the system was ready to put into production. Like Nikola Tesla, he could clearly see his designs in three-dimensional color in his mind's eye. He was confident he could have the design to the machine shop by late that evening. He would request one more prototype for testing and then he was sure that they would be able to put the system into production. He was also inordinately proud of the fact he had, for the first time, managed to fire a gun. Lowboy had helped him a lot by suggesting he think of the gun as just a big firecracker launcher. As silly as that sounded, it seemed to have worked.

Jonas had designed the system so that almost no training was needed to operate it—it was almost fool proof. Jonas did not believe that anything was truly fool proof because fools often seemed to do the impossible without even knowing it. Anyone who had ever played a video game and fired a shotgun would be able to use the system easily, though.

The next version would look exactly like an unmodified single barrel shotgun, with the batteries and fold out controller built into a compartment in the stock. As far as he knew, single shot firearms were still legal for hunters to use. He had heard a few comments about some declaration by the president about some kind of coming gun confiscation, but he never bothered himself with that sort of stuff. He was far too busy designing technology that he hoped would put his patriots on an equal footing with the feds.

Chapter 22: THE BATTLE

"An idiot is someone who believes a politician's promise." John Debrouillard

<u>Washington, D.C.</u>

Mr. President. We have identified a target town in North Carolina for gun confiscation."

The president stood slowly and turned to face the secretary. "Tell me more about this town."

"Yes Mr. President, Sir. The town is named Bent Pine. It has a population of 2,705. The median income is $27,000 per year. It is difficult to know how many guns the residents of the town have, but there seem to be only a few hunters and no shooting range near the town. Based on the relatively low median income, we surmise that very few of the residents have been able to purchase semi-automatic, high capacity rifles. Therefore, we suspect that few citizens will be able to provide much resistance."

"Also, the houses in the town are fairly well spread out, with only a few close concentrations of housing units, so that when our people strike there will be few close neighbors to realize what is happening and try to assist their neighbors."

"The town is also located between two mountains and was built between the river and a mountainside. There is only one major highway running through the town, so it will be easy for us to close off access at both ends of the town once we occupy it. We should be able to control the situation very easily"

"That sounds reasonable," the president said. "What percentage of the people in this town voted for me?"

"Almost none, Mr. President," the secretary said. "The town is very conservative and so is the state. You did not even carry the state."

"Good," the president smiled. "Will 5000 men be enough? We want to make sure this goes our way."

"Yes Sir, Mr. President," the secretary nodded his head. "I believe it will be more than enough. Our people are trained in clearing houses and have the aptitude for this. We are using DIS people exclusively. No one who has ever sworn an oath to defend the Constitution will be involved in this operation, only those who have sworn an oath of fealty to you, personally. We are also backing up our people on the ground with helicopters and drones. This will be a bloodbath for any citizens who resist or own guns."

"What about the local police force?" The president asked.

"They will not be informed. On the website of the town the local sheriff states that he is a constitutional supporter. I suspect he and his staff will not survive the strike."

"Excellent," the president said. "Be sure to collect some videos for me."

"Yes Sir. As always Sir," the secretary nodded.

Bent Pine, North Carolina

Tom Coy sat high on the mountainside with his binoculars. Tom was 31 years old, a fit and recently mustered out army veteran with two tours in Iraq and two tours in Afghanistan. He had been a sniper.

He was now a member of the Bent Pine militia. Today, as usual, he wasn't wearing his militia uniform. His scoped .308 Winchester leaned against the tree beside him as he periodically scanned the highway that led into town. This was boring work, but the town and the militia had decided only nine days ago that it should be done because the sheriff had a friend in the current administration who warned him that something might be coming his way. Tom's employer, the owner of the local lumberyard, had kept him on full pay for sentry duty and the owner himself was in the yard right now running the forklift that Tom usually ran. Tom now had sentry duty three days a week.

The local sheriff, Merle, was now in his late sixties or early seventies and was a Marine Corps veteran who had served three tours of duty in Vietnam. Merle had been wounded twice and Tom knew he had been awarded a silver star, even though he had never heard Merle mention it, or anything else about the Vietnam War for that matter. What he knew he had learned from his boss at the lumberyard.

Merle, and the leaders of the militia, which included the mayor, were worried about the government. There had been much talk of gun confiscation in Congress of late, and they were concerned that it might come to pass. And then of course, there was the recent illegal executive order from the president stating that he was banning all civilian firearms in the U.S. Apparently, few, if any, in Bent Pine were willing to give up their guns. Tom had sworn an oath as a military officer to defend the Constitution from all enemies, both foreign and domestic, and he was not willing to give up his second amendment rights either.

The mayor was also worried about the possibility of an economic collapse and eventual martial law being declared. He, as were the rest of the militia, was determined that no federal police would ever be needed, or even allowed in Bent Pine. The mayor felt that having militia sentries keeping an eye on the approaches to Bent Pine made sense, especially since he and the city council had started to stockpile food and supplies (including guns and ammunition) for the citizens of the town and county just in case.

With the talk coming out of Washington, the mayor said he wouldn't be surprised if the feds might even come after Bent Pine's stockpile of food someday, even though everything had been purchased for cash and very quietly. Worst case, he thought, having sentries wouldn't hurt a thing.

When Tom mustered out of the army, he didn't know what to do with himself. The civilian world now seemed strange, and somehow unreal to him. He had horrible nightmares almost every night. There were two nightmares that were often repeated. The first one was where he was hunting in the woods and there were many small white bunnies hopping around. Since he was squirrel hunting, he ignored them, although he wondered what they were doing there. At some point in the dream, the fluffy white bunnies morphed into resistance fighters and started shooting at him. When he tried to return fire with his double-barreled 20-gauge shotgun he found that he had no ammunition. It was at that point that he usually woke up in a cold sweat with the sheet and mattress under him drenched and frigid.

The other dream was one in which everyone he passed on the street had the face of one of the people he had shot in his official duties as a sniper during his four tours of duty. Every time he awoke from this nightmare he threw up. He slowly lost weight until he looked to be a pale ghost of his former muscular 210 pounds on a five-eleven frame.

After only a month at home with his parents, he just up and left one day and set out aimlessly across the country in his Jeep CJ5. He had no destination in mind. He just wanted to get away from the home that now seemed so strange and the people he could no longer talk to, even though he loved them as much now as he had when he left. He thought that it was probably a good thing that his fiancée had sent him a Dear John letter a year before he left the Army. He had changed. He knew that. He often wondered if he would ever see the return of his old, happy-go-lucky self.

When he rolled into Bent Pine, he was struck by the beauty and serenity of the town, and how friendly the people were. While having lunch in one of the cafes, Tom met Merle. At first he had answered Merle's questions guardedly, wondering why this small-town sheriff was interested in him. Then, as he learned that Merle was a fellow veteran, he opened up a bit more. Soon he was telling Merle about his war experiences and finally broke down in tears for the first time since he had joined the army. Merle just hugged him and told him that it was going to be all right. Soon one of the older waitresses came over and hugged him too.

They put him up in the spare room at Merle's house. The next day, Merle found him a job at the lumberyard. The owner of the lumberyard was about Merle's age with white hair and a closely trimmed white beard. He showed Tom around and told him that he had been in the service with Merle and that they both understood very well what he was going through.

After working in the lumberyard for six months now, Tom was getting better and had gained weight. The nightmares still came, but with ever-decreasing frequency.

He now had a room in a downtown rooming house. He had no idea that any of these old fashioned rooming houses still existed, but he discovered he loved living there.

He was slowly making friends around town; friends he could talk to, many of whom had served in the military themselves, and many of whom had not, but who still accepted him as he was, without judgment.

What he liked best were the fishing trips to the river where they just sat in comfortable silence and fished. He always brought his catch back to the rooming house where Mrs. Samuels cheerfully fried them up for a meal. The other roomers and Mr. Samuels always thanked him for catching the fish.

No one even minded the fact that he kept his guns in his room. In fact, Mr. Samuels even offered to clean them for him if he didn't have the time.

So far, today had been just as boring as every other day Tom had spent on sentry duty. He was at one of the five sentry posts that the town was now keeping manned 24 hours a day. The mayor even provided night vision goggles for those on the night shift.

It was a beautiful, clear morning with a tangy chill in the air. It wouldn't be too long before was too cold for the fishing trips, but Merle had promised to take Tom deer hunting, and he was looking forward to that.

Tom heard the sound before he saw them. At first it seemed to be a single helicopter approaching town from the east above the highway. The sound was too loud for a single helicopter though. When he looked through the binoculars he saw that there was a line of black helicopters—a long line of black helicopters—headed toward Bent Pine. Tom was on the radio in a flash.

"Merle, This is Tom, over."

A few seconds later, "What's up Tom?"

"We have a line of black helicopters coming in from the east along the highway. There are also a lot of armored trucks and black vans coming along the highway towards Bent Pine. It looks like there are also some sort of drone transport trucks, kind of like we used overseas for smaller drones."

"Roger that, Tom. Are you sure?"

"Hell yes, I'm sure."

"How many men do you think and who are they?"

"I am guessing over a thousand, and I can't even see the end of the convoy yet. There could be several times that many. I think they are feds. I didn't even know there were that many of them."

"Well, I guess that fucker in the White House was serious when he said he wanted his own million-man-army right here in the United States."

"It sure looks that way. Do you think they are coming after us, or just passing through?" Tom asked.

"I don't know. I have Betty here in the dispatcher's office calling the feds right now. We better assume they are hostile, but we need to let them fire the first shot just to be sure. Damned if I know why they are here. We are going to block the highway and I will meet them and ask who they are and what they are doing in my county. Jimmy is headed up there to relieve you right now. Can you take a position to cover us at the roadblock? We are setting up by the junkyard. I will take my hat off if it goes hot. If you see that, fire at will."

"Got you covered, Friend," Tom said. He looked back down the trail and he saw Jimmy drive up in a cloud of dust near where Tom had parked his Jeep. Tom picked up his rifle and pack and trotted down the trail to meet Jimmy.

Jimmy was carrying his deer rifle as well, and waved to Tom when he saw him. Jimmy was a deputy and was still wearing his uniform.

"It looks like some deep shit coming," Tom said.

"Feds?"

"Yeah, I think so."

"I don't trust those greedy bastards as far as I could throw a tank," Jimmy smiled and spat a wad of chewing tobacco at the ground.

Tom waved and ran to his Jeep.

Kansas City, Missouri

Lorne entered John's office and walked up behind him. John was concentrating on various maps and government documents and didn't hear him come into the room. Lorne put his hand on John's shoulder. "John, there is major trouble in Bent Pine, North Carolina. We have to go there now. The feds are attacking the town."

"It is most likely a preemptive gun confiscation move on the part of the president," John said. "That is his style."

"The grace period in his executive order isn't even over yet," Toni said from where she was standing behind Lorne.

I am ready," John stood. "Let me get my rifle."

This time the helicopter was much larger. Lorne slid into the pilot's seat and John climbed into the front passenger seat. Toni, Doc, and Peggy got into the rear seats. While they were loading the helicopter, a car swiftly drove up and squealed the brakes slightly as it stopped. A small, lightly built, hooded figure got out carrying only a laptop computer. The car left and the hooded person got into the back of the chopper with Toni, Doc, and Peggy. Peggy nodded to the figure and he/she nodded back. John looked quizzically at Lorne. "Don't ask," he said.

"If that is who I think it is, we need to talk." John turned and said, "Toni, can you change places with me? I think our guest and I really need to talk."

"You bet," Toni said, with a glance at Peggy. The rest of the trip John and the hooded figure were deep in conversation. Peggy and Doc hardly got in a single word.

Bent Pine, North Carolina

Merle stood alone in front of the roadblock, armed only with the 1911 Colt in his holster. Behind him were seven huge dump trucks from the quarry, several smaller dump trucks, and the road grader from the city yard, as well as a couple of bulldozers from various nearby construction sites. None of the vehicles had keys in the ignitions, and they formed an effective barricade across the highway that the federal armored trucks and vans were unlikely to be able to pass through or drive around. The nearby rooftops and second story windows were lined with as many men who could get to their rifles and get there on a few minutes notice. There were also five or six men scattered throughout the junkyard on Merle's left. The word had now spread throughout town for everyone to take cover and arm themselves.

The federal trucks and vans approached to about 200 yards from the barricade and stopped. The lead helicopter landed on the pavement in front of Merle. The other choppers either continued on or circled. Merle didn't think that looked good at all. A man stepped out of the chopper. He was followed by six feds dressed in SWAT gear.

"What is the meaning of this?" He shouted. "Who the fuck do you think you are?" The men with him immediately pointed their M4 carbines at Merle.

"I am the sheriff of this county," Merle said. "Who are you people and what is your business here?"

"We are Federal Agents. Get those vehicles out of our way. What we are doing here is none of your business." The man seemed to become increasingly agitated with every word.

"I am here to protect the people I serve," Merle said.

"Oh fuck you," the fed said. He drew a pistol and pointed it at Merle. Before he could pull the trigger his head exploded. A microsecond later Merle heard the rifle shot and the fed's lifeless body collapsed to the ground. The six feds with him seemed shocked and confused. Merle took cover behind a bulldozer blade and drew his pistol as another of the feds dropped, shot through the head.

"Thank you Tom," Merle said under his breath as he shot at the remaining feds himself. Rifle fire was now coming from the junkyard and buildings that bordered the road. The pilot of the chopper was shot through and through and the Plexiglas windshield of the chopper crazed and partially collapsed. "I think that was a big fifty," Merle said out loud. "That must be Deputy Gator."

The trucks down the highway spilled SWAT-costumed feds onto the tarmac and they began firing their M4s. At that range, the accuracy of the M4's with the 14.5-inch barrels favored by the feds for clearing buildings was not particularly good. The return fire from Bent Pine was mostly .270, .308, and 30-06, fired from bolt actions and a few semi-auto hunting rifles. The feds were dropping with almost every shot, their low-bid body armor mostly useless against the heavy rifle rounds.

Merle was worried. He knew the militia men were on the way, but the helicopters, though small, could set their troops down anywhere and those troops would soon be able to flank them. Merle studied the helicopter closest to him considering if a shot from his 1911 would have any effect, when he saw the chopper's windshield craze, and the chopper spun out of control and crashed to the ground.

"Wow." He muttered. "That must be Tom. Man, he is good." Once the first chopper went down, some of the men with deer rifles also began to target the choppers that were close enough. In short order, three more crashed and the rest flew in all directions out of range. It looked like there were at least a dozen helicopters left in the air.

For now it was a standoff. It wouldn't last, Merle thought. They were out-gunned and outnumbered. There were more feds out there on the highway than there were townspeople, let alone armed men, in Bent Pine.

Merle was sure the feds had snipers as well so he got on the radio and got word out for everyone to keep their heads down and only fire when they had a good target.

About then that big fifty of Gator's began firing at a rate of about one shot every 2 seconds. Merle knew that Gator couldn't fire that quickly with any accuracy, but off in the distance the feds were dropping, one after one until the 20 round magazine was empty. Several shots shattered the front windows of armored trucks and killed the drivers. That created a traffic jam as the feds all tried to retreat at one time, the armored trucks often leaving before their squads could get back inside. Merle thought it looked like an old slapstick movie and he would have laughed if this were not so serious.

The big fifty continued firing as the feds retreated and one after another they dropped as they ran. The feds didn't stop until they were almost a mile away. "It must be Tom on the big fifty." Merle said. "He is the only trained sniper in town."

Tom lay prone beside Gator. Gator's .50 cal Barrett was cradled against his cheek. He carefully worked out the range and drew a bead on the chopper hovering over the feds on the roadway almost a mile from where he lay. The day was almost windless. Tom grinned, "An easy shot." He fired and the chopper whirled and spun out of control, the pilot shot through the heart.

This time Tom felt his actions were right. He was defending his friends and fellow Americans from tyranny, not trying to control dissidents in another country so a few corporations and government crooks could make a profit from spilled American and local blood.

The crash of the chopper caused the feds to pull back another half mile. Tom motioned to Gator and they both moved to another position. In a few minutes Merle flopped down beside them.

"Damn, Gator. I'll never make fun of you for buying that big fifty again. I never thought there would ever be a need for a rifle like that here in the USA."

"Neither did I," Gator replied. "Neither did I."

"They can be quite useful," Tom said. "I can still cause some damage to those feds from here if need be."

"Shit, I can't even see that far," Merle said. "No, hold off a bit. I want to know what is going on. I am going to get on the phone to D.C. and see what I can find out. Shoot if they come at us though." He looked at Gator. "How many rounds do you have for that thing, anyway?"

"About a thousand, Chief," Gator grinned. "All match grade. I keep two hundred in the squad car. A couple of the guys are fetching the rest back to us."

"Holy shit," Merle smiled. "Remind me to buy you a steak dinner when this is over."

Tom looked at Merle, "Be as quick as you can. They have drones and they are getting them ready to launch."

The Farm, North Carolina

Porter found Jonas in his private lab fiddling with an apparatus that had no obvious purpose Porter could discern. "Jonas," he shook his shoulder. Jonas' mind slowly returned from the lost world within his head and he said, "Huh."

Porter gave Jonas a couple of minutes to normalize, as Jonas referred to his process of becoming aware of his surroundings once more, and then said. "Jonas, how many of the mini-missiles do you have ready to go right now?"

"Uh, I don't know for sure. I haven't been in the assembly shop today. Maybe 15."

"How about the drone jammers you were working on?"

"Uh, 257 here now. We shipped 500 to Kansas City yesterday."

"That's good. We have a problem over in Bent Pine, about 20 miles from here. The feds have attacked the town with a contingent several thousand strong. So far, the people in Bent Pine are holding them off, but they need some help. No one knows why the feds are there. The feds refuse to communicate with the local sheriff and mayor, but John in Kansas City said that it is probably a pre-emptive gun control confiscation strike by the feds intended to create fear and feelings of helplessness in the gun owning population. Kansas City is sending some people to help too, but we can get there much more quickly."

"Cool, I have been wanting to try some of my stuff out. I can be ready to go in fifteen minutes," Jonas said.

"You can't go," Porter replied. "We need your talent too much to risk you in a gun battle."

"I'll go with you or without you!" Jonas asserted.

"Yeah, you are just stubborn enough to do just that," Porter grinned. "Ok, let's go."

Bent Pine, North Carolina

"What do you mean that you can't tell me why your DIS cops are shooting at us?" Merle shouted into the phone. On the other line, the mayor was shouting something to a high-ranking state official, but Merle didn't pay attention to what was being said.

"Well, fuck you then," Merle said into the desk phone. "We will just kill every last one of your damn federales. Then we are coming after you personally, you idiot." Merle slammed the phone down and turned to confer with Sean Donald, the commander of the Bent Pine Militia.

"All the men have reported for duty. We have all the approaches to the town covered; we are turning travelers on the west highway approach around and sending them back to safety. Most of the men are moving into position to back up everyone already at the road block."

"Sean, let the boys know that they have drones. I don't know what kind yet but prepare for the worst. Tom saw some through his binocs. I suggest you set your best shots to sniping the helicopters, and ask Tom to see if he can get the drones with that Big Fifty."

"Already covered, Merle," Sean smiled. "I had a word with Tom on the Radio."

"They will be the quad-copter drones, I'll bet. They will probably have predators on us very soon as well," Sean said. "We will spread out and dig in."

"I need to get back to the road block," Merle said. "But first..." Merle took a scoped FN/FAL from the gun rack on the wall and picked up a sack of loaded magazines for it. He smiled, "Maybe I can't reach out and touch them the way Tom can, but I'll get some lead into some of them."

"Oh stop asking silly questions, and just let us through," Jonas quietly said to the armed guard at the edge of town.

Lowboy was looking around for helicopters. He heard some but couldn't see them yet. Most of the other 20 or so people who had come with them were outside the bus doing the same. All were armed.

"There's one," Myrtle pointed at a helicopter.

"One of yours?" Jonas asked the guard. "It isn't one of ours or we would have communication to that effect."

"No, it belongs to the feds. You folks better take cover. They have been shooting at us. They have shot several of our guys so far; two that I know of are dead.

Jonas quickly walked back to the bus, got something, and then walked back to the guard. He was carrying an old 12-gauge single shot shotgun.

"What do you think you are going to do with that?" The militiaman asked.

"Just watch," Jonas said and aimed at the helicopter flying almost half a mile away. He pulled the trigger and launched the mini-missile. When it was two hundred feet from Jonas, the built-in rocket engine fired and the mini-missile quadrupled its speed in a flash of light. Jonas twisted the stock of the shotgun and a screen and joystick popped up. Jonas used the joystick to fly the missile to its target. The flash that destroyed the helicopter was as bright as a miniature sun.

"Whoa," the guard shouted. "You guys better get up to the front. I think they need you there."

Jonas was lost in thought again. He was busy trying to figure out ways to improve the mini missile system. Porter took the single barrel shotgun and the backpack full of missiles from Jonas and Lowboy led Jonas to the bus. In just a couple of minutes they were headed toward the front.

"Hey look Boss, we got reinforcements."

Merle turned and saw a band bus headed their way. The bus stopped well behind the roadblock and people poured out of the bus armed with various rifles and other assorted gear. One huge fellow carrying a scoped deer rifle trotted up to where Merle was crouched behind a concrete barrier block, and crouched down beside him.

"How's it going, Sheriff?" the big guy asked. "My name is Lowboy."

"Well," the sheriff said. "We're holding them off for now but I don't think that will last for long. Take a look." The sheriff pointed to where the DIS police were bunched up about a mile and a half down the highway."

Lowboy looked where the sheriff pointed. He saw more than a dozen quad-copter drones headed their way. "I think we can handle those." Lowboy said. He turned and waved his arm at the bus and another huge guy came trotting up to where they crouched behind the barrier. "Hey Myrtle," Lowboy said. "Can you get Jonas to use some of those drone jammer things that he made?"

"You bet," Myrtle replied and ran back to the bus. Soon, Myrtle and another fellow trotted back up to the barrier to join the Sheriff and Lowboy.

"Jonas," Myrtle asked, "can you shut those drones down from here?"

"No, the jammers need to be closer," Jonas frowned. "The jammers I have with us only have a range of about 200 yards."

"Well," the sheriff said, "if we could get them closer."

"I think we can do that," Lowboy said. "Do you have a vehicle I can use?"

"Yeah," the sheriff said. You can use my squad car."

"Turn some of those jammers on and give them to me Jonas." I'm gonna take them down the road a bit."

"That is suicide," Myrtle said.

"Well, I don't intend it to be," Lowboy replied. "But you may have something there."

"Well, You ain't gonna go without me," Myrtle grinned.

"Well, let's go then."

The Sheriff watched the two huge men get into his squad car, pull around the barrier with the help of a dozen men who almost carried the car over the ditch, and start toward the feds massed to the East on the highway. The squad car was flying down the road toward the feds as fast as it would go, and Myrtle was tossing jammers out the window every so often. The sheriff watched as the drones grew closer and closer to the two huge men in the squad car.

The crowd at the roadblock cheered as the first drone got close to the car, faltered, and crashed. Apparently the jammers worked. Jonas appeared to be lost in thought, as if he was figuring out a better way to accomplish things. The sheriff smiled and pulled the young man down into a crouch behind the concrete barrier. Jonas didn't even notice.

The sheriff got up and went over to where Tom lay with the big fifty. "Tom, can you hit those drones from here?"

"I can try, no guarantee."

"Okay, you give it a try."

Tom settled in behind the scope. One of the drones had now stopped about 200 yards away from the squad car, just out of range of the jammer, and was hovering as if readying for a shot. Just as the auto pistol attached to the quad-copter drone begin to fire, Tom squeezed off a round from the big fifty. The drone shuddered and slid sideways a bit and then regained its equilibrium, it's gun still firing. Even at that distance Merle could tell that some of the shots hit the squad car. However, the squad car was turning around. Tom squeezed off another round and the drone shook and then spun out of control and crashed.

"Great shot," the sheriff smiled. "Hang in there. I need to make a phone call."

The sheriff got one of the militiamen to give him a ride back to the mayor's office, where the mayor was still trying to reach the white house on the phone.

"Any luck yet?" Merle asked.

"They have me on hold," the mayor said. Just then they heard a chopper approaching from the west. It came quickly, at a much higher speed than the DIS choppers were capable of. Merle thought it landed in the parking lot. He did not hear any shooting, so he stayed in the mayor's office, trusting the militia to handle things outside.

A man soon strode through the door. He was about six feet tall and looked kind of familiar to the sheriff. Another man only a little over five feet tall followed the man. The smaller man carried an old Garand rifle with a familiarity that told Merle that he undoubtedly knew how to use it. Another odd individual followed the two of them. This one looked to be a young adolescent in a hoodie, but Merle couldn't tell for sure if it was a boy or a girl. The figure in the hoodie was carrying a laptop with a large antenna.

"Is that the White House?" The six-footer asked gesturing at the phone,

"Yes," the mayor said. "They have us on hold."

"May I have the phone?" The taller man requested. Without a word, the mayor handed it to him. The man put it to his ear and said, "I know you are listening. This is John Debrouillard. Put me through to the president, immediately."

A voice came on the line, "Yes Sir."

A little later a voice said, "This is the president. You are a damn hard man to kill John."

"I wish I could say the same for your feds here in Bent Pine, but it isn't true. You have five thousand of your federal police out there, stymied in an illegal gun confiscation attempt by a small town sheriff and a few deer hunters. Your people have taken a number of casualties, almost a hundred according to my intel, and more than half of your helicopters are down, as well as several of your drones. We have film of the entire fiasco and we have reporters on site and in the surrounding mountains filming everything that is happening."

"John, I am the president of the most powerful and influential country in the world. You can't go against me."

"I already have, Mr. President. Just remember, you started this. Oh, and by the way, you might want to reconsider that tactical nuke you are planning on hitting Bent Pine with in a few minutes."

"Why is that John?" The president asked. He smiled as he spoke, knowing that the person he was talking to would be vapor in a few minutes.

"Ask your people to tell you where your missile is now targeting?" The president turned to the Secretary of Interior Security and the Secretary of Defense. "Where is the missile headed?"

"The secretaries both spoke into their phones. The secretary of Defense got the information first and said, "Mr. President, it is headed right at the White House. We have lost complete control of the missile. It has been hacked. That has never happened before."

The president's shoulders sagged a bit and he spoke into the phone. "OK, John. What is it you want?"

"Mr. President, you can't win this one even if you call for a major military strike on Bent Pine. The word is out and, if you try, you will soon find yourself hanging by the neck from a tree on the lawn of the White House. You may get me and a few of the citizens here, but the rest of the country will hang you for treason, Sir, and deservedly so."

"Remember, the people of the United States of America are the single largest standing army in the world, with over 300 million guns, and the will to use them. Your underpowered assault rifles and body armor are no match for a typical American deer hunter with a 30-06, and I doubt our military will support you in killing American citizens. I suggest you cancel gun confiscation unless you want to start the largest and bloodiest revolution this continent has ever seen. One I add, that you will not survive."

The president paused for almost a minute. John suspected he was conferring with his staff. "All right John, you won this one. I will rescind the gun confiscation for now and recall the Department of Interior Security people from Bent Pine," he paused. "You will redirect the missile to somewhere harmless?"

"It is being done now as we speak," John signaled to the hooded figure and he or she did something on the laptop and then gave John a thumb's up.

"John, this isn't over," the president said. "I will get you and I will have my way with this country. I always get my way, no matter what. This is just a small setback. No one, and I mean no one, ever bests me!"

"Mr. President," John said, "have you considered that We The People may get you first?" and set the phone back in its cradle. He turned to the others in the room, "Gentlemen, this incident is over. We won," he paused, "but the revolution is just beginning and it is going to get really nasty before it is done."

"I do not trust the president," the mayor said.

"Neither do I," Merle said. "Hey, now I know you. You are the guy in the video; the one who the feds were after with the quad-copter drones."

"Yes," John said. "That was me."

"I am sorry about your wife," Merle said.

"Thanks. Me too," John wistfully replied. "We still have a lot to do. We have to evacuate as many folks as we can from Bent Pine and get them to safety."

"Do you think the feds will try to strike again?" The mayor asked.

"Yes," John said. "But I think we have a week or more. They will have to do political damage and spin control before they will attempt a strike. We already have the story of this attack out on the internet and some of our folks are gathering more film and interviews and getting more material on the internet—mostly hosted on foreign servers—as fast as they can. We dealt the government a serious blow today, thanks to you folks in Bent Pine. However, they will not quit until they are all dead."

"Neither will we," Merle said, "and there are a lot more of us."

Chapter 23: MONTANA

"Galt's Gulch is a state of mind." John Debrouillard

Montana

Peggy looked over the 7,000-acre ranch from the hilltop. From her vantage point she could see the roads and houses being built, and the construction in the old mine pit which would soon create an underground citadel that would lie directly under center of the town they were building. Of the 2700 or so citizens of Bent Pine, 2,500 had come to Montana by ones and twos and in various raggle-taggle groups. Most of the rest had moved elsewhere. Only a very few diehards had stayed behind in Bent Pine.

The council had purchased the ranch for $30,000,000 and donated it to the cause. The council also had several deals underway to purchase large adjacent tracts of land.

John said that it might have been better to disperse the residents of Bent Pine in smaller enclaves throughout the country, but no one wanted to do so. New identities and local bank accounts with long local histories were being created for all in the hopes that the government could be confused long enough for the people to win the revolution.

Everyone who settled here from Bent Pine was deeded two acres to build on, if they wanted it, or a house in the town with lot large enough for a garden and chickens, if possible considering location. The council provided the cost of materials but the labor was left up to the residents. No one complained about the work. These were true Americans who would have made the Founding Father's proud.

This was a planned settlement with room for gardens and greenhouses, agricultural land, and small-scale commercial hydroponics and aquaponics operations, as well as pastures for hay and grass-fed beef and space for small-scale manufacturing. The goal was to make the town and surrounding area as locally sustainable as possible.

The town, which everyone has simply started calling Home, was also laid out with a strong eye to defense. One of the Bent Pine folks was a retired General from the Vietnam era. Though now in his late seventies, he had put together a team to design the town's defenses. He had also requested that every household in town be armed with true full auto assault rifles and everyone old enough taught how to use them.

An impromptu gun range had been set up, and it was to date the most popular activity in town. No one had any problems in defying the old ban on full auto rifles and a few full auto guns had appeared and more than a few ARs had been modified. Peggy smiled when she remembered the ten-year-old girl she had seen at the gun range consistently placing three round bursts in the center of a target at 100 yards with a M-16. That child would grow up to be no one's victim.

All of the houses built so far had basements, and most were earth-sheltered as well. More than 90% were bulletproof. The federal invasion of Bent Pine had convinced most residents that bulletproofing was good.

Peggy glanced at the slight, hooded figure beside her. She still did not know the girl's name. The girl was a member of the hacker group that Peggy had managed to contact. She was the liaison between the hacker group and the resistance.

"You like him, don't you?" The hooded girl asked.

Peggy was a bit surprised. "Who?" she asked.

"John," the hooded girl said.

Peggy stared into the girl's dark blue eyes. "Yes," she replied, "I do."

"So does Toni," the hooded girl replied.

"I know," Peggy said with a hint of forlornness in her voice.

"You think you can't compete with Toni because she is beautiful?" The hooded girl asked.

"Well, that thought has crossed my mind," Peggy replied. "Toni is drop-dead gorgeous."

"You are smarter than Toni," the hooded girl said.

"Toni is smart," Peggy replied.

"Yes, but not nearly as smart as you."

"What are you saying?" Peggy asked.

"You know what I am saying," the hooded girl smiled. "I like Jonas. I am going to marry him even though he doesn't know that yet."

"But you are sixteen and he is twenty-five," Peggy protested.

"That doesn't change what will happen," the hooded girl calmly stated.

"What if Toni is determined to have John?" Peggy asked.

"Toni is determined, but not as determined as you, or John for that matter. You and John are a match just like Jonas and me. This I know."

Peggy stood, wordlessly thinking about what the slight, young girl said. It was not Peggy's style to chase after a man. Besides, they would probably all be dead soon if the government figured out how to get to them. However, the young girl's words brightened Peggy's mood. To change the subject she asked. "Do you think you can really hide this place from the feds?"

The smile under the hood grew wide. "Oh yes, it is already being done. We have hacked into the satellite feeds and drone feeds and all data for these coordinates are being replaced with our own data, which shows only an undisturbed landscape. This location is also not on any regular flight paths of commercial or military flights, and we are quite remote and located in a very lightly populated area. Plus, the town and habitations are being built so that the town and surrounding area will not obviously stand out from above."

Peggy smiled. "I hope you are right."

"The resistance will win, and this place will be just fine. This is where Jonas and I will raise our children."

"But you haven't told him yet?"

"Of course not. He is not ready for that concept," the thin young girl smiled under her hood. "He will be when I am ready, though."

Washington, D.C.

"The entire town is empty! What do you mean the entire town is empty?" The president asked.

"Just what I said, Mr. President," the secretary of Interior Security replied. "Almost all of the residents have just up and moved out of Bent Pine, including the mayor and the police force. None of the remaining people there have any idea where they went. They walked away from their jobs, their homes, and their businesses. We have interrogated several of the few residents who stayed, with prejudice, I might add, and they truly do not know where the people went."

"Where did they go? Do you think they all went to the same place?"

"We think somewhere in the West. We haven't been able to track them. All of the RFID chips, and GPS systems in their vehicles are dead. We suspect they all went to the same place, but we are not sure."

"How many people are we talking about?"

"Approximately 2,500, Mr. President."

"Are you drunk, blind, or just plain stupid?" The president almost shouted before regaining his composure. Then, more calmly, he said, "There is no way that could happen."

"Mr. President, we were able to go back into our satellite data and find pictures of the people leaving. They left in small groups using trucks and trailers for the most part to move their stuff. They all went west. Somewhere around Kansas we lost them in our imagery. All of them, one by one; they just disappeared. They were there in one frame and simply gone in the next."

"How could that happen? Do they have some sort of Star Trek style cloaking device?"

"We don't think so Mr. President."

"Then what?"

"We think the data streams from the satellites were hacked and all trace of these people removed before the data reached us."

"No one can do that," the president said.

"Nonetheless, that is our best guess about what was done."

"That would mean that our entire surveillance system has been penetrated."

"Yes Mr. President, I am afraid so."

"Could it have been that hacker group, Unknown?" The president asked.

"No Sir, Mr. President. We have moles in Unknown. They tell us that not only did they not do this, but that they are simply not capable of doing this at the scale which it has been done."

The president's face grew very somber. "I think we may be up against a very formidable foe."

"I think you are right, Mr. President."

"However, we have the entire might of the federal government on our side. We have my DIS army that I built of people with loyalty only to me. We have numerous federal agencies funded by taxpayer dollars that do my bidding alone. There is no way that these people can beat us.

"I hope you are right, Mr. President."

Home, Montana

John stood on the edge of the precipice looking out over the stunningly beautiful terrain and the town below. Peggy was on his right and Toni was on his left. Nearby stood Doc, Merle, Lorne, Gwen, Jonas, Tom, Myrtle, Lowboy, Porter, and, slightly separated from the rest, a slight, hooded figure. Leon was sitting in a wheelchair close to Doc holding Peggy's cat Loco. His cancer had spread to his bones and walking was now difficult for him. Nonetheless, he had a smile on his face and a lightweight carbine rested across the arms of his wheelchair. All the rest were armed as well, except the hooded figure, who held a laptop, and Jonas who still pretty much feared guns. The sun was setting and casting a reddish glow across the mountaintop.

Toni took John's left arm and Peggy took his right arm. They both stood close to him as the evening chill grew. Gwen was standing between Myrtle and Lowboy and all three were in animated conversation. Most of the rest were as lost in thought as John.

"I do not know what the future holds for any of us," John said looking around at the group gathered around him, "but I am honored to fight for our country with the finest group of people I have ever known." He paused a bit. "Some of us, perhaps even all of us, may not survive what is to come, but I have no doubt that We the People will win this revolution and take back our country. Our traitor-in-chief has vastly underestimated the strength and will of We the People. We will prevail."

At that, ten rifles, one .380 pistol, one laptop, and one empty fist were thrust into the air and the cheer echoed off of the mountains.

PREVIEW

DRONE WARS TWO: FLINT AND STEEL

By

Mike Whitworth

Look for it soon on www.docspress.com

Chapter One: The Far North

"The combination of raw determination, knowledge, and creativity is man's most fearsome weapon, bar none." John Debrouillard

Somewhere in the Far North

I stood naked in the snow facing the man who had ordered the murder of my wife—and me. My hands were tied behind my back with doubled plastic wire ties, and it was cold, really cold. The sun shone brightly in the clear blue sky. One security goon had a grip on my arms and five others had guns pointed at me.

"You are no longer the thorn in my side, John Debrouillard. I have you now," the president said. "Simply killing you is not enough. I want you to suffer for the trouble you have caused me."

"Mr. Pretender to the Throne," I said, spitting blood from my mouth, the result of being beaten by the president's goons. "Someday, I will kill you for murdering my wife; and for the destruction you have wreaked on our Constitution and our country. You have my promise on that."

"Not likely, John," The president smiled. "We are going to turn you loose here. It is 20 degrees below zero right now and it is just going to get colder tonight. It is more than five hundred miles from here to the nearest civilization. You won't last until morning and I will be able to say in good conscience to the American People that I did not have you killed. I will simply say that I do not know for sure what happened to you."

I spat in the president's face. He stood there, shocked at first. I don't think he had ever been physically threatened during his entire protected life. Then he wiped his face, and turned his cold, reptilian eyes on me. "Bind his feet, too," He said to his goons.

The man behind me pushed me face first into the snow and, with two others, held my legs so one of them could bind my ankles with a pair of plastic wire ties.

The president laughed and trudged through the snow back to his waiting helicopter. His guards followed. I managed to roll over on my side and watch them board the chopper and take off. Now I was starting to get mad.

I once watched an internet video where a fellow showed how to break plastic wire ties binding your wrists with a powerful, sudden movement of the shoulders and arms. I struggled to my knees in the foot-deep snow and had a go at it. At the second try, the plastic wire ties broke and my hands were free. My wrists were bloody where the plastic cut me, but I didn't care at the moment. Once my hands were free, I used both my legs and hands to break free of the restraints around my ankles in much the same way. In less than a minute I was free and leaving bloody tracks in the snow as I made for the trees on the edge of the open area where the helicopter had landed.

I knew that getting warm was my first priority. I needed fire, yet I had nothing but the broken plastic wire ties I had salvaged. I was completely naked and barefoot. I had no clothing, no matches, no knife, and no food or water. I was in a fix that even my Paleolithic ancestors would have feared.

Moving as quickly as I possibly could, not the least worried about sweating while shivering naked at 20 below, I headed into the trees and down slope toward what I hoped was a creek. I paused to tear huge handfuls of tinder fungus from several birch trees as I passed them. That task was a lot tougher than I thought it would be. Once more I was thankful for internet videos on wilderness survival, which I had watched by the hundreds.

I knew from reading that the tinder fungus should be dried before use, but I didn't have the time or a fire for that. I was just hoping I could somehow use the fungus as it was to start a fire.

One thing I learned as a boy was to never quit. I came from a neighborhood where no one went to college. I went to college and earned three degrees in spite of that. It wasn't in my nature to lie down and die. So I didn't. Nature would have to kill me all by herself. I wasn't going to help her even one little bit.

At the base of the slope was a small stream. It was completely frozen over, but I could see cobbles and pebbles through the clear ice. I looked around the bank and found a twenty-pound rock that I wrested free from the snow, and then smashed through the ice to get at the cobbles and pebbles below. There was one I had my eye on. It was brown and looked little different from many of the others. I was pretty sure that this one was a chert cobble, though. My study of rocks at the university and my time collecting them as a child might pay off now.

I smashed the brown cobble with my large rock and it cracked in half. It was a nice chert, almost four inches across. I then chose a smaller rock and, after a few tries, knocked a large flake from the chert. My distant ancestors could probably have done much better, but my flake had a single sharp edge and I was pleased.

I chose a good spot under the trees and made a large pile of the abundant small dead twigs and branches. Then I shredded some of the tinder fungus with the sharp chert flake and piled the tiny, dust-like shreds in a hollow in a large piece of tinder fungus.

To strike sparks to start a fire, I needed not only the chert, but also a piece of steel, or marcasite as the Indians had used. My chances of finding any steel or marcasite in the next half hour were approximately zero. I needed another way to start a fire and I didn't have the hour or two it would take me to make a bow-drill fire starting set, especially since I had never made one before. I just knew about them from watching online videos.

Then I thought, why not make a magnifying glass from some of the three-inch thick clear ice on the small creek? I broke a piece of clear ice free and, using the chert flake started shaving it into the shape of a large bi-convex lens about eight inches in diameter. I was greatly hampered by intense shivering and freezing fingers, but, under threat of death, persevered. When I was done, the surface of the ice lens was too cloudy to pass light effectively. I needed something to polish the surface. I tried rubbing the surface with my hands, but my body was shutting down the blood flow to my extremities and they were cold. I knew I didn't have long left now, so I held the ice against my stomach and used what little remaining body heat I had to melt the surface ice. In about ten minutes I had a passably clear ice lens.

I carefully held the lens, bracing my shaking arms against a stick, and focused the light beam on a small pile of shredded and powdered tinder fungus. In about 90 seconds, a small tendril of smoke rewarded me. By blowing carefully and adding larger shreds of tinder fungus, I soon had a small fire going. I huddled over it as I slowly added larger twigs and then small sticks. Soon, I was warmer, but by no means warm. At least though, as long as I had the fire, I was in no danger of freezing.

As I sat naked by the warmth of the fire, my butt on a pile of bark and my back almost against my small lean-to made from dead branches, weaving strips of bark into crude boots and a robe, another fire in my belly hardened my determination.

It might take me a while, maybe a year, maybe even three, but I promised myself that I would one day kill the president, with my bare hands if possible; if not, then maybe with a drone. The president was a man who lived by the drone and I thought it fitting that he might die by the drone as well.